DarkFront Witness Book 1: Haunted

A.J. Morgentstern

DarkFront Witness
Book 1:
Haunted

A.J. Morgenstern

For Laura. Logan lives.

Foreword

Hey guys,

I'm Abigail Linhardt, one of the authors of The Dark-Front Trilogy you are about to begin. I wanted to start this novel with a bit of a trigger-warning and my own thoughts on dealing with this kind of subject matter—even though I'm not a warning type of person.

I wrote the original short story "November: Jasper and Huck" very soon after the death of my own brother. The story was born out of some guilt I held, which I won't discuss here, and the feelings of loss and helplessness that comes with a tragedy like this. There is no way to convey the thoughts and emotions my family and I went through after his death. If you know, you know and I am so sorry.

This novel deals with suicide and depression the best way I know how: through a story. But I wanted to share some other thoughts going in.

First, if you are suffering from depression and/or thoughts of suicide, please seek help. I know first hand it's not easy. Why, you may ask? Because it feels like attention-seeking thanks to TV shows and other entertainment that have wrongly and immorally glamorized mental illness and suicide. If I mention that I have sever depression or other issues to people, their eyes glass over and they tune out. They simper robotically and say, "I'm sorry, that sucks." They don't know how to deal with it, for one, and they don't want to, secondly. You have main-character syndrome if you tell someone you have issues like that. You want attention. You don't really have a problem. Just be happy. Do things that please you.

If only it were that simple.

Asking for help is not easy for these and so many more reasons. I've disclosed personal things about myself before and had them used against me by coworkers or people I thought were friends. So I try not to tell people about it, any more. That's another reason. I used to think the surefire way of knowing someone actually had a mental illness was that they wouldn't talk about it. They wouldn't disclose that information. That could still be true. It's still true for me.

Secondly, to our sufferers out there: I want to tell you that if you use your illness or suicidal thoughts to manipulate others, you are a garbage person. That's all on that topic.

Thirdly, to the ones who know people who suffer: I know it is annoying to listen to them whine all the time and talk about how sad they are. But if they are talking to you, it means (as you can see from above) that they trust you and are being vulnerable with you. If you have no idea that one of your friends is suffering from depression or suicidal ideation, it's not necessarily your fault. This has been my personal experience. Some sufferers just don't want to burden others with their issues. Please, keep an eye out for those you love who may be at risk.

Another word to those who are friends of these tortured souls: you don't have to fix anything. When we come to you, we just want some company, a shoulder, to tell SOMEONE what is going on in our heads. Depression is very, very lonely. Supporters, it's also ok to tell a sad person that their constant doom and gloom is wearing on you so long as you say it with love and not in a way that says, "Please STOP coming to me." Just tell them you need a break, too. Or better yet, suggest something that will be a break for you both. There is nothing better in the world than when someone is there for me. Who keeps inviting me to things even though I say no all the time. Please, keep inviting me. Don't discount or forget about your ill friends just because you "know they won't come." Going isn't the point. The point is someone still wants us around.

Think about that: I got invited. Someone wants me here.

That thought goes a long way with people with suicide ideation.

I think that's enough for now. To those suffering, please reach out. Find your local or national help line, call, talk to someone. Take a chance and reach out to someone on social media. Play video games online just to be around people. If you are like me and have/are struggling, I am so sorry and I wish you weren't. I pray you magically find the courage to reach out for help. To the supporters, if someone you know seems to be begging for attention: give them attention.

You have been sufficiently warned: this book is a work of fiction and might seem silly to some, but it deals with very real, very present problems in our world, drawing heavily from my own conclusions of my experience. I hope you either find this trilogy entertaining (which is completely fine and the point of the novel) or helpful.

Either way, thank you for being a witness.

Chapter 1:

Ghost In The Blood

The door at the end of the hallway slammed, making everyone jump. The green metal walls of the abandoned school made it echo long and loud until it faded into the lightless darkness.

"The wind," Huck said, smiling at the wide eyes of his best friend, Jasper.

"Or a ghost," Mark, his identical twin whispered, half smiling. Huck and Mark were mirror images of each other, down to how they wore their black hair fringed into their eyes. The only difference was Huck's eyes. He had a blue and green one. Mark had blue eyes.

"Or a ghost pushed by the wind into the door," Jasper laughed from behind the shoulder mounted camera he peered in to.

Their guide, an older man in army green pants and a denim jacket, sighed and shook his head. He placed his hands on his hips and paced back a few steps. "I told you kids, this place is off limits. We can't go down any further. I shouldn't have opened the front in the first place."

Huck sensed the man about to retreat. "Mr. Halstead,

you're the premier historian in town, right?" he said, changing his tone to be flattering. "We wanted to go to—what was his name, Mark? The one with the skull in his office?"

"Mr. Dangerfield," Mark supplied, quickly picking up on Huck's tactic. "His name would have looked so cool on our thumbnail."

Halstead grimaced, confused.

"On the internet," Huck cleared up for him quickly. "Imagine it. *Dangerfield and the Haunted School*." He shook his head, faking regret. "Damn, Mark, we missed a golden opportunity. He really wanted to come, too. Said he'd show us the boiler room."

Huck glared at Jasper as he snickered into his hand, stifling his laughter. Jasper quickly pressed his lips together and pushed his tasseled blond hair out of his face.

"Look, kids," Halstead started again, going for the ring of keys on his belt. "I don't care what Dangerfield said he'd do. The building is old. Dangerous."

"Just how dangerous, Mr. Halstead?" Mark went on, stepping in front of the camera and angling himself and Halstead at a perfect three-quarter view to the lens. "We did some research, heard about the kid who was bullied here, and took his life in the basement. It was a real nightmare for the town. When was that?"

Huck smiled at his brother's simple but effective way. Mark was like magic when it came to conversation. Something about his big, blue eyes behind his black forelock made anyone—guys and girls—open up to him. Talk to him. Huck didn't mind since he wasn't too into talking to people face to face. In front of the camera, though? That he could do. That he loved.

"Well, Mr., uh," Halstead replied, emphasizing the mister.

"Derringer," Mark and Huck said together.

Halstead's eyes flicked from one twin to the other. "Does this gimmick get you viewers?" he asked, pointing to each brother in turn. "Twin stuff is, uh…"

"Ew," Jasper moaned from behind the camera. But Huck could see his perfect, white teeth smiling under the lens.

The older man shrugged. "My granddaughter was the one who wanted me to do this. She watches you two. Among other things on that damned phone of hers."

Mark smiled understandingly at the older man. "That's great, sir. We'd love to send you home with a signed t-shirt. But more than that, I'd be in your debt if you could just answer a few more questions for us. We won't go downstairs."

Halstead shifted, then nodded. "You are right about the boy. His name was Able High. In fact, after he hung himself and the curse set in—"

"Curse?" the three of them echoed. Huck stepped into view on the other side of Halstead so he was framed by him and Mark.

"We didn't read anything online about a curse," Huck went on. He looked into the lens and spoke to his future audience. "This is entirely new information, guys. While we knew the school was ironically called Able High after the kid who was killed here, we didn't hear anything about curses." He turned back to their guide, who stood awkwardly while Huck chatted to the invisible audience. "Mr. Halstead, what do you mean curse? Did something happen after the tragic suicide of the boy?"

Halstead shifted and looked around, as if something watched him from the walls. "Well, yeah."

"Look into the lens," Jasper whispered from behind the camera. "It's unorthodox, but gives our show its unique feel."

"Uh," Halstead stammered, looking for the lens and wincing into the camera lights.

Jasper tapped the glassy surface right below the red recording light.

"Oh, I see," the older man said. He squared up. "Yes, once Able High took his own life, unfortunate events began to happen to the students who had made his four years of high school a total torment. You see, Able hung out with a... questionable crowd."

"Witches," Mark supplied to the camera. "We've heard about covens of witches in these small, midwestern towns. Does any of that hold up in this story?"

Halstead nodded. "Many think Able's friend, her name was Nancy, cursed his tormentors. And cursed Able, too."

Huck and Mark exchanged glances.

"Nancy cursed Able to never rest," he went on. "Cursed his spirit to come and exact revenge on the bullies. But..."

Above them, something fell. Jasper gasped and turned to look. Even Huck's heart hammered in his chest.

Not real, he told himself. *It's never real.* He looked up, the hair on the back of his neck suddenly standing up. An involuntary shiver rippled down his spine. Something rolled across the floor above them.

Mark reached across Halstead and gripped Huck's arm. Huck looked into his brother's blue eyes. Mark's face dropped all performance. He frowned slightly, tilting his head and mouth, *what?*

Huck cleared his throat, taking Mark's hand off his shoulder. "Why did she curse Able? Didn't she have feelings for him?"

"No," Halstead sighed, shivering. "Able liked Nancy in a way she'd like him. So she wanted to keep him restless, they say. To do her bidding."

"Ah," Mark said, his black brows going up in understanding. "So while we thought we were dealing with Able, an angry spirit, we may in fact be dealing with an old witch's curse?" He smiled into the camera. "Mr. Halstead, does that explain this?"

Mark held up his phone for the old man to see. All the color drained from Halstead's face until it glowed gray as a ghost in the camera light.

"That symbol," he began. "Where is that?"

Huck smiled at Mark's shrewdness. "We found that symbol repeated twice," he said. "Once on the roof behind the old door and another near the back exit of the girl's restroom. We thought it might be to lock Able's ghost inside. That would create a haunting we call a loop."

Mark took over. "A loop is when a ghost haunts the same place and goes through the same actions over and over. Usually pretty harmless. But a haunt with intention is different. That's when the ghost is here, active, and looking for something. But this seems to be the case of a noun haunting: that's where something—usually a witch—binds a spirit to a place until it finishes a task." He turned to look at Halstead.

"You—what I mean is—no," Halstead stammered.

The building creaked. A shift in the air touched Huck's cheek. He gasped, his breath turning to white clouds before his face.

"Cold spot?" Jasper whispered.

Mark's face turned serious again. "What the hell?"

"Cut it out," Huck ordered. The other two always assumed whenever something weird happened, it was indeed ghosts or demons or something. But Huck, no matter what, had to convince himself it wasn't real. He couldn't start believing. Believing would make the things they hunted real.

"Mr. Halstead," Jasper suddenly asked while the twins

held up their EMF readers to the walls, "how do you know Nancy didn't fancy Able like he did her?"

The older man's lip trembled and his eyes bulged. "Nance?" he whispered, eyes locked down the dark hallway.

"Guys," Jasper hissed, grabbing Huck by his black jacket and spinning him to face Halstead. "He sees something."

Huck took a step back behind Mark. Mark didn't mind, taking the lead and protectively putting this arm out in front of Huck.

Jasper switched his camera to night vision. "I don't see anything."

"Keep recording," Mark whispered. "Mr. Halstead?" He took a step away from Huck towards the petrified man. "You knew Nancy Claymore, didn't you?"

"Damn you!"

The older man spun, swinging his heavy ring of keys at Mark. Jasper and Huck screamed, leaping out of the way as the man flailed his arms, landing blow after blow on Mark's face.

Huck's brain went into overdrive. He shouted, lifting his leg and kicking Halstead hard in the center of his chest. Mark fell to the ground, crying out in agony from the keys that tore his face.

"This asshole is nuts!" Jasper shouted, dropping his camera from his shoulder and hauling Mark to his feet.

"Run!" Huck screamed.

Huck pulled Mark down the stairs, praying Alisha—Mark's girlfriend—was waiting outside like she promised. She was, but was on the phone, giggling and blushing. Her eyes shot up from where she leaned against the driver's side of the car. Her red hair caught the cool, setting sun as she jerked up.

"Start the car!" Huck shouted. Mark cried, hands over his

face as Huck stumbled over the gravel, dropping some of his equipment.

"Holy shit, what happened?" Alisha gasped, quickly stopping her call and stowing her phone on her pocket.

"The psycho who said he'd give us a tour?" Jasper gasped, diving into the back seat. "Turns out, he knew the victim we're here to investigate."

"Oh, shit," Alisha hissed again, jamming her keys into the ignition.

Huck fell into the passenger's side seat, pulling Mark with him. He clutched his twin hard. "Drive!" he screamed when Alisha stopped to take in her boyfriend's bloody face.

Crying now too, Alisha slammed her foot down, peeling out on the gravel with the car in reverse. The doors to the abandoned school burst open and Halstead glared in the door way looking something like a ghost himself. He scowled and dived down the concrete steps towards the car.

"Drive, damn it!" Jasper cried, buckling up.

Finally, the car revved and spit gravel up into Halstead's face as he bore down on them. The car, belonging to Mark, was an old black Chevy Corvette from the 90s. He and Mark had matching ones given to them by an old friend of their mother's. The things ancient engine ground and gasped, but finally got them onto the black asphalt hall glittering in ice.

Catching his breath, Huck slid out from under Mark to the back seat and joined Jasper. He reached into one of their packs and pulled out a first aid kit. It held a few bandaids and some disinfecting wipes. Huck handed them up to Mark, who had stopped bawling now. Huck reached up, taking Mark's hands off his face, and pushed his hair out of his eyes.

"I think you're probably in more pain than you have damage," he said reassuringly. Huck knew their good looks were half the reason they had the views they did. "Scars are cool, though. So don't worry."

Mark winced, wiping away the blood. He nodded, getting his brave front back. "Yeah. Damn, I should have known an old creep like that had something to do with the haunting."

"What happened?" Alisha interrupted. She looked around for her phone that fell out of her pocket when she sped off.

Jasper took over for Huck since he still gripped Mark's shoulders over the back of the seat. "We just asked questions. Turns out, that old fart had the hots for Nancy Claymore back in the 80s. He must have known her pretty well. Damn old idiot needs to get out of town," he added.

Huck caught his mismatched eyes in the mirror as Mark pulled down to better see the damage. Mark saw Huck looking and smiled at him in the mirror.

"You were right. It hurt a lot more than it did damage," he said.

Something vibrated. Huck looked around and saw Alisha's pink phone on the floor under her chair. He reached for it.

"No, don't!" Alisha cried, jerking her head up to look at Huck in the rearview mirror. "Huckleberry Derringer, give me my phone!"

"Calm down," Huck mumbled, preparing to toss it into Mark's lap. He stopped. The name that glowed on the caller ID froze him solid.

"What?" Jasper asked, leaning over to look.

"Cut it out!" Alisha screamed, jerking the car hard to the right as she reached back and tried to snatch the phone. "Huck, give it to me!"

Huck instead shoved the phone into Mark's hands. Mark, blinking through the last of the blood on his face, looked down. Huck saw his eyes dim.

"Daemon?" Mark rasped. His blue eyes instantly filled with tears. "Alisha...I thought."

Alisha gripped the steering wheel harder, glowering out the window at the darkening road. "Thought what, Mark? Thought the rumors that I was blowing him behind the gym were false? Yeah, I know, remember? You accused me in the middle of first period!"

The phone started to ring again, Daemon's name appearing on the screen.

"Then why's he calling you?" Mark asked, emotion stuffing up his voice.

Huck felt bad for Mark. Everyone had heard how Alisha had hooked up with Daemon right at the start of the school year. For his brother's sake, Huck hadn't believed it. Alisha and Mark had been waiting for three years. Rage sparked in Huck's chest now. Alisha had some nerve to cheat on someone like Mark. As far as Huck was concerned, Mark was perfect. Huck had a high opinion of himself, but Mark? Mark was smarter, more charming, calmer in hot situations, and was the one behind every good idea the three of them had.

"What the hell, Alisha?" Jasper added. "Well? Did you?"

Alisha glared into the backseat, eyes flashing. "Yeah. So?"

Mark gasped, a new wave of emotion making him sniffle. His lips parted and fluttered, lost for words.

"Damn it, Alisha," Huck snarled.

"Hey, don't you damn me, ghost boy!" she snapped. "Daemon has five times as much going for him than you and your stupid ghost show." She snapped her head to Mark. "Well? Say something."

Huck watched, distraught, as Mark just looked away, tears tracking down his scared face.

"Hey," Alisha snapped. "Look at me, Mark." She raised her hand and slapped Mark hard across the face.

Huck shouted and reached up to grab her arm. Alisha dodged, and the car jerked.

Everyone screamed.

The world went dark around Huck as the back of the old Corvette spun. Alisha screamed, cranked the wheel hard, and the next thing Huck knew, the world went upside down. Metal screamed, grinding on the road. Glass shot inward, cutting Huck's arms as she covered his face. He swore he saw Mark shoot out the front window as Alisha screamed and the car slammed to a sudden, fatal stop.

RED and blue flashes blinded Huck. His head throbbed so hard he wished whoever was shouting would shut up. Someone lifted him roughly, jarring his body. Something plastic went over his nose and mouth and the red and blue was replaced by the blinding glare of a too-bright white light.

"He's losing too much blood," someone cried over the other two rapid-fire voices.

Huck's brain went into overdrive. Was it him who was losing blood? He had to say something.

"O…" he gasped. The thing on his nose fogged up.

"He's conscious," someone shouted, leaning over him. He couldn't make them out besides brown hair and a pink face mask. "Can you hear me, kiddo? What's your name? Can you tell me your name?"

"Huck," he wheezed. "I'm…I'm O-negative."

"Shit," someone else hissed. "We're in luck. Hey, Huck?" A man leaned over him as the entire room Huck laid in jerked into motion.

An ambulance. He was in the back of an ambulance. Holly, their adoptive mother, was going to pitch an absolute fit.

"Huck, can you hear me?" the man asked again, appearing with a white mask over his face and blood-stained blue latex gloves.

"Mark?" Huck called, suddenly afraid. "Where's Mark? He went through—through the window." Panic took hold, strangling him. He tried to sit up, but something strapped him down. "Where's my brother? Please, where is he?" he cried.

The lady leaned in close and whispered. "He's fine. He's right here. But Huck, we need to know if you're ok."

Huck nodded, feeling more and more awake ever second. He looked down at himself. He wasn't bleeding. The blood wasn't his. "Mark's AB-negative," he offered. "Is he—is he ok?"

The lady smiled under her mask. "He is now. You're going to save your brother's life, ok?"

"Jasper?" he asked next. He looked around, his eyes flowing with tears.

"Huck, calm down," the lady whispered. "I need you calm."

Something pierced the crook of his arm. "Mark?" he cried. He finally turned his head and spotted his twin just a foot from him. His entire head was black with blood. "Mark!" he screamed.

Chapter 2:

The Change

Huck watched Emily's eyes. They were glued to the laptop screen. She took in the shaky camera footage, eyes wide. Like most viewers, she looked for any shape or shadow out of the corner of the camera's angle. The lens showed a dark hallway, white dust floating in and out of the sides. Two sets of breathing echoed down the hall from the guys behind the camera. Emily glanced up from the screen to Huck and the other senior behind the laptop screen.

"It's so nerve-wracking," she whispered, hoping to not talk over a mysterious noise. "How do you get the guts to go into these haunted places?"

Jasper stood next to Huck and bit his lip nervously as he waited for the criticism on his latest edit. Jasper was the camera man and editor for their videos. Huck stood more confidently, arms crossed and a full blown smirk on his smooth, angled face. He knew Emily loved his face and his thick black hair that he constantly flicked out of his eyes. That's why he and Mark were the front men of his and Jasper's ghost hunting web series. The girls in his class, and several thousand on the internet, loved him for his angelic features. And his neon, mismatched eyes.

Emily looked back to the screen, watching as a door off to the side slammed open of its own accord. The Huck on the screen jumped back, cursing. Jasper held the camera, off screen. Emily frowned.

"Where's Mark?" she asked.

Huck sighed and dropped his arms. "At home. He's been refusing to come to school since..." He glanced over at a table full of pretty girls and their too attractive boyfriends. "Since the accident."

Emily and her friends, and Jasper and Huck, all looked over at one girl with too-straight red hair and a million dollar smile. She had a broken nose and bruises across both eyes but that didn't stop her followers from fawning over her. If anything, it made them even more unbearable.

Good, thought Huck, glad to see she didn't walk away untarnished. He hadn't actually seen Alisha since the accident.

"What exactly went down with that?" Emily asked, looking to her friends Kate and Aaron. She paused the video to draw attention back to Huck.

Jasper didn't reply, waiting on his best friend to explain. Huck clicked his tongue and sat down, closing out of the video on his laptop. When the player shut down, his own website glowed green and black back at him.

"Oh, wow," Emily said, seeing the interface. "New website for the ghost hunting series? Looks really professional."

"Thanks," Huck beamed, smirking again. "With the videos monitizing finally, we've been able to afford a few upgrades."

Jasper leaned over the table, looking at the website upside

down. "I did the graphics. You don't think it's too much? Kind of cliche?"

The girls shook their heads, blushing. "You're so talented, Jas," Kate said much to Aaron's annoyance.

"You look good on screen," Emily said to Huck.

"I know, right?" Huck beamed. "My face was made for this."

A giggle from the red-haired girl drew all their gazes back.

"So?" Emily asked, covertly pointing back to her. "What did Alisha do?"

Huck chewed the inside of his cheek, trying to find another distraction. All the eyes were on him. Taking advantage of the opportunity to be in the spotlight, he sighed and gave in. "You know that rumor about how she was," he mimicked a motion, fist in front of his mouth, "with Daemon?"

The girls grimaced, nodding.

"Turns out it was true," he sighed. "She was cheating on Mark."

Talking about Mark made the cafeteria of Boaz High suddenly feel huge and ominous. He missed having Mark at his side 24/7. "So Mark finds out while we were coming back from that hunt last week."

"Oh, you didn't go to the concert?" Emily asked, crestfallen. "That's why I didn't see you."

Jasper shook his head. "We were shooting, but Alisha was helping us out."

Huck elbowed Jasper for interrupting his story. "So the dick calls her on our way back and Mark sees his name on the phone, right? She tried to play it off, but you know how perceptive Mark is."

They all nodded.

"They were arguing and we hit a patch of ice when she hit him." He stopped talking. The image of Mark in the ambulance flashed into his mind's eye in a blur of red and blue. He was bloody, unconscious. Holly, their foster mother turned adoptive mother, had been screaming when they got to the emergency entrance of the hospital. "They needed blood for Mark. He's AB negative so..." He shrugged, touching the mark on his arm where a needle had been stabbed into him.

"Universal donor," Jasper jeered, ruffling Huck's hair.

Huck smacked Jasper's hand away, reflattening his hair. "Yeah."

"Wow," Emily sighed, reaching back out to the laptop to click on another video. "That's intense. He's fine though, right? Why's he not back in school? He can walk right?"

"Yeah," Huck said. He didn't elaborate.

Mark had turned into a recluse ever since coming back from the hospital. He hid in his room all day. He used to hang out with Huck and Jasper, going with them on ghost hunts, making the web series, and even doing some editing work. He did most of the research so that when they visited older places, they could talk about the history and other incidents that had happened there. But now he'd been locked away, sulking for almost two weeks.

"I wish he'd get over her," Huck sighed at last.

Jasper gave Huck a look that said he was disappointed in him for talking that way about his twin. Huck ignored him. Yeah, he loved Mark and they did everything together. But the moping needed to stop. Alisha wasn't worth this much heartbreak.

The video that played now was one done just before the accident. Mark and Huck walked in synch down a graveyard path. Mark excitedly talked, walking backwards and telling the story of the old man who haunted the graveyard and how they hoped to catch him on video that night. Huck watched his brother, missing that version of Mark. Jasper had focused in close on Mark's face. They were identical twins except for one feature: Huck had been born with heterochromia. Supposedly, their birth father had it too. Huck and Mark had not seen so much as a picture of their birth parents. He didn't care; they gave them up as newborns. They'd been brought up in the system. Landing at Holly and her husband Richard's house was the only constant in their lives. They used to eagerly await the times they got sent there. Holly and Richard loved them like their own, keeping a room open for them.

Mark in the video smiled a lot, making jokes at Huck's expense. Huck hated teasing but put up with it from Mark and Jasper. Mark had a gap in his teeth Huck didn't have. It gave him a charming, boyish quality he lacked.

"20K followers?" Emily scoffed, pointing to the follower and subscriber counter at the bottom of the video. "Please, I have 50K follows on Bang-Bang. Why don't you have a Bang-Bang?"

Huck had been hearing this for a year now, ever since the stupid video app became popular. "Bang-Bang doesn't monetize," he started. "You may have 50K followers, but linking VOD to my own website allows followers *and* monitizes. And subscribers pay. I may only have 20K followers on VOD, but 12K of those are subscribers who pay each month for the backstage footage." He smiled arrogantly to drive home his point.

Emily backtracked quickly at this, pulling her hand away from the screen. "You should let me do an episode with you," she said with a nervous laugh. "My viewers might come to your website if I'm in it."

Huck saw right through her trick. He glanced at Jasper whose grimace begged him not to saying anything spiteful. He ignored his best friend's plea. "Emily," he said, slapping the laptop closed, "I'm not stupid. I know you want to use *my* fame and success for your own numbers. But trust me, no matter how many you have on that dumb app, you don't make money." He winked at her, clicking his tongue to emphasize his point. He picked up his backpack and marched away, knowing Jasper would follow.

Jasper whispered an apology then ran after him. "You didn't have to be mean about it," he said. He was the only one allowed to give Huck a piece of his mind who Huck didn't retaliate on with the full force of his popularity.

"I won't be used by some high school junior for fame," Huck snapped back. "She can do it on her own, like I did."

"*We* did," Jasper reminded him. He waited a beat then shook his head, smiling. "Why do I put up with you?"

Huck didn't know but he was glad Jasper stuck around. Holly and Richard fought hard to adopt them when they turned thirteen and it had taken a year to legalize everything. Unfortunately, Richard passed from cancer shortly after. High school had been the start of Huck's life and he'd not have traded Jasper's immediate friendship for anything. Or his editing skills. Really, thanks to Jasper, their series, Dark Front Witness, took off the way it did due to his natural talent for marketing and editing.

"I do have a big head sometimes, don't I?" Huck admitted. His phone went off and he checked it. Mark's pale face and blue eyes showed up on the caller ID. Huck groaned. "Hold up, Jas, it's Mark." He slid into the boy's room and motioned angrily for a freshman to get out. The boy did, recognizing Huck and Jasper. He answered. "What?"

Mark's voice wavered, breathing quietly on the other end. He didn't say anything.

"Mark?" Huck stopped and turned the phone onto speaker for Jasper to hear. "What's wrong? You ok?"

"H-huck," Mark's voice trembled like he shivered. "It's looking at me. It's got white eyes. It's in the closet. Just like you said. Come home, please."

Jasper grabbed Huck's arm.

"No, no," Huck whispered, shaking his head. He'd seen a shadow in that closet almost every night for the last four years. He'd described it once to Jasper. But not to Mark. Didn't everyone have a monster in their closet they swore they could see?

"Yeah, it's there," Mark whispered. "Huck, it's making a sound. I-I think it's calling my name. It's angry at me. I don't know what it wants. Please, come home."

Then, Mark screamed so loud the speaker crackled.

Not waiting, Jasper grabbed Huck's arm and pulled him out into the parking lot where his car waited.

"He's just freaking out," Huck tried to reason. "He's on too many pain meds or something." But he got in and let Jasper peel out of the high school parking lot. "I've seen shadows and ghosts as long as I can remember." Saying it out loud sent a shiver down his spine. "They're not real," he said more to himself.

"Like that time you had a panic attack in the basement?" Jasper asked. "We do this series to catch stuff like that and put it out into the world. Don't you believe it?"

"No," Huck growled, digging his nails into his thighs. The time in the school's basement made his hair stand on end just thinking about it. He thought he'd seen someone hanging from the pipes, a boy about his age. But he'd blinked and it was gone. "It's not real," he murmured.

JASPER FOLLOWED Huck as he walked slowly into the house. Holly was gone at work at the hospital. The house was empty.

"Mark?" Huck called. He shivered. His breath rose in hot mist before him.

"Cold spots," Jasper whispered.

"Shut the hell up," Huck groaned, making his way to the back of the house where their bedroom was. But the hairs on the back of his neck wouldn't lay back down and the tension down his spine grew. "Mark?"

He quickly shoved the door open. The moment Huck opened the door, Mark collapsed onto his bed like he'd been standing on it. Mark gasped, sobbing loudly.

"Leave me alone!" he begged, scrambling to press himself against the wall, away from the foot of the bed.

Huck's eyes shot around, looking for an intruder. Nothing moved but for a few hanging pieces of clothing in the closet that swung slightly. Had he seen a slight depression at the foot of the bed? *No!* he chided himself. *Not real.*

Seeing his twin, Mark dashed across the room to him, throwing his arms—one wrapped in a hard cast from the crash—around his neck. He sobbed into Huck's shoulder, shaking like a wet cat. Jasper rubbed his back gently.

"Ok, ok. Relax, Mark," Huck breathed, leading his brother out of the room. The house suddenly felt much warmer. "Jasper, will you make that coco stuff Holly has hidden on the top shelf?"

Jasper ran ahead while Huck practically carried Mark to the kitchen table. Shaking still, Mark sat down, eyes trained on Huck like he feared Huck too might disappear into a dark corner.

"I saw it," Mark whispered, his face red from crying. Huck spotted bruises around his neck. "That shadow person you used to talk about," Mark went on, reaching out to take Huck's hand.

Huck let him but didn't move to comfort his twin. "Mark, all kids see monsters in their closet. I told you it was never real."

"But you said it was," Mark begged. His eyes rounded with terror. That's when Huck noticed that they were no longer blue. One had turned a vibrant green. "I've seen it ever since I came back from-from the accident," he stammered. "You saw them too, you said you did!" His voice mounted, pleading with Huck to admit it. "Remember when we-we filmed at the dam? And you said you saw that drowned woman?"

Yeah, he remembered. He'd been terrified. But he wasn't about to tell Mark that.

Mark swallowed so hard Huck heard him gulp. He still shook. "And the time the shadow was in the curtains? And when—"

"Yeah, well it's not real." He doubled down. He rubbed Mark's forearm and felt something wet and sticky. Looking down, his heart skipped a beat. Blood covered his hands. Turning Mark's arm over, he found a huge, long gash going from Mark's palm to the crook of his elbow. "Shit! Jasper, call an ambulance!" he shouted.

The world tilted around Huck then. The kitchen spun and the ground moved so he could barely stand up. "Mark, what did you do?" he asked, panic straining his voice.

"We'll drive him," Jasper shouted, dropping his camera and running to grab Mark as he started to pass out.

The world whirled around Huck.

Chapter 3:

Brother's Keeper

Holly ran to the emergency entrance and scooped Mark from Huck's arms. Tears flooded down her passive, numb face.

"Are you all right?" she asked Huck as more emergency staff came to load Mark onto a bed.

Huck nodded. "I'm fine, Holly, but he needs some professional help. He wants to kill himself over some girl?"

Holly glared at him as the staff rushed Mark through the swinging doors. "You don't mean that, baby." Her hand was bloody as she gently touched his cheek. "Jasper, watch him, will you?"

She ran after her son, her blue scrubs blending in with the faded powder blue walls. Huck waited a minute then headed to the exit.

"Where are you going?" Jasper asked, running after him. "Don't you want to wait to hear if he's ok?"

"Not really," Huck said as aloofly as he could. "If he wants to be like that, over some girl, he can."

Jasper stopped in his tracks. "How can you be like this? He's your brother."

"Yeah," Huck snapped, turning on his heel to glare down at Jasper. "I'm not his keeper. What he does with himself is up to him. I tried to be there for him for the last two weeks. He cut himself off from us, ok? He wanted to be alone. So he can."

He shoved open the hospital doors and marched toward Jasper's car. "You going to drive me home or do I have to order a rideshare?"

Sighing sadly, Jasper went around to the driver's side door. "I'll take you home. But you have to listen to me on the way back."

Huck braced himself for whatever sermon Jasper had prepared and hardly heard a word the entire way home. Jasper went on about how they'd been through so much together and that just this once, Huck needed to try to be a little selfless.

"Remember when you first showed up at Holly's?" Jasper asked. He drove deliberately slow and took a rout around the park since the drive would be too short for him to berate Huck as much as he wanted otherwise.

Huck frowned out the window. A light rain began, spattering the glass and making the streets morph into odd, glowing shapes. "Yeah? Vividly. We had everything we owned in black trash bags. She was horrified."

Jasper smiled for a minute. "I forgot about that. But not that. You ran away."

Now he knew where Jasper was going. He collapsed a little into the seat, his ego taking a blow. "Yeah. I did. I was ready to hate them because everyone said foster parents were evil. We were maybe eight?" He couldn't remember. That life was so far removed from the last four years of his life.

"And who found you?" Jasper asked.

"Sheriff Logan," Huck quipped. "I was hiding under his cruiser. He'd just got the job as the captain of the Ad Astra

Rangers." He smiled. "That state trooper guy—what was his name?—was so mad." His smile slid off his face. "I tried to break into the cruiser. Thinking I could sleep in it. Logan came out and caught me. Shit, I was so scared."

Jasper nodded, waiting for him to go on.

Huck looked down at a black leather bracelet on his wrist and fiddled with a fraying bit. "I begged him not to call Holly and Richard. He didn't. I don't know how, but he found Mark wandering the streets. He was looking for me." The memory overtook Huck. The chill of that night came back. It had been raining then too. Mark was soaked, lips blue, and face pale.

"Logan thought it was me," Huck went on. "Thought I'd escaped his house while he was scouting around. But Mark explained everything. Logan knew Holly, so he knew exactly where we belonged. But he let us stay. I think he called her and told her what was going on, but lied to us, saying we could bunk down."

They passed under a light that didn't match the other street lights. This one bright blue while the others still glistened yellow.

"Mark was...upset with me. I told him he didn't have to come after me." He laughed, shoving the memory away and the feelings of shame that came with it. "Holly was pissed. Richard was always the calmer one. I thought they wouldn't care if they lost me. They still had Mark."

"You have a habit of using those around you," Jasper said. This drew Huck's attention to him as they pulled into his driveway.

"That sounds like something you want to complain about," Huck said, opening the door.

"Wait," Jasper said, grabbing Huck's arm. Huck sat back down in the car.

"I'm the front man for Dark Front, Jasper, and that won't change."

Jasper hammered his palm three times hard on the steering wheel. "Damn it, Huck, that's not what I'm talking about! I'm fine being tech on our show. Your lack of concern for Mark is what actually freaks me out. Do you ever have anyone else's well being on your mind? Ever? What if I was in danger somewhere? Like, if a serial killer was chasing me with his creepy mask and chainsaw? Would you just up and leave me?"

Now Huck smiled, but Jasper's words hit him deep. "What am I supposed to do for Mark?" he asked. He was shocked to hear genuine concern in his voice. "I tried to be there for him. He just kept turning me away."

"Then just hang around," Jasper offered. "Sometimes people are so wrapped up in their grief and their demons, they don't know what to do. The don't choose to be like that. You can't leave them alone."

That didn't sound like a good solution. With Mark out of the videos, they'd lost views and a few subscribers. For some reason, the viewers liked Mark more. They even talked about Jasper in the comments more than they talked about him. But it was his show. It was his idea to do high-quality ghost hunts and stupid things like buying cursed objects off the internet.

"Ok, well, let's look into that abandoned manor again," he suggested. "I'll ask Mark to come along," he added quickly.

His best friend licked his lips and stared out the front of the window. "I don't think that will be enough, Huck. I think you need to stop making episodes for a bit and hang out with Mark. He's going through some stuff and needs support."

"Jasper," Huck said, fixing his hair in the rearview mirror. "Don't worry so much. He'll be fine."

"You heard him tonight, right?" His voice dropped. "You

only told me about the shadow man. He described exactly what you said to me not four years ago."

The tiny hairs on Huck's arm stood up. He shook the feeling away. "Damn paralysis demons," he laughed. He shoved the door open again and left Jasper behind in the rain.

Chapter 4:
Down the Road

"**M**ake sure you get my new haircut in good light," Huck said with a wink and a smile as Jasper danced around a hole in the rotting floor. "And get one side with my blue eye and another shot with my green."

Jasper tried desperately to keep the camera on Huck as they walked down the abandoned house's halls and around corners.

"You're walking too fast," Jasper grunted, taking a wide step over a suspicious white patch of wood floor while holding the large camera on his shoulder. "And it's three in the morning. It's dark. No one can see your hair."

Huck stopped so suddenly Jasper almost ran into him; he clutched the camera, losing his balance from trying to not run into Huck.

"Good thing this isn't a livestream episode," Huck snarled. He looked into the camera and said "Cut," loudly, telling himself for later where to edit the video. "What's the point of our 100K subscriber special and the new camera if they can't see me?"

Jasper patted the new piece of tech on his shoulder,

looking at it lovingly. "I guess I could mess with the settings. See if your black hair will stand out in this black house." He looked up with just his eyes. "Holly said to be back by now. We still have an hour drive home. And I have a Spanish test tomorrow. Er, today."

Huck didn't smile back. He motioned for Jasper to start recording again.

Jumping right back into his part, Huck smiled broadly and gazed into the lens. "It's almost three in the morning, and if legend holds true, the ghost of Lady Wentwal will appear sometime within the hour. The locals say she took her life on the top floor." He looked down the dark hall to the winding Victorian stairs dramatically. "We have a ways to go. And with all the rot and mold, this is a dangerous journey with or without ghosts."

"What are you doing?" Jasper groaned, dropping the camera from his shoulder.

"Narrating for our viewers?" Huck shrugged, smoothing his manicured eyebrows. "Trying to build suspense? What are *you* doing?"

Jasper sighed and rubbed his eyes violently, looking away from his co-host into the dim light from the window. "You're doing something weird with your lips and squinting too much."

"It's called a look," Huck argued, making sure his t-shirt was untucked just right from the side of his designer jeans. "Makes my cheek bones look sharper. Plus, makes me look boyish." He smiled at Jasper and pointed finger-guns at his friend. "Ratings and views! We've almost made it, we have to up our game now."

"The stuff we capture on camera gets us ratings and views. Just like always." Jasper reached forward to adjust the mic clipped to the front of Huck's shirt.

Huck scoffed. "Maybe I'll think about quitting again? Leave you and your scrawny ass to film, investigate, and edit alone?"

"Mark will feel like hunting again, just you wait." Jasper didn't even flinch at the threat. "I know this whole ghost hunting thing is a joke to you, but my thing is honesty. I need your stupid face. We're making enough for college, now. Can you at least pretend you like your job like the rest of the world?"

Huck pulled his pewter talisman necklace out from under his shirt. "We'll need to do another take. I forgot to have this out." He didn't look up, but heard Jasper sigh. He waited a beat, then said, "I don't know if Mark will ever want to hunt again after…" He quickly avoided eye contact, casting his head up and down the hallway. "Holly brought him home today."

Jasper's mouth popped open. "So that's why you insisted on coming today. Shit, Huck. Shouldn't you be home to see him?"

"Nope," Huck quipped back.

Just then, Huck's phone vibrated, and he jumped at the opportunity to look at the alert rather than watch his best friend's disappointed face.

The text from his twin brother went on for several screens. The punctuation was all over the place and nothing made sense. Like Mark was drunk texting. Huck groaned and scrolled through it quickly, only catching bits here and there. There was only one sentence coherently typed: Please come home.

Huck quickly typed, "Figure it out, Mark. I'm working. I don't have time to babysit you." He sent the text, and looked up at Jasper's face. His friend had a way of looking sad, eager, and pushy at the same time.

Huck smiled. "Let's go find the lady of the manor, shall we?"

THE SETTING MOON splashed a deep blue and white across the sky as the boys loaded up their static cams, mics, and other equipment. The dew made the air taste clean, fresh.

Huck went to his side of the car and stood in the open door. Remembering the text from his brother, he opened his phone. He had a voicemail. He hadn't even felt his phone vibrate. Curious, he held the phone to his ear and listened. It was Mark. The first few seconds were just Mark breathing into the phone.

Finally, his voice broke in a quiet sob. "Leave me alone," he begged something.

A tiny trickle ran down from the nape of Huck's skull. His hair stood on end. He'd felt similar sensations when a supposed spirit or ghost made something move or spoke in the spirit box while they filmed. The feeling didn't always accompany those instances. Only sometimes. Those were the times he hated most.

"What is it?" Jasper asked, leaning over the car top. "Excuse the colloquialism, but you look like you've seen a ghost. Are you sick?"

His gut turned like it did when he ran a red light. A surge of adrenaline raced up his spine now. He swallowed hard and looked over at Jasper. His friend's eyes danced between his dual-colored ones.

Closing the door, Jasper came to his side. "What the hell, dude? What's the text about?"

"Wait," Huck whispered. His lungs wouldn't take in air. "Something's wrong."

Mark's voice shuddered. "I can't anymore. I don't know what's happening." He inhaled sharply then screamed, "What do you want from me!"

A high, shrieking call came over the phone, followed by a string of curses from Mark. Then, a clattering sound told Huck Mark had dropped the phone.

Around them, the crickets and other night creatures faded into the mist. Silence fell.

A jolt ran up Huck's arm from his phone. His arm dropped and he staggered back against the car. Every inch of him grew clammy. He knew what had happened before he could say it. His chest constricted and he couldn't breathe. Jasper rushed to his side. Confused, Huck wonder how he knew what had happened. Like some part of him was gone now. Forever taken away. Unsure why, a tear spilled down the corner of his right eye.

The vibration tingled his too-sensitive fingers. The phone screen glowed with the name "Holly" followed by a heart and the eye-roll emoji.

Jasper sighed, growling loudly. "What happened? Huck? Are you ok?"

Huck took a couple of breaths before answering the phone. He tried to laugh off the fright and sat in the passenger side of the car. "Hey, mom," he wheezed, running his hand through his thick, black hair.

"Huck, baby?" she managed between gasping sobs. "I need you to come home, okay? Mark, he... Hun, your brother, he..." she couldn't finish.

It didn't matter. His lips went numb and he couldn't reply. His arm, though it was heavy as a bucket of stones, didn't drop his phone. It wouldn't move from his ear as his mom continued to beg him to come home, telling him how she found Mark. The details blurred together in a monotone.

Eventually, he hung up. His throat went so dry he could barely reply to her.

"What is it, Huck?" Jasper whispered. He hadn't started the car yet, kneeling outside the passenger side.

Huck hadn't noticed him there. The pressure in Huck's face tricked him into thinking they had been moving at a high speed for the entire conversation with his mom.

"We have to go home," he croaked. He looked down and touched the dark screen of his phone. "Mark..." Dare he say it? He'd felt it before Holly said it. He'd known. How? "Mark's dead."

Jasper immediately reached out and put his hand on Huck's limp arm. "Damn, Huck, I—I..." Jasper gulped. "What happened?"

He fixed his eyes outside the car. "Took..." His voice caught. He cleared his throat, eyes falling to his phone. "Took his life. She found him..." He couldn't go on. Holly didn't deserve that. How could Mark do that to her? His face burned.

Shocked into silence, Jasper didn't move. "What can I do?" he whispered.

Huck sucked in his lower lip and nodded. "Drive."

Jasper got up without a word and slid into the driver's side. "Huck, we shouldn't have gone. I knew we should have stayed—"

"I get it!" Huck snapped, finally meeting Jasper's eyes. "Shut up and drive."

OF COURSE it rained the day of the funeral. Typical October weather in Kansas. The muscles in Huck's brows hurt from glaring hard for the past three days while Holly ran around making funeral arrangements. She'd not said a word to him now in almost forty-eight hours. He'd not spoken either. He'd always addressed her as Holly. Mark called her mom. He wanted to call her mom now, but didn't want to hurt her even more. She always said Richard was the only one who could tell their voices apart. If he called her mom now, it might break her to hear Mark's voice.

When he got home from the ghost hunt that night, he'd gone to his room but couldn't sleep in it with Mark's bed empty. He'd gone to the bathroom to wash up before sleeping on the couch but had frozen in the bathroom doorway. The bathtub was stained red. The rugs were gone, no doubt soaked in Mark's blood. The shower curtain had red smeared all over it. Part of it was ripped down like Holly had gripped it to steady herself. She'd found Mark here. He hadn't known that. The house was empty when he got home because Holly had rushed Mark's already lifeless body back to the emergency room. When Jasper came over the next day, he called for a cleaning service to come and remove the blood. He hadn't spoken. Holly didn't say a word. So Huck didn't speak either. Jasper took care of everything. Huck had never been an emotional boy, but he knew he owed Jasper.

Now the three of them stood together as the priest said some final words and lowered Mark's coffin into the ground next to Richard. Jasper's parents left him to stay with Huck and Holly but he hardly noticed his best friend there. Holly had fought to not cry in front of Huck but he heard her at night. During those nights, he didn't even check his phone, hearing it buzz every few minutes with Emily or Kate trying to reach him. He'd not been back to school since.

Logan, the sheriff, came to the funeral too, even though he worked night shifts. He'd known both boys for the last four years, having been a safe adult to go to when they got in trouble with Holly and Richard. He didn't press Huck to talk and left with the rest of the crowd, squeezing Huck's shoulder on the way out.

Holly's eyes were hidden under large black sunglasses. Huck couldn't guess her mood. Her full lips were pressed together so hard, they turned to thin lines. Jasper held her hand, stoic and quiet. One of the service leaders handed a shovel towards Holly so she could toss the first of the burial dirt onto her son's coffin. She didn't move, unable to reach out and take it. Jasper nodded to Huck.

Forcing his stiff body to move, Huck took the shovel and shoved it into the pile of graveyard dirt. He held it for a second, looking down at the silver coffin. Somehow, tossing the dirt onto it made it seem real. Final. No going back. But there was already no going back, right?

With a shuddering breath, he heaved it into the pit. It sounded so loud when it thudded against Mark's coffin. Unable to wait for the man to take back the shovel, Huck tossed it to the ground and shrank away like it might attack him. Jasper gripped his shoulder with his other hand to steady him.

"Mrs. Derringer?" a weaselly voice said from behind them.

Holly turned around, quickly swiping at her eyes under her sunglasses. She wore them even though it was raining. "Yes?" she asked.

Huck faced the guy too. He wore a gross, brown suit with a yellow tie. Everything was too big for him. He didn't carry an umbrella, his hair slipping over his bald head to show his shiny scalp underneath where it thinned. He held a manilla envelope in his stubby fingers. Holly stiffened.

The man handed her the parcel. "You've been served," he mumbled. He nodded to the priest then looked at the casket in the ground. "Apologies. But I knew you'd be here today."

He left. Huck's constant glower deepened. He didn't know what was inside, just knew it was legal business. Only someone who works for the government could look that bad.

Holly cursed. This startled Huck. He'd only heard her curse a few times in his life. "He's suing us," she said, speaking for the first time in days. "That bastard."

"Who?" Jasper asked when Huck couldn't manage to speak.

"That jerk who..." She swallowed, "who Mark and Alisha hit. He wants to sue us for over sixty thousand in damages."

At this, Huck's heart fell. Holly didn't make near enough. She hadn't had a savings account since he'd known her. How could someone sue a single mother just after she buried one of her children? Huck was at a loss for words.

"Settle out of court," Jasper suggested. "Isn't that what they do in the movies?"

Holly sighed despondently. "If he will."

"We'll pay in full," Jasper went on. He nudged Huck. "Right? DarkFront's bank account has enough."

His mouth fell open at this and even Holly took a step back. "I can't ask you guys to do that," she protested. "This is...adult stuff. You don't need to worry about it."

"That was our college fund," Huck murmured to Jasper.

"Does that matter right now?" Jasper said. He gave Huck a meaningful glance then nodded towards Holly.

Black tear tracks flowed from under her sunglasses. She'd tried to hide her sadness from him, be strong for him.

"Yeah," he said finally. "Mom, I'll pay it if he'll settle outside of court."

Something lit under Holly's Black skin when he called

her mom. She smiled and her cheeks turned red. She sniffled. "Thanks, baby." She pulled him into a hug. "He better, or else."

JASPER SPENT with Huck the night after the funeral. He and Huck sat on the floor in the living room with only one yellow lamp on, both working on their laptops. A pile of sandwiches sat uneaten on the coffee table where Holly had placed them before going to bed.

"We need something big," Huck sighed, searching for popular haunted places near their county.

"I'm thinking multiple episodes," Jasper suggested. "Like a mini series. We can film it all over a few days then release an episode every three days? Skipping weekends."

Huck nodded, listening to the back of the house. Holly had stirred and he heard her grabbing her robe to come out. He shot up, ran into the kitchen and nabbed the bottle of vodka he'd found that afternoon when they got home from the funeral. Jasper was about to ask him what he was doing when Huck shoved it under the cushions of the couch and then sat on them. He motioned for Jasper to hand him his laptop, which he did.

Holly came out, red-eyed from crying and walked past them like a zombie. She went right to the cabinet Huck had just pilfered and opened the doors, scanning the inside. She sighed. She leaned back to look at them and Huck lowered his eyes quickly. Not finding the vodka, she went to the fridge and took out an entire casserole a neighbor had brought over and traipsed back to her room.

"How'd you know?" Jasper asked.

"Logan told me," he confessed. "He said it wouldn't be

wrong to take it from her." He fiddled with a sticker on the laptop that was coming loose. "I've seen enough in the system to know I don't want her near that stuff. Especially right now."

Jasper nodded. He stood up and joined Huck on the couch. "I don't want to make anything weird," he started, "but I'm here for you, ok? Like, anything you want to say, you can say to me. Even if it sounds stupid."

Just as Jasper said that, the familiar sound of the latch on his closet door clicked open. A taste of metal filled his mouth as the hairs on the back of his neck stood up. He swore something whispered behind him.

"Coven Wood," he said, shaking off a shiver. "That entire town is haunted. It's a good drive from here, but that's ok. I don't think anyone has ever covered it before. Especially around here."

"All right," Jasper agreed. "I'll get started on the research." He eyed Huck. "If you want to back out, just let me know. Should we wait till Holly's a little better?"

Huck nodded. He focused on a dark corner of the living room. Was something breathing there? Watching him? "Don't worry, Jas," he whispered. "This stuff isn't real. I can handle it." Now more than ever, he needed a distraction.

Chapter 5:

Coven Wood

"There's probably a gas station in town," Huck sighed, looking down at this phone, trying to track their progress.

"Can you search?" Jasper asked, unwilling to take his eyes off the road that wound through the tightly packed forest. The dirt road was so narrow that if another car came in the opposite direction, they'd have to swerve to avoid a collision. Not that they could see another car coming; the road twisted and turned so much Jasper had slowed to a crawl.

"Service sucks too much," Huck replied. "There is something there though, I can see the white outlines of a city or something."

The two boys sunk back into the silence that dominated their trip so far. The long drive from Boaz to the spot marked on their map close to the northern state line had only been broken by calls from Holly and the stops they made along the way.

They passed the boundaries of the forest. Ahead, the darkening sky glowed with the white light that only comes from a city in the middle of nowhere.

"See? Coven Wood," Huck smiled. "Let's get a place to sleep and get our bearings. Service might be better too."

"Hey," Jasper piped up, his voice rising more than it had since they left Boaz. "Remember that guy who reached out to us like two months ago?"

Huck could hardly remember a time before the car accident that started the Autumn from hell. He stayed quiet, knowing Jasper would go on whether he said he remembered or not.

Jasper pulled a colorful sticky note out of his pocket. "Valon Gabriel," he read. "He has that exorcism show on day time. I got an auto reminder that I haven't replied to his email. Should we? Could be a potential break for the show. Bigger audience. Coupled with the numbers we hope to get from this mini series, it could really replenish our bank accounts."

Huck rolled his eyes, remembering the cheesy TV show host now. "That message was so shady, I cannot believe you are bringing it up. And no one with their sanity intact calls themselves an exorcism show." Huck leaned his head back and closed his eyes. "Maybe later."

"It's time for DarkFront to get sponsors," Jasper tried again. "He's bigger than we are. We deal in shady," Jasper pointed out before trailing off. "What the..."

Huck opened his right eye and looked sidelong out his window. "The hell?"

They broke into a clearing from the trees where the hills that rose up to the right dissolved into white mist seemingly oozing up from the earth. The trees barely peeked out from the sudden haze. Both boys leaned to the right and squinted to get a better look.

"Jasper!" Huck screamed, pointing out the front.

In a moment of sheer terror, Jasper screamed and cranked

the wheel to the left, peeling out on the damp asphalt. The car spun twice, tires screaming and burning rubber, before it jolted to a stop. Huck gripped the dashboard and his head smacked the window when the car jolted to a stop. Their panting filled the silence.

"What?" Jasper gasped, grabbing his friend's arm. "Why the hell did you grab the wheel?"

Huck didn't answer. He hadn't realized he'd grabbed the wheel and turned the car. His eyes danced back and forth between the high beams before them. He couldn't say what he'd seen. *Jasper, I saw a woman in white, completely made of smoke, hit the hood of your car.*

"I don't know. I'm sorry," he managed. Spinning around, he fixed his eyes on the misty hills again. Were those three pyres of fire behind the trees? Was that where the smoke came from? The more he watched, the more cultish vibe he got. One of the pyres looked to be in the shape of an upside down star.

Jasper flung open the car door and ran to inspect the front. Not seeing anything, he snapped his head around to see if he could catch anything fleeing.

"What are you doing?" Huck cried, a shiver running up his arms. Something screamed at him, warning that Jasper needed to get back into the car. They needed to keep moving.

"I thought I felt us hit something," Jasper called. He leaned in, the beams illuminating his pale face. "There's a small dent."

It's not real, Huck thought to himself, eyes glued to the fire behind the trees. The shadows of the trees beamed down the hillside. If someone was up there, there was no way they missed the screaming car tires and flood lights. "Get in the car, Jas," he called. Something was coming.

The moment that thought hit him, he felt a dozen pairs of eyes turn on him. "Jas, get in the car," he ordered.

Jasper knelt down, disappearing under the front of the car, looking for whatever they had hit.

Something came towards him. It wanted him. It was running at him, calling up something to track him down. "Jasper!" he screamed.

The sensation took him. A metallic tingling down from the nape of his skull. An involuntary shiver. He all but saw something watching them out of the trees. His brain said eyes were on him, but he couldn't spot them.

His friend ran inside at the terror in his voice and slammed his door shut, looking around. The light lit up the meadows around them and part of the trees approaching on the other side. Nothing moved.

"What's going on?" Jasper asked, facing Huck. He looked earnest, willing to believe anything Huck told him.

"Get us to a hotel," Huck whispered. He pushed the lock in. "We'll continue later. In daylight."

"I lost the city," he apologized.

"Then go back," Huck snapped. His palms were so clammy, he had to wipe them on his jeans. Whatever had run towards him, scaring him, laughed now. He sunk his head into his shoulders and looked around. "Drive."

Jasper took them back the way they'd come and spotted Coven Wood not a few miles off from where they guessed they'd gotten lost. In silence, they found the one motel in town and got a room. The lady who checked them in didn't say a single word to them as they paid. Jasper showered but Huck couldn't make himself move from the squeaky bed once he'd sat on it. The old feeling of being five years old and thinking a monster lived under the bed washed over him. He wrapped his arms around his knees and waited for Jasper to reemerge. When he did, Huck laid down and tried to sleep. Jasper let him alone but it was well past three in the morning before sleep finally took Huck.

"IT WAS a cannibalistic cult possessed by the ghosts of aliens," Jasper said, smiling, as he chased Huck around the back of the car where he loaded up their bags from the motel they stayed in. "I looked it up last night. I had to pay big bucks to use the computer in the office and their dial up since there's no service, but that just adds to the weirdness of Coven Wood. How is it not interesting? On top of that, this town is basically New Coven Wood. The old town was deeper into the forest and was absolutely emptied. Just like Roanoke. It was in 1915 or so."

"Get to the good part," Huck said, slamming the trunk closed once he'd replaced all the equipment in it. They never left their expensive tech in the car over night.

"Cannibal, alien-worshiping ghosts!" Jasper repeated. He'd gotten all his spunk back in the light of day after a night of sleep and motel TV.

"That's too many boxes to tick," Huck said. "Our audience will laugh us out. And this Coven Wood place is giving me the shivers. I don't like the way the people just look out from behind the windows. Remember that movie *House of Wax*?"

"Remake or original?" Jasper asked. He glanced around at the shops that were opening on the same street as the motel. A few eyes glanced out of windows towards them.

"Remake," Huck shot. "That's exactly what this feels like."

Jasper stopped. His hands fell to his side. "Why did you

even drag me over here, then? You're a god-awful, stubborn skeptic. And you run a ghost hunting series."

To avoid answering, Huck glared at Jasper over the top of the car. "Stop trying to make me feel bad." The shiver that accompanied his lies cooled his flesh. He knew he could easily manipulate Jasper that way. It worked.

"You're right. I'm sorry," Jasper sighed, tapping the top of his car. He pulled a map out of a bag of snacks he'd bought at the convenience store. "Let's head down the road. Crone's Trail is nearer that national forest. We can get some filming in of the surrounding area before our night session."

IT TURNED OUT, the road wasn't marked on the map. More than once, they pulled over to rub mud off a road sign to see where they were. The signs claimed it was Highway 89 but that wasn't on the map. Huck couldn't even remember a Highway 89 in Kansas. Other signs were covered in graffiti of badly drawn runes or unreadable letters. The same vandal had marked almost every sign they came upon. The boys got turned around again and again—every time they thought they were close. Before they knew it, noon came and went. Finally, Jasper suggested going back to Coven Wood for directions. Annoyed, and tired of being in the car, Huck agreed.

But they couldn't find it.

"These damn trees!" Huck shouted, pounding the trunk of the car when they pulled over near five in the evening. "We can't see anything."

Jasper took his pack out of the trunk. "Let's walk a bit. If we don't find anything in an hour, we can turn back."

"Sun sets in an hour and a half," Huck sighed, checking

his phone. "And it's supposed to rain tonight. Temperatures will drop."

Jasper shrugged. "We'll sleep in the car, like real ghost hunters. C'mon, Huck. Go on an adventure."

Something inside Huck turned a cog. Looking into Jasper's pleading green eyes, he suddenly got the feeling that if he said no, he'd regret it for the rest of his life. He could give his friend this. Almost smiling, he shook his head and opened his mouth to reply.

He froze. A feeling, like recalling a dream, said that if he said yes, he'd never see Jasper again.

No, that was weird talk. He didn't believe in that kind of feeling or vibration or whatever. He was just creeped out about the events from the night before.

"Fine," he smiled, heaving his pack onto his shoulder. "Into the woods to look for alien ghosts."

Chapter 6:

Taken

"I see a sign with lights!" Jasper crowed in delight. The sun went down about half an hour ago, and Huck didn't care enough to argue with his friend with the cold rain starting to soak their clothes. "That has to be a gas station."

"Good, I'm dying of thirst," Huck sighed through his chattering teeth. They'd taken off their packs and held them in front to try to keep the equipment dry.

They came into a gravel clearing after breaking through the trees. A soft, white glowing sign several yards away read, "Coven Wood Bed and Breakfast" with a vacancy sign blinking half-heartedly. Blocking their view of whatever lay beyond was the most ancient house Huck had ever seen. It had that old south kind of facade, a big porch, and every window was dark.

"A bed-and-breakfast?" Jasper asked. He looked around. "How did we end up back in Coven Wood?" He squinted back the way they'd come, looking for signs of the small town. The glare and fog from the rain cut off anything beyond the first bend in the road.

Every window of the motel offered only a black square of

nothing. No light. Not even a set of yellowing blinds. Huck doubted it was operational. Up a hill to the left, an even older house sat overlooking the gravel parking lot and sign.

"Hey," Huck laughed, pointing. "It's the Bates Motel."

Jasper sighed and punched his shoulder. "Don't even joke about that right now. This place is checking off everything on the creepy list I keep in my head."

He followed Jasper down the gravel parking lot, their foot falls overly loud, echoing up into the cold night air.

"Hey, there's an old general store." Jasper's tone was way more delighted than it should have been.

A structure off to the left and slightly hidden behind the bed-and-breakfast appeared from the mist. A few old-style gas pumps stood at attention in front of the shop. The lights inside somehow looked on and off at the same time. No movement came from the inside, but the pipes on top steamed. Not so much as the laugh track on an old black and white sitcom came muffled from the inside.

"It looks *really* dead, Jas," Huck mused incredulously. Despite saying this, Huck found himself drawn up the steps of the bed-and-breakfast.

"I bet the front desk is in the store," Jasper said, grabbing Huck's arm and pulling him towards the little shop.

The door opened, and not so much as a bell signaled his entrance. The air inside was colder than the November chill outside. "Hello?" Huck called into the foyer. In the corners of the room, cobwebs gently lilted on the draft. It was painted that odd hospital blue with chunks of drywall scraped out. The shelves were sparsely filled, and the products were dusty.

"Two?"

The high, ecstatic feminine voice made them both jump. A short woman with waist-length brown hair appeared from a back room. She wore too many hemp necklaces around her thin neck and had moon and star tattoos on her fingers.

"One room if it's ok," Jasper asked, still cringing from the scare.

"Sure," she smiled. "It's easier that way."

Huck frowned.

"Two in one room is just more convenient," she said again, handing them a dusty set of keys. Her eyes lingered long on Huck's face. "So happy you're here." To Jasper she said, "You're not bad."

She spoke whimsically, like she was looking into somewhere else while speaking to them. Like she saw past their flesh to their souls beneath. "The Mother Beldam will be so happy you're here. She rarely comes down from her manor when she visits, but I'll tell her you're here. You'll want to go into the house. The others are there."

"Right." Jasper gingerly took the keys. "Do you know anything about the history of this place? We're looking for Crone's Trail."

"You're on it," the girl replied sweetly. "Old Coven Wood is all around us."

Huck checked his phone. His map showed he was in the middle of nowhere and kept trying to find service to refresh.

"You may have heard of us?" Jasper went on. "We're Dark Front. We make a web series that's pretty popular a few counties over. We wanted to film if that's ok."

Her eyes glassed over even more, her teeth showing behind a false grin. She wouldn't stop looking Huck right in the eyes.

"The web series?" Huck supplied awkwardly. "Ghost hunters?"

The girl nodded. "So you're the one. Tell the guys in the bar. They love that kind of thing. The bar is off to the side of the foyer. Most of them play pool and drink this time of night."

Huck scoffed and looked at the empty, dark parking lot. "Thanks, lady."

The rain slowed when they exited the office, allowing them an easier walk across the empty parking lot and to get their equipment safely inside. Sets of old stairs crawled up the side of the ancient house, allowing each room private access without going through the entryway. Their room was on the bottom floor, though. The room key took some coaxing, but they got inside.

"Oh, wow," Jasper said slowly. He dumped his pack out and immediately prepared his equipment. "Did you see that place?" he gleefully hissed. "This room is no better." He took out a small, handheld camera and started to point it into the corners. A thin layer of dust covered everything. All the furniture and the wallpaper looked like it hadn't been touched since the 80s. "Get the black light," Jasper said, almost too excited to stand still. "There is no way someone has not been murdered here."

Huck grabbed the long black light and flipped the switch. It clicked, but none of the purple light flooded the room. "Dead batteries," he sighed. "I forgot to change them after the Wentwal episode." He looked around, then picked up the recorder. "Let's do some chatting with the locals, then I'll take the batteries out of here for the light."

"Sounds good." Jasper handed Huck the laptop. "Do a search on the place. See what you can find."

"There's no service," Huck said after trying a few times to connect his laptop and phone to anything remotely close. His face lit up. "That's perfect. Roll the camera, get a shot of our phones with no service, and get some shots of the motel room." He pulled out his spirit box and a smaller camera. "Let's go to the bar when we're done."

"IT LOOKS *REALLY* EMPTY," Jasper said for the fifth time as they trekked around to the front of the house. "There are no cars out here."

"You live for this stuff," Huck sighed. "Take it in, go on an adventure, blah-blah-blah."

"But I don't want to die for it."

Ignoring his friend's remark and the tingling at the base of his skull, Huck pushed the door open. The ancient metal hinges creaked, announcing their entry to everyone inside. A heat wave and slow version of *Carry On My Wayward Son* by Kansas pushed into their faces where they stood in the doorway. The sound of pool balls clacking snapped over the chatter and ruckus. A couple of eyes turned to look at them.

Huck spun around to take in the empty parking lot again. Shrugging it off, he led the way in.

The foyer was wide open, with sweeping sets of stairs at the very back. The room was dark with light coming from a dim chandelier far above them. Like the woman said, a pool table stood off to the side in front of an old west bar. Chairs and a few small tables littered that area for socializing. The man behind the bar, staring disdainfully at a tray of glasses, looked up. His blue eye glimmered in the yellow light from the over-hanging light. His green eye continued to glare in the opposite direction. A man at the pool table quickly ran his hand through his long greasy hair, glaring at Huck.

"I'll chat to the guy in the Canadian tux behind the bar," Huck whispered. "Guy playing pool is giving me the death stare. Don't forget to ask them if we can record before you do," he warned Jasper.

"He's just jealous of your good looks," Jasper said good naturedly before parting ways.

They split up, each heading to their designated interviewees. Huck saddled up to the bar and opened his mouth before he knew what to say.

"I'll have beer, shaken, not stirred." He grinned at the bartender as if they shared a secret joke.

"What?" The man's glower deepened, killing Huck's smile. "ID?" he grunted, barely opening his lips.

"Really?" Huck sighed.

"Try me."

Huck pulled his wallet out of his back pocket and tossed his driver's license onto the bar. The man picked it up. Around his forearm, a looping tattoo of what looked like runes circled all the way around. It was old and faded. Some green ink underneath made a phrase in Latin he couldn't make out. The man glared down his bulbous nose at the offending piece of plastic.

"Eighteen. And only just." He sighed, tossing it back. "Shame. You're so young."

"What does that mean?" Huck asked.

The man's blue and green eyes focused on Huck now. "We were all young once." He tilted his head as if to get a better look at Huck. His face fell even more. "Blue and green," he murmured. With that odd statement, he bowed his head and rapped his knuckles on the wood. "Hell, the women are out, so why not?" He turned around and grabbed a beer. Slamming it down, he added, "I'm not shaking it, kid."

Huck looked into the man's mismatched eyes with his own. "Don't see that often," he offered, more humbly than previously. "Holly—my mom—said it meant I was gifted."

To his surprise, the man didn't turn away. He watched Huck half-heartedly as he spoke. "That right, kid?" He picked up an already dry glass and started to rub it with a hand towel. "Shit, I was told the same thing. But sometimes, being gifted ain't enough." He checked out the window into the dark parking lot for something. "Sometimes you gotta know how much you can take."

Huck fought to pry the lid off the bottle. "I guess. It's good for my ratings, at least."

The man nodded. "The witches'll be back soon. They like weird stuff like you."

"Weird?" Huck asked. "Witches? No, I don't believe in that stuff. I just use it for the web series." He pulled out a digital recorder. "Do you mind if I record?"

The man narrowed his eyes. "Sure." He took the beer, used a knife to pop the cap off, and set it back down.

Huck started by talking about the web series and said they were just here to get some shots before moving on to find old Coven Wood. The longer he spoke, the more the bartender seemed uninterested, but would not break eye contact. He polished the same glass for ten minutes.

"What you boys yapping about?" The man from the pool table, who Jasper should have been talking to, joined Huck at the bar, once again flipping his hair back. Up close, Huck saw how once the man must have been attractive, but now used his long hair to cover a growing bald patch. He wore bedazzled jeans and had the same tattoo as the bar tender but with a different word smudged out from age. Huck hoped he never looked as pathetic as this guy.

"Not a thing that concerns you, Simon," the bartender growled, his green eye glaring again. "Mother Beldam is going to want to see this one."

Huck set his beer down, cringing at the taste. "Sorry?"

"You ever done anything nasty, kiddo?" the man named Simon asked with an oily grin. "I've done some messed up shit."

"What do you mean?"

Simon smiled and picked at something between his front teeth. "We are drawn to a certain type, that's all. And, phew! Your friend is a saint."

A rumbling drew both Huck and Simon's eyes back to the bartender. *Was he growling?* Huck thought. Simon threw his hands up in mock surrender.

"Um, yeah. Jasper's the better half." Huck shrugged. "I just like to look out for number one. I don't sugarcoat things. If that's nasty, then I guess I'm the bad guy of the duo."

A new guilt welled up inside him the more he spoke. "I could be nicer, I guess."

A gravelly chuckle emitted from the bartender. "Don't say that. We like 'em tough. You gotta be to make it by. But not so tough as to not break." He smiled so darkly Huck thought the man might eat him whole. "The dirtier the soul, the harder they are to break. The better they crumble when they do. It's delicious."

"Right," Huck smiled nervously.

"Do whatever it takes to survive."

"Yeah." Huck pushed the beer away. What was he thinking? He'd never drank before. The front of his brain fogged over and, for a minute, he thought the barstool he sat on swayed. "Where's my friend?"

The bartender put down the too-clean glass he'd been wiping. "Good question. Byron?" He looked over Huck's head outside, towards the gas station windows.

Jasper shouldn't have left alone. Huck turned to look, too, wondering where he went. He shouldn't have left him alone.

What if he got lost in the dark? Or one of these creeps took him and did awful things to him.

A scream shot up from the back of the house, faint and distant. Huck sat up straight, grabbing the digital recorder. "Did you hear that?" he said, glancing around.

"Damn Byron," the bartender sighed. He flicked his head and two other patrons slinked out the back quickly.

"I should go," Huck said, sliding off the bar stool.

Chapter 7:

Sacrifice

"This place has tunnels, you know," Simon the pool player said, leering down at Huck. He slammed a hand down in front of Huck, cutting off his escape. He checked out the window the same way the bartender had. Not seeing what he looked for, he huffed. "Old house like this has more secrets than rooms, and more rooms than the eye can see."

The bartender glared at Simon.

"Yeah?" Huck asked casually. "Could be cool for a few shots." None of them seemed concerned about the ruckus that had come in from outside. "I gotta find Jasper, though."

"He went to the tunnels," Simon said quickly. "What's this?" He leaned a little too close to Huck and prodded at his spirit box.

"Picks up EVP," Huck explained. "That's Electronic Voice Phenomenon. I think it's kinda kitschy, but Jasper is a big believer in this kind of thing. He's kinda a kook really—"

Both men suddenly stood up, pushing away from the bar. Huck looked around, unaware of whatever drew their attention. "The Mother Beldam," they all whispered in perfect unison. Without warning, they all filed out the front door, leaving him alone.

"Ooh-kay," he sighed. With them gone, he decided to look for the tunnels and find Jasper. He might think every-thing was a big crock of malarkey, but Jasper would love it if he got some shots of a tunnel under the old house. He took his camera, spirit box, and started to snoop around. He checked his phone but had no texts from Jasper or missed calls. Also, still no reception. Had Jasper tried to call?

Making sure to point the camera into every shadowy corner he could, he slowly walked between the set of stairs. Underneath the right set, an old wooden door waited to be opened. He lifted the black iron latch and peeked down. It was darker than where he stood. Not scared, he started down the stairs. He didn't find a tunnel, but he did make his way down to what he thought were rooms converted into offices. The cramped space reminded him of creepy basements he'd encounter in foster homes. It even had an eerie, invisible darkness hanging over it.

Curious, he whipped out his spirit box and turned it on, slipping large headphones over his ears. The white noise filled them. He hooked an AUX cable into his digital recorder that was still going. He carefully stepped over a few odds and ends until he found a set of stairs leading deeper underground.

His hair stood up, and the tingle buzzed at the nape of his neck.

"Is anyone there?" he asked more quietly than he normally would.

The spirit box continued to scratch. He was about to turn away when it skipped.

"What?" he asked the darkness again. His ears pricked up.

"We... down.... ere...." the staccato reply came over the box.

"You are what? Give me a sign, or whatever the hell Jasper always says."

"Ee... r... own... ere..."

"'We are down here'?" he asked.

The pit of his stomach dropped away. The box droned on with its white noise, but he heard beyond it. Underneath the static and skips, a sound rose. Normally, when the box picked something up, it skipped. This time, it just came up under the static. A cry of a thousand voices came from behind a thick black veil.

His senses kicked in like never before. A force inside him shouted for him to leave. Yes, something was down there, something that wanted him. He needed to go. Now.

"Go!" all the voices screamed.

Turning, Huck bolted back up the stairs, a cold sweat making his hands slippery. *This isn't real!* he screamed in his mind, but didn't take the chance.

At the top of the stairs, he pushed the door open back into the lounge. He stopped dead in his tracks.

The room was full again. All eyes on him. None of them moved or spoke. Behind them, the front door hung open. A single sound cut through the silence. Someone panted in sheer horror, choking on blood. Simon, the pool guy from before, stepped aside. Huck's mouth went dry.

Lying across the pool table was Jasper, bloody, crying. Huck's feet froze to the floor and his stomached dropped out.

"We don't typically do this," the bartender said with a grunt. "But the Mother Beldam is coming. We need to be ready."

"And we'll get in trouble if we don't seize this chance," Simon said, crossing his arms like a sulking child.

To the right, in a room that looked like a large dining room, the girl from the store lit black candles on a table covered in a red cloth. She mumbled something, holding an old book in her other hand. She didn't look at Huck or Jasper.

"I've stepped into something you didn't want me to see," Huck wheezed, his entire body shaking. "We'll go. We won't say anything."

"We like dark souls. And yours has blood on it," an old man he hadn't seen before, covered in Jasper's blood, said. "But we need you. Your darkness will just entice the offer. But we still must break you."

Huck took a step back. "Blood on my soul? I've never killed anyone." He couldn't make himself look at Jasper.

The old man hobbled up beside Simon. Dried blood painted his lips bright in his pale face. Had he bitten Jasper? "Lies," he growled like a wolf. "We know a guilty soul when we see one."

The bartender reached back and pulled Jasper forward by his hair. His friend cried in pain. Huck could see now Jasper's leg bled, cut from glass like he'd leapt through a window. So Jasper had been the scream he'd heard before. Bite marks bled on his neck.

"Tell him, kid. Who'd he kill?" the man said, grabbing Jasper's tear-stained face.

Terrified, Huck locked eyes with Jasper. "I haven't. Jasper, you know that. Let us go!" he begged to the still crowd.

Simon snickered. "He is a dirty soul. Not even asking if you're ok." He patted Jasper's bloody face.

"Huck..." Jasper whispered feebly.

"What do you want from me?" Huck shouted, eyes darting to behind the gang to the windows. The front door stood ajar. Just as he plotted his run, he spotted it. Behind the trees, walking slowly towards them, was a woman in black. Her entire figure was hidden behind a black veil.

"Tell us who you killed," the bartender grunted softly, running his fingers over Jasper's face. He forced Jasper's lips open with his fingers so his sobs were louder. "I'd love it if you told us before the Mother Beldam gets here."

Shaking his head, Huck clutched his spirit box, the voices still echoing in his skull. "No one. Never. I'm just a kid!"

"M-Mark," Jasper managed to say. Saliva and blood dribbled from his mouth as he started to lose consciousness.

Ice filled Huck's veins, stopping his heart, and rooting him to the spot. "I didn't," he whispered. "He killed himself."

"That's what I want to hear!" the old man cheered, slamming Jasper's face down with a thud. "Time to go now, boy."

Huck knew immediately that they wanted to hurt him. To kill him. Then it happened.

Black blood oozed slow and thick from the corner where the ceiling met the wall. It stretched down until it pooled on the old wood paneled floor. Huck's eyes snapped from the creeping blood to the inhabitants of the bar. Their flesh moved before his eyes over their bodies: stretching, snapping until it was pulled so tight he could count every rib. Their gaping maws opened in silent, hellish screams and their eyes flamed, now turned to red pits like an endless tunnel to hell itself. Around them swarmed hundreds of black shadow people, flickering. A ghostly red stream pulsed out from each of them, snaking up above.

One of them—almost indistinguishable from the others now—snapped his fleshy, skeleton face towards him. "See something ya like, kiddo? Are you witnessing right now? What does it look like?" The voice sounded as a hundred damned screams and a chorus of devils all at once. Hovering over Jasper, like it waited for his blood, a black, formless shape congealed. Its red eyes locked onto Jasper, waiting for the sacrifice. A long, spidery hand reached down to his best friend. All the ghostly red trails from the people led to this shadow.

Huck blinked, and it all vanished. The oldest man caught the change in Huck's eyes and squinted maliciously. "You did. You witnessed."

"Shit." Huck turned to run.

"Don't run, boy!" the bartender roared, for once raising his voice.

Huck bolted down the stairs the way he'd come. He ran so fast his voice cut out the snapping and static from the spirit box, but once he reached the offices again, he went deeper into the creepy basement. He ran down two sets of three steps. Down here, the basement was unfinished. Concrete. Cold and dark. He ran, realizing he'd found the tunnels.

The network of tunnels froze him for only a minute. They'd know them better than him.

Right... the voice of a young man whispered from nowhere.

This bodiless voice guided him down several twists and turns. A new one chimed in now and then to give him directions. He didn't want to stop and think about it. He just wanted to get out. If he stopped, something behind him would catch up. Something shapeless. Something that wanted him and his screams, to bring him pain. Something that wanted him to believe he'd killed Mark. He could smell the shapeless black. Like burning, molded eggs.

Without warning, Huck ran headlong into something solid. It knocked him off his feet. Looking up in the darkness, he made out the rungs of a ladder. He gripped it, ready to climb.

"Huck!" Jasper's voice cried out from above.

He gripped the wood so hard he thought his fingers would break. There were too many of them. He had to go. He could get help. Digging up the last of his strength, Huck climbed up. He would swear later something grabbed the hem of his jeans and tried to pull him back down.

Breaking the surface, he found himself in the woods again, several yards behind the motel. Knowing the car was close, he scrambled to his feet and ran. He shot a glance around, but no one had left the house. Laying on the ground outside the hotel, beneath a broken and bloodied window, was Jasper's camera. Crying out, Huck ran and grabbed it. It was recording.

"Huckleberry," a sweet, feminine voice sang from the other side of the bed-and-breakfast. A single light in the manor on the hill was lit. "You're the one we need. Come back."

He had to leave everything.

Everyone.

He ran until his lungs burned and his legs went numb. He prayed to any god that would listen that he wouldn't see the fires in the woods again.

The trees remained dark.

Screaming in agonized relief, he caught sight of the car on the side of the dirt road. He didn't slow down, allowing himself to smash into the driver's side door before pulling it open and getting inside. He locked the door and started the car with his own set of keys. He gripped the wheel, shaking, his breath a rasping quiver. He sat, waiting for the shapeless black to appear. For something to run after him, slam into the window.

For the first time in his life, a feeling like black chalk coating his skin covered him. Guilt. Pressing his forehead onto the wheel, he allowed himself to sob.

"I'm sorry, Jasper," he moaned, stepping on the gas. "They wanted me. I should've been the one on that table. They were right."

The tingling he'd felt since going into the basement subsided. He didn't like it. He bit down hard on his bottom lip, denying the sensation as hard as he could in his own head. This was not how he wanted to live his life. Not with this. Seeing the nightmares that others only had to witness in their dreams. He lied to himself for four years about seeing those dark things. But Coven Wood was too real. Jasper's wide, terrified eyes were too real. It was like that place and those people had awakened something in him. Or had they shown him to something?

Maybe that's what drew them to him? The... thing... inside him was what they wanted.

"I'm not foul," he pleaded, hitting the wheel savagely until his palm hurt. Jasper would tell him he wasn't. His friend's bloodied face loomed before his shut eyes.

Should he call the cops? Would there be any use in it? Could they find the devilish motel? He couldn't even tell them where it was. Down some road in the woods. Coven Wood. His arms wouldn't stop shaking. He closed his eyes again, trying to conjure the house in his head. Was there a road? Could someone get *back* to it?

The sun's first rays peaked over the hill and through the branches. Huck sped down the hill towards a small town visible below. A bright slip of paper in the seat next to him caught the morning sun. Looking over, he saw the sticky note with Jasper's handwriting on it. The name of that tele-exorcist written on it: Valon Gabriel.

Whipping out his phone, he quickly searched for the name of the town. Nothing. Then he tried Coven Wood Hotel.

Nothing. Highway 89? Nothing in Kansas, anyway. His phone told him he was on Highway 281 in Smith County.

Everything was gone. Screeching to a halt just outside the town's main road, he dialed 911 and waited. The operator asked him where he was. He couldn't say. He sent his location. He was in Kansas, for sure. When he told them his coordinates, they told him he was in a small town near Lebanon, Kansas.

"No, I'm not," he sobbed into his phone. "I'm west of there, I swear! You have to help me. My friend's been hurt. I-I think they want to kill him."

After that, he couldn't remember what the operator said. He cried into the phone, head down as the quiet town woke up around him. His mind went completely blank. It didn't show him images of the night before, it just turned off. He came to when a gaggle of cop cars surrounded him, lights flashing, and a few curious onlookers squinted at the car. A red-haired woman in a blue uniform approached the window and tapped on it, scaring him half to death.

He got out and found half the town staring at him from behind a line of cop cars and flashing lights. He wrapped his arms around himself and looked around.

"You look confused," the cop mused, pressing her lips together.

"Did you find the house?" Huck asked hoarsely. "What are you doing here? It's back on Crone's Trail."

She frowned. "This is the coordinates the dispatcher gave us, kiddo." Her eyes ran down then up him, taking in his pale, tear-stained face. "Sheriff Savage is on my phone," she offered a little more kindly. "Your mother asked for him to come out when we reported your call to her. Says he is an old friend of the family?"

"Logan?" Huck choked, feeling hope for the first time in days.

"He wants to talk to you," she confirmed. "Damn Ad Astra Rangers think they can just slide into any report. This is my county." She eyed Huck. "Make sure he knows this county's got a sheriff and we don't need the Rangers down here."

Besides being the Sheriff of the county, Logan also was a captain in a special state-wide division of Rangers, giving him powerful jurisdiction anywhere in the state.

Huck grabbed the phone. "Logan?" he croaked. "I'm not lying. They've got Jasper, they took him!" A fresh wave of grief roiled up in him, making him sob. He'd never felt so emotionally broken before in his life. "I think they killed him. They killed him!"

"Listen, kiddo," Logan's calm, deep voice came over the phone. "I know you're freaking out, but it's going to be ok. Once you're back in town, come see me. Cooperate with Sheriff Clark, ok? She'll fill me in on everything you said and anything they find."

He didn't want to hear that. He shook with a disappointed sob. "It's called Coven Wood," he begged his old friend. "Please, please look it up! I can't find it because my phone's not working. We found it before coming up here. They were acting all cryptic and weird. I think they were a cult. They said…" He choked and stopped before saying they wanted him.

"Huck," Logan's voice said sternly. "Take a deep breath. You've been through a lot."

"Logan, they'll kill him!" he begged again. His knees gave out, and he fell to the ground. Sheriff Clark, the red-haired lady, appeared and knelt by him, rubbing his arms comfortingly.

"I swear," Logan said steadily, "we will look into it. The cops are there now, right?"

Huck nodded, sniffling before remembering Logan couldn't see him. "Yeah," he said. "There's a bunch of them here."

"Good," Logan sighed. "Work with Sheriff Clark. She's good people. Then come home, all right? Do you need me to pick you up?"

He'd already had a break down and didn't want to seem as destroyed as he felt. "No. I have... Jasper's car. I can drive home."

A moment of silence fell between Logan and Huck. "Logan, tell Holly I'm fine."

"You got it, kiddo," he promised.

Huck stopped the call and looked up at Sheriff Clark. She didn't simper at him or coo. Her face held stern and solid. "Let's get you off the ground," she said, hoisting him up and taking her phone back. She steered him over to the group in uniforms.

"You look like you've seen a thing or two," Sheriff Clark started, after the EMT planted Huck in the back of the ambulance and swathed him in a blanket. She half-heartedly followed his eyes into the woods, then back. "We combed this place. Nothing like what you said is around here. But we'll keep looking."

Huck shook from the cold and raw fear. His clothes were still wet from the rain the night before. His eyes watered from not blinking. He swore if he blinked, something would come out of the woods in the millisecond his eyes were closed. "It's out there," he croaked.

The woman patted his shoulder kindly. "Sorry, kid. If we find anything about your friend, we'll call you. Sheriff Savage gave us his number and your mother's. In the mean time, we'll file a missing person's report. Now, we need to get you home. You look like you might be ill."

She walked away into the crowd of white cars and flashing lights.

"It's there," Huck repeated. "You just can't see it."

Chapter 8:

Six Months Later

Huck's breath filled the space under his blankets with poisonous exhalations, and his head spun. He'd have to open the blankets to breathe clean air if he wanted to live through the night. No, it'd be better to not look into the corner of his room. That dark corner behind his closet door he stupidly left open. That's where it hid. That's where it had always hid since Mark. They told him it was called a paralysis vision. They started to appear here and there—always when he was stressed out or in a new foster home. For a minute in high school, they vanished long enough for him to convince himself that they were not real. Now, ever since Jasper, they came back in full force.

Clenching his eyes shut, he threw the blankets over him wide, letting in fresh air. Then he slammed his fist down so hard, he punched himself between his eye and the bridge of his nose. His eyes instantly watered, and he was sure he felt blood running down his lip.

Get it together, Huck, he moaned to himself. *You're an 18-year-old man. You shouldn't be scared of ghosts.*

The thing with most people not afraid of ghosts was that they couldn't see them. Safe from the visions, they had nothing to fear. Huck wasn't sure he saw ghosts or if he was damaged by the events from six months ago. Mom told him to think about seeing a therapist. He didn't want one. He didn't need one. He just needed time. Right?

Something pressed down on the foot of his bed.

Huck jerked his knees up to his chin. The queen-size bed was huge to him. Holly's was the first home he'd lived in that offered him a bed this size. He'd loved it as a lanky, too-tall fourteen-year-old. Now it felt too big.

He shuddered, his breath filling the covers again. His head went heavy and his vision darkened despite the lack of light. The thing at the end of his bed took a step, tilting the mattress down towards it. It headed for him on all fours, slowly. One more step and it would be inches from his hiding place under the blankets.

A hand, outside the duvet, gently pressed down over his ankle. Its long, spindly fingers started to close over his ankle. His breathing picked up, suffocating him. A guttural crackling softly rumbled over the topside of the duvet. The hand clamped down over his ankle hard.

With a high-pitched scream, Huck threw the blankets off. Terror froze his heart in his gasping chest.

Nothing was there.

Sweat poured down from his long, black strands, sticking them to his neck. His head snapped back and forth, his vision black and white from lack of oxygen. He looked down at his ankle. Nothing, but it throbbed like he'd hit it against the hitch of a truck.

The crackling reverberated from above. Snapping his head up, his eyes landed on the shadow figure above him. Sprawled like a spider over the top of his ceiling, its formless face looked down at him. Huck screamed, paralyzed with fear as it slowly descended the wall behind the headboard. Its darkness engulfed his vision. With the unmistakable slam of wood against wood, the shadow figure zoomed past him toward his closet. The bedroom lights burst on, blinding him, but he saw it meld into the shadows of his inner closet.

"Baby?" Holly gasped, rushing in, baseball bat clutched in her hands. She spun on the spot, her long, decorated cornrows slapping her back as she searched for the intruder. "What is it, Huck?" She glared at the window. Without waiting, she marched over to it, ready to swing.

Unable to form words in his dry, searing throat, Huck choked on his swallowed sobs and pointed to his closet. Embarrassment waited behind his other reeling emotions, ready to burn his face once it got its turn.

Holly dashed to the closet, kicking the door open and raising the bat. Her long, satin pants almost blended into the darkness inside. When nothing moved, she poked at the hanging clothes with the bat.

"I dare you!" she screamed into the closet. "Give me an excuse. This may be Kansas, but I ain't scared of you!"

Huck focused in on the shadows of the closet until it swam before him. Nothing moved. It was gone.

"Mom, it's ok," he choked, sniffling. "I'm sorry, I thought I saw…" A shadow? A ghost? Stupid. "I'm so sorry," he bawled, covering his face.

His ears scorched. There was the embarrassment, heating him up and burning him alive from the inside. Diving into the duvet, he tried to bury his shame and tears.

"Oh, baby," Holly cooed, setting the bat down against his night stand and joining him on the bed. She wrapped him up in her long arms. Against his too-white, too-skinny arms, she looked healthy and strong. "It's ok." She kissed the top of his head. "It's ok. They said this might happen."

She didn't understand. Yes, the experts said he'd experienced trauma and that could manifest in many ways. Nightmares mostly. But this hadn't been a nightmare.

She rocked him back and forth, petting his hair. Pressing her cheek onto the top of his head, she hummed gently. "I'm so sorry, Huck baby. I wish I could take away all the bad thoughts. I wish I could protect you from all this loss."

That's what she used to say when he first came to her house. He and Mark were five when Holly first met them. They'd been placed with her in an emergency situation. Their first foster house, that he could remember, had been more than a little rough. The system constantly moved them around. His first solid memory was Holly hugging him and Mark one night during a thunderstorm. She'd promised to make them safe. Forever.

I'll take away all the bad, she used to say.

Inhaling slowly, Huck let out a shaky breath onto her neck. "I guess it was a nightmare," he sighed, eyes still locked on the closet. "I'm sorry."

Holly shook her head. "You have to stop saying sorry, baby. I told you, it's not your fault."

Yes, it was. They'd told him it was. He wouldn't have believed it before, but not now.

He couldn't stop the shaking. It came back in full force, vibrating the entire bed. Holly gripped him tighter.

"I have something that might distract you," she sighed after a moment. "I didn't want to show you."

"What is it?" Huck asked, eager to have something to distract him. He pressed his palms into his eyes, wiping away the last of the tears. His eyes had been red-rimmed for the last six months. Now they ached like sore muscles.

"Wait here." She stood up and walked out of the room.

Huck kept his eyes on the closet. Nothing moved. These damn things never did come out when more than one person waited beyond. Were they afraid? No, that couldn't be. He glanced down at his bedside clock. Four in the morning. He needed to sleep. Summer was basically over and the move to the university loomed before him. His suitcase, boxes, backpack, and bags of filming equipment sat at the other end of the room, waiting to be packed up and driven to a prestigious private university on the other side of the county. Holly had used every systemic pull in the book to get him in on all kinds of grants and scholarships since he'd not made back what they paid the loser that had sued them. She wanted the best for him, and he felt he didn't deserve it.

Her long-legged, heavy steps announced the reappearance of her tall frame. She clutched a piece of white paper in one hand and a tissue in the other. She handed him the tissue.

"For your nose," she sighed.

"Oh, I forgot." Embarrassed again, Huck took the tissue and wiped at his nose and upper lip. Sure enough, blood soaked the tissue. "Shit," he moaned into it, pressing it against his nose.

Holly sucked in her cheeks, chewing her lip in hesitation before she spoke. "Did you do that to yourself?" she asked.

"What? No." He held his breath. "Well, yeah, but it's not what you think."

Her eyes pleaded with him.

Sighing and rolling his head, he said, "I accidentally hit myself while trying to pull the covers up."

A bit relieved, Mom took a deep breath. She tapped the paper with her long, clean nails.

"I debated about showing this to you and Mark." She stopped to swallow. Saying Mark's name always brought a tear to her eye and a stab-wound to Huck's heart. "They reached out months ago."

"They?" Huck asked, turning on his bed to face her.

Holly nodded. "The bios."

Huck's heart skipped a beat, then tumbled over in his chest. "Our biological parents?" He still hadn't gotten in the habit of saying *my*. For eighteen years, he'd always referred to himself and Mark. *Our*. Not anymore. "My parents?" he corrected a little too late.

Holly nodded. She bit her bottom lip, playing with the edges of the paper. "They tracked us down. Sent an email back in April. We had some back and forth."

Do they know about Mark? What do they want? The questions, theories—and even some disdain—rattled through Huck's head.

"Are you mad at me?" Holly asked, joining him on his bed again.

"No," Huck quickly shot back, eyes boring into the printed email. "I'm just... confused. Why did they reach out now? I've not heard anything about them, from them, or seen a picture of them. Ever, I think."

She shrugged sympathetically in reply, handing him the folded email. She gently gripped the side of his neck, making him look her in the eyes. "Read it with care, baby." Leaning in, she kissed the top of his head, lingering there. "I love you," she whispered before getting up off the bed.

"I love you, too," he called after her.

She stopped by the doorway, motioning to the light switch.

"Leave it on, please," Huck replied.

Nodding, she left.

The sudden silence filled his ears until they hurt. Stuffing the tissue into his bleeding nostril, he unfolded the email. He skipped the body, looking at the name in the signature.

Marion W.

He'd never known his biological parents' first names. But he knew the last name. "W," he mumbled out loud. Winchester. But he and Mark had never really been called by their names. They were case number 6359. Or The Twins, as the system in Boaz called them. When Holly and Richard first started to try to adopt them, he and Mark took Richard and Holly's last name: Derringer. They'd insisted the kids at school and the teachers call them by that name, even though it wasn't theirs.

Pushing the memories away, he read the email.

Dear Miss Derringer,

This is what comes from letting a single woman with your background adopt.

Huck's indignation on Holly's behalf flared up instantly. He'd never liked his mother for giving him and Mark up. Now he gave himself permission to hate her. Marion Winchester didn't know crap about Holly Derringer and had no right to judge her like that.

My husband and I have reached out to you several times in the last year. Your quick retorts, despite what you think, are not humorous. I suggest you keep who you are dealing with at the forefront of your mind.

Simply put, as you may remember in my last email, we'd like the opportunity to meet the boys. Rest assured, we are not looking to part them from you. Being nearly 18 years of age at this point, we'd hoped they'd be on their own, but we found out through our own means that they still reside at your address.

Kindly supply their contact information so I may speak with
them directly. We simply want to meet and have a chat. Please
realize that soon the boys will be legally adults and, should it
come to it, you cannot stop them from meeting us.

   Kind regards,
   Marion W.

Huck held his breath while reading the first words he'd ever heard from his biological mother. She wanted to meet him. Them. She wanted to meet them. Quickly checking the date, he saw this particular email came in the middle of October. No wonder Mom didn't reply. They'd been busy burying Mark. Then they'd been working on their out of court issues. Then filling out police reports. He'd been questioned, psychoanalyzed, in and out of offices of doctors, police, investigators. Jasper's parents even hired a private investigator. It had been a bad end to the year.

Gently folding and unfolding the paper again, he re-read the first line. A disdain for this woman—his birth mother—roiled in his gut. She didn't know Holly. She had no idea what the woman he and Mark called mom did for them. Marion sounded pretentious. Mean.

Just as the tangle of new emotions rose in Huck, something to his right flickered. He didn't have to look twice to know the shadow was reemerging from his closet. Choking back a sob, he dove back under the covers and cried until he fell asleep.

JERKING AWAKE WITH A SHOUT, he tossed the blankets off and looked around. Sun filled his room despite his ceiling light still being on. The smell of bacon, pancakes, and eggs floated up lazily from below. He quickly scanned his room for the shadow. Nothing.

Slipping a shirt on, he left his room and entered the haven that was Holly's kitchen. With wide-open windows looking out onto the tree-lined neighborhood, the kitchen was soaked in sunlight. Flowers, herbs, collections of tea cups and pots, and little signs of faux worn wood expressed words like joy, laughter, and the classic home sweet home. Holly excelled at basic home comforts. She stood behind the hanging cabinets, frilly apron snug around her hips, flipping pancakes. Her laptop stood open on the round dining room table on this side of the counter top.

Huck slid into his regular seat and chugged the glass of orange juice she'd poured for him.

"Did you get back to sleep?" she asked, coming around the hanging cabinets and plunking down a plate utterly laden with pancakes, cheesy eggs, and several strips of bacon. "Your GED certificate came in the mail yesterday, by the way." She lazily pointed to a huge, white envelope on the table. "The university got their copy before us. Typical mail system."

Huck nodded. Taking another drink, he choked when his eyes caught the syrup she drowned his breakfast in. The regular brown maple syrup glittered with gold.

"What… the…?" he gagged, coughing on the juice.

"Found it online," Holly beamed. "I couldn't resist."

"Of course you couldn't," he sighed, taking in his now glittering breakfast. "At least it matches the grout in the bathroom."

"That was an experiment," she chirped.

"But why'd you have to experiment in *my* bathroom?"

She tasseled his hair roughly. "Because I knew you love me and would forgive me. When will that happen?"

"When the glitter phase is over," he replied as good-naturedly as he could. He knew it was just one of her ways of dealing. He couldn't shame her for it and just had to endure everything from a sparkling pink shower to gold glitter on his breakfast.

"Oh, hush, it tastes the same," she snapped, pointing at the golden syrup. She turned back to the stove.

He dug in anyway, hungry after the frightening night, and ignored the academic mail. He glanced up at the screen of her laptop. His hand, holding a pile of glittering eggs, froze halfway to his open mouth.

A familiar website of black and green filled the screen. The banner read: DarkFront. An old video of his played on mute. His own, white face danced in the frame as he looked into the dark hallway he explored before turning back to quickly rattle off some trivia about the haunted place. The camera—operated by Jasper—jerked to the side as Mark said something. He and Huck both laughed on the screen. The Huck on the video stopped, looking to the side of the camera. His heart sunk. Jasper must have said something, and he didn't listen. The Huck on the screen laughed, eyes crinkling so hard they closed. Mark doubled over, hand on Huck's shoulder to steady himself as they guffawed.

Watching himself, he gave a tiny, sad exhale of laughter. He didn't even know what Jasper said, but he'd give anything to hear him again. He may have been the face of their web series, but Jasper was by far the viewer's favorite after Mark. The man behind the camera.

He hadn't watched back any of the footage yet. Hadn't been on the website. His monetization had suffered badly.

Curious, he scrolled down to the comments on the video. He instantly lost his appetite.

> Fake news. Jasper's not dead.

> It's a stunt, you guys. They are doing this for views. Stupid prank. Probably Huckster's idea.

> How do you think he convinced the police to give a report? And the newspapers?

> Anyone think that maybe Huck offed his partner out of jealousy?

> Or Mark's suicide drove him mad lol

> Watch him try to monetize off this...

He wanted to puke. Was this really what his loyal followers thought? For over three years, he'd curated this web series. He'd met fans at cons, small though they were. No, that wasn't the issue. They insulted Jasper's memory by even thinking his death was a fake.

They were right about one thing: he'd always been jealous of Jasper.

Sick, he dropped his fork and pushed his plate away. Holly came back around, carrying her own plate. She sighed happily, sitting next to him. She followed his gaze to the screen.

"I was just checking," she mumbled, taking his hand.

"They hate me."

"Does it matter?"

"Yeah. Or no?" He looked over at her. "I thought maybe I could come back to it. Maybe." His throat tightened. "I don't know, mom. I'm supposed to try to go back to normal, right? But I can't. I can't do this without him. Them. I can't come home without Mark. I can't… I can't!" he shouted, burying his face in his hands.

Holly slammed the laptop shut and shoved it away. "I shouldn't have opened the website. I'm sorry." She took his face in her hands. He could tell she wanted to say something else: This was the only way she could hear Mark's voice. "But you're right. Maybe try something else?"

He looked up, sniffling. "What do you mean?"

Adjusting to face him square on, she licked her lips and said, "Go find your other friends. Emily and Aaron stopped by on Friday to see if you wanted to hang out. Go and spend time with them. Then, maybe, look for a job?"

"Ugh," he moaned, leaning back against the chair.

"Just for a bit, baby," she said over his groaning. "I checked the statements. Your series is not bringing in the money you used to make."

"Because I haven't made new content," he said, almost begging her. "Let me make a video."

Grimacing, Holly stroked his forehead and tucked his hair behind his ear. "I'm not stopping you, Huck."

Of course she wasn't. But she wasn't exactly encouraging him to go out and film ghost hunts again, either. He knew she didn't want to encourage that lifestyle right now.

"I just don't want you to go down a path that might lead to… more hurt," she offered. She tilted her head. "Try other steps before jumping back into what you used to do."

He couldn't stand the pleading look in her brown eyes. Inside, he knew she wanted him to enjoy his life, to get back to normal. And he knew he should. But the how seemed stupid. Elusive even.

"I don't…" He swallowed to loosen his tight throat. "I don't want to disappoint you."

"Oh, baby." She sighed, taking him into another tight hug. "You won't. If all you do is try, I'd be happy."

Over Mom's shoulder, he caught sight of three family pictures. One with him and her. Another with him, her, and Mark. And the last: just her and Mark. He'd not only lost his brother, his twin, she'd lost her son. She hurt too.

"Ok," he said in a low tone. "I'll go out today and find the guys."

Chapter 9:
Shadow People

After breakfast, Huck got dressed. Unwilling to be recognized in their small town, he pulled a black hoodie over his shaggy hair and covered half his face with sunglasses. Late condolences for Mark still came in, remembered now that his best friend had also gone missing. People liked Jasper. Of the three of them, Jasper was the town's favorite.

"Really?" Holly asked as he slinked towards the front door. She took in his look.

"I…" He stuttered. He stopped and swallowed to clear his nerves. "I just don't want people stopping me. To talk."

Holly sighed, grabbing her work bag. "The point is to talk, Huck honey." She surveyed him hopelessly, knowing anything she said wouldn't make him change. Instead, she jumped forward, kissed his pale forehead, and pushed past him out the door. "I have to work a double. Be good and lock up. Say hi to the guys for me."

He nodded, watching her leave. Something in his chest hurt every time she left now. Like she might never come back. Maybe she'd leave him. Her obligation to him was over: he was eighteen. The system spit him out and didn't pay her to take care of him any more. But she did.

Locking the door, Huck ducked into his own car—an old, black 1995 Chevy Corvette—and drove into town. The small city of Boaz, Kansas boasted a meager twenty thousand citizens. A few people spotted him and waved sadly at him. News had gotten around that the search for Jasper was winding down. They were quitting. So the sympathy poured in again. He ignored them and drove to the darker northern side of town. Sheriff Logan worked the graveyard shift, but told Huck to come by if he ever needed anything. He'd find his friends later.

Max Logan Savage lived at the edge of town near the largest graveyard on the perimeter. It was attached to an old church that no one really used anymore, except for wakes and maybe at Easter. He drove past Logan's house twice before getting the courage to park on the street under a tree whose roots pushed up the street. Logan would be asleep since it was late morning. Would he be mad that Huck woke him up?

Holding his breath, Huck knocked on the chipped, dark red paint of the front door. To his shock, Logan opened it, standing back from the sunlight and squinting.

"I saw your old junker roaming the streets," the sheriff said with a tired smile. His long blond hair ratted up the back of his head in a sloppy bun. "Come on in, kiddo."

Logan led Huck into the tiny, yellow kitchen and sat him down at the rickety dining room table. He moved a hospital cooler out of the way and motioned to the coffeepot on the counter. "Coffee?" he asked. "All I have is black."

"Thanks, Logan," Huck sighed, taking off his glasses. He kept the hood on. "You said I could come over whenever I wanted. If I needed something."

The man nodded, pouring Huck a mug but not taking any

for himself. He sat down and yawned. "Any time, kid. So what's up?"

Huck chewed the inside of his lips. He tapped his thumb on the side of the mug. "They're not looking for Jasper anymore, are they?"

The sheriff frowned sadly, tucking some stray strands behind his ear. "It's... been winding down. Even the Rangers are cooling it. I'm-I'm really sorry, Huck."

"I don't blame *you*, Logan," he replied. What did he want then? To ask meaningless questions? Talk about his night-mares? Explain how lonely he was?

Logan cocked his head and looked at Huck with sympathy. "I mean it, kiddo. I know you've had a tough year."

"Jasper wasn't like Mark," Huck said suddenly. "Someone killed him. He's still missing."

Mark had taken his own life. "Mark got distant," Huck went on, clutching his coffee. "At first, mom and I thought it was the car accident that made him that way. But the weeks before, he got real bad."

"We all handle trauma differently," Logan supplied, gently laying his cold hand on Huck's arm. "You two were close."

"We were twins." Huck scoffed sadly. "Went through the system together. Everything. More often than not, we were all each other had." A memory popped into his head and he couldn't stop the gentle grin it brought with it. "One time, when we were separated into different houses, he ran away and stole this guy's vespa to come get me."

Logan smiled wearily, his eyes still red from lack of sleep.

"The guy reported that his *motorcycled* had been stolen," Huck went on. "So they didn't find us for a week." The smile faded. "He always looked out for me. Same as Jasper."

"They loved you," the sheriff said. "You know I got your back too, right? We've been buddies since your mom took you in. Before she adopted you. You've spent a lot of nights sleeping in my cruiser. Little run away." He smiled endearingly at Huck.

Huck nodded. "You're a good friend, Logan."

The older man nodded, too. "A tired one, too. Why don't you go see the guys in town? They're still hanging out at the supermarket downtown."

"Losers," Huck joked.

"We've all done it," Logan added with a wave of his hand. "Try to hang out with your friends, kiddo. Ok?"

"Ok."

AARON, Kate, and Emily waved at him from the bed of Aaron's truck in the parking lot. True to their habit, they sat in the back eating snacks and drinking various fizzy liquids to while away the day. Emily waved enthusiastically and motioned him over.

"Guess what," she started, dropping the tailgate for him to climb up.

"It's amazing," Kate added.

Aaron rolled his eyes. "Please, not more about the mortician guy."

Huck hopped in and took a proffered orange soda. "The old man who runs the funeral home? Did he finally buy that old church from the city?"

"No," Emily droned, a giddy smile pulling her lips too high up her face. "Turns out, he has a grandson who is visiting town."

"Holy shit, guys, no one cares," Aaron snapped, kicking

out at the girls from where he perched on the side. They giggled and flinched away, undaunted.

"You're just jealous," Kate said snidely.

"Why?" Huck asked. "Not that I believe them, Aaron," he added quickly.

The girls giggled again, covering their mouths.

"He's *so* strong," Kate offered. "He helps dig graves, apparently."

Now Huck got it. Aaron was average looking. Huck had never thought about it, but he supposed they were all average looking. But of course, there was a time he thought he was the best-looking guy in their school. That mindset seemed a lifetime ago. "People in this town get too excited about new things," he offered. "That's all."

A second of silence drifted between the friends. "We're glad you came out to hang," Emily offered, touching his knee lightly.

"And now you can spend more time with us!" Kate said, raising her arms in the sunlight. "We thought we might not see you all summer."

"What do you mean?" Huck asked quickly. "More time?"

"Shit, Kate," Aaron mumbled, taking a drink from his glass bottle. "You didn't have to say it."

"Say what?" Huck asked.

The girls exchanged glances. "We always felt second rung compared to Jasper," Kate mumbled. "Especially after you started that DarkFront show."

Emily playfully shoved Huck. "Yeah, share the fame, would ya? Some of us have been trying to reach influencer status for years now. When are you starting again, by the way?"

A strange feeling crept into Huck's gut. "Is that all you want to know?" he asked.

"It is the coolest thing our school has ever produced," Aaron added. "You were cool."

Huck leaned back against the side of the truck. "I don't want to do it again, guys."

"But you should!" Emily crawled up onto all fours and took a few seductive steps towards him. "With us?" She smiled and bit her bottom lip. "That'd be fun."

For one second, Huck almost said he'd think about it. Then he stopped. "What if I don't?" he asked. His heart sunk, knowing the answer.

Aaron shrugged. "We'd find something else to do, I guess. We thought it would be fun to all do it together. You've got a huge following. Why stop?"

DarkFront was his, Mark's, and Jasper's thing. It almost felt like an insult to their memory to start it up again with different people. Especially these three. They were just after his fame.

"Let's just hang out?" Huck asked. "We can do other stuff."

Emily sighed, rolled her eyes, and sat back on her feet. "See? I told you he wouldn't let us in on it. Your moodiness is aggravating, Huck. You're no fun anymore."

"Screw you, Huck," Kate pouted. She grabbed her purse and stood up, hopping over the side. "Come by my place tonight, Aaron. My folks aren't home and it seems I'll be bored." She glared at Huck.

Desperately trying to save his only friend group, Huck said, "Guys, we can still be friends. Don't leave."

"Nah, we're out." Aaron stood up and scratched his side through his shirt. He looked disappointed. "See ya around, Huckey."

THE TRUCK SPED off around the store, leaving him alone in the parking lot. The summer hadn't heated up yet, so he pulled the sleeves to his hoodie down. The rumbling of Alex's old motor faded away. He didn't remember them being that harsh. But then again, he'd had a lot of friends when his web series took off. He'd been full of himself, self-confident, unable to see others around him. It had been lonely then, too. Except for Jasper. Jasper put up with a lot. Then, at home, he had Mark.

Sadness taking over, Huck climbed back into his car and drove around town again until he came up to the old backside of the graveyard. Mark was here. He got out and slipped through the rickety black iron gate. Taking the shaded pathways through the headstones and past the few larger mausoleums, he found his brother's marker. Not yet a year old, some drying flowers lay over the new grass. Mom must have been by a week or so ago.

Huck sat down next to Mark's grave and fiddled with his shoestring. He'd run out of things to say a while ago. He never had to speak much with Mark. Mark just knew things.

"I wish I could talk with Jasper," Huck sighed. "You knew him. He had advice for everything. He was the better of us."

He looked up into the trees across the field of the dead. He blinked, and a dark shape flickered into view. Gasping, he sat up straighter, ready to run. Like a moving mist, it formed more and more to look like a man.

"No, no," he begged, rubbing his eyes. "Not again."

A tingling at the base of his skull started and crawled up

until it rang like metal in his ears. He even tasted metal in his mouth.

"It's not real!" he hissed, covering his ears. The ringing almost sounded like voices, grating and calling from somewhere far away. He locked onto the form. It had eyes now. White, empty, glowing things that bored into him.

He heard it breathing, like it blew right into his ears.

Just when he thought the noise would escalate too much, a soft voice behind him said, "Huck?"

Screaming, he spun. Something touched his shoulder.

Nothing there. His chest constricted with fright so much, his gasping hurt. Snapping back to the trees, he looked. The black thing was gone.

"Shit," he gasped, leaning against Mark's headstone. Looking down, he saw something had trampled the grass; it curved over like someone had just dashed over it. He'd taken the gravel path. Shaking, he pushed himself up and sped back towards his car. He slipped through the gate and slammed his car door once safely inside.

Gray clouds covered the sky, and an icy wind blew through the new leaves on the trees. He gripped the steering wheel hard. His eye scanned the graveyard. Nothing moved.

Chapter 10:

Something's There

The next weekend found Huck staring blankly at his own website. He scrolled through even more of the comments. Everyone thought the same thing. He'd quit. Jasper and he broke up, fighting over production. It was a stunt. A few people linked articles and videos to news reports of the police investigation and the little coverage a missing boy from Boaz got. Before closing out his website, he checked his followers. It had gone down by over one thousand every few days.

"You need to get a job, something to distract you while you wait for university to start," Holly kept saying.

Only one place had accepted him: Boaz State University —or BSU, as the kids called it—a large institution right on the edge of the county near one of the bigger cities. It wasn't far, but it would be a step up from the small town.

The acceptance letter peeked up at him from a drawer in his desk. Sighing, he pulled it out. A bright sticky note clung to the front, crumpled from being shoved in. Water marks and stains from mud covered parts of it. Curious, he plucked it off. It was that name, written in Jasper's handwriting: Valon Gabriel. Remembering the big-time paranormal internet personality, Huck typed his name into the search bar quickly. Maybe he'd watch some videos, get inspired, and get back out there.

"Oh, good grief," Huck chuckled.

Valon Gabriel's website looked hokey. Outdated graphics sparkled with blood and ghostly fonts. The layout was not clean. A video auto-played the moment the page finished loading. A crappy guitar rift shot out of the speakers and an over the top male narrator grunted, "Are you ready to believe?" before going into a long-winded trailer for the series.

Skipping past the cringe, Huck looked for the start. They showed the seance in black and white. The camera showed a wide open, empty room with a round table in the center. The only visible light came from a candle in the middle of the table, but the entire screen lit up with staged lighting. Huck scoffed, noting the cheap effects. A man sat at the center of the table, long brown hair gleaming in the candlelight. His eyes waited, closed. Once the intro music cut out, he opened them with a dramatic snap.

"Hello, believers," he said in a deep, charismatic voice. "Tonight, we are holding a seance for a dear friend." He held his hand out, motioning a weeping woman in from off camera.

Huck shook his head as he watched. Everything was scripted. He even spotted the smoke and wires effect that made the table move the longer the seance got. The woman moaned and pretended to be possessed by a ghost and call out some cryptic messages. If he hadn't been into production himself, he could see how others would buy it. At the end of the episode, Valon slung his merchandise, selling bottles of branded holy water and a book of prayers. Huck sat back in disgust.

Then it hit him: it was almost like watching himself. Valon gloated, preened on camera, and held poses in flattering light. Just like he used to. It was all a show. Valon believed nothing he said, just like Huck. Jasper had been the believer between the two of them. Huck just did it for the views. The following. The cash. And the adoration. The audience loved him. He got fan mail on their website, even the occasional creepy comment on the videos. Sure, they loved Mark, and Jasper had his fans. That never bothered Huck because the entire show was his idea and he rested easily knowing that. He'd been so self-absorbed. That Huck seemed forever ago.

He casually flicked through a few other videos on Valon Gabriel's website, watching a minute here and there. Every episode glittered with over-production, gilded in glamor. A few had live chat replays where they donated to "bring power to prayer." He'd never wanted to do a live show. Jasper did. Maybe it would be worth it? But he'd need a partner. Running DarkFront on his own would be overwhelming.

Leaning back in his chair, he surveyed his desk before him. Camera bags, a few pieces of lighting, and their body mics sprawled out before him. He'd not gotten around to organizing ever since November and Jasper's disappearance. No. His murder.

Groaning, he let his face fall into his hands. "What am I supposed to do?" he moaned out loud.

Just then, something slipped on the upper shelves of his desk. A heavy object clattered beside his right elbow. Opening his fingers, he peered down and saw one of his handheld cameras. The screen had flipped open when it fell. A black canvas waited to be turned on. He picked it up and stood up to look at where it fell from. It had been sitting far back on the shelf; he could tell from the dust. He could even see the track where it had scooted across the shelf and fallen down.

The tingling down his neck started, and he tasted metal in his mouth.

"Oh, no," he whispered.

Just behind him, a cold spot spread. The hairs on his arm stood up. As it crept into his bones, he swore something breathed down his neck. Eyes touched the back of his head. Agonizingly slowly, he turned his head a little, then used his eyes to look behind. Nothing there.

He flipped open the camera all the way and turned it on. He didn't hit record, turned the screen to face him, and held the camera up. Just over his shoulder, a set of red eyes met his in a pure black face.

Screaming, Huck dropped the camera and spun around. Again, nothing there. At least, not that his eyes could see.

"Leave me alone!" he shouted into his empty room.

Nothing moved, but he physically felt the cold drift away. Looking back down at his camera, he gritted his teeth and set it up. He plugged the camera into his computer, opened his website and set up a live stream. He angled the screen so he could see himself, sat down, and went live. Staring into his own eyes, he took deep breaths while a few viewers appeared in the righthand side of the screen on his computer.

"Hey, guys," he sighed. Out of habit, he shoved his shaggy black bangs out of his eyes with long, pale fingers, like he'd practiced a million times in the mirror over the years. "It's me." He forced a smile that quickly devolved into a sad grimace. "I've read your comments and, to be honest, I get where you're coming from. I don't blame you."

He stopped, pressing his lips inward to stop the overwhelming emotion erupting onto his face. Tears heated his eyes, stinging them. He forced them to stay open. If he blinked, they'd fall. His reflection looked manic.

The view counter suddenly hit twenty. Hearts bubbled up from the bottom of the screen and random emotes from other uses peppered the chat box.

Forcing an exhaled laugh, he said, "Sorry, guys. It's been a while. I am going to be uploading again. Just me." His heart wouldn't turn to stone. Instead, he looked down.

The chat lit up with white words.

Where have you been?!

WTF, where's Jasper?

What did you do to him, you jealous monster??

Huck is back!

Are you ok?

Did you find a real cult?

Lies, nothing in the news in months...

OMG, do we get new episodes again??

"I know you don't believe what happened to Jasper." He glared at the camera, holding back his rage. "No one does. But that's why I need you guys to believe in me. I know I was the skeptic. Ghosts and hauntings were Jasper's thing, and Mark was really into it. But recently, I've experienced some things that have me questioning. This sounds fake, I get that. Like I'm shilling for views. But, guys, I'm genuine. I saw things last year that rocked me. I have to make sense of it."

As he spoke, he began to believe himself. Something inside finally switched on.

Going on ghost hunts again??

Praise the gods!

Is this a good idea?

Don't go anywhere at night alone.

"If I can investigate again," he said, eyes trailing over nothingness, "maybe something will make sense. I can't just sit here and wait for life to get better. Because it won't." He locked eyes with his lens. "It won't. It just got worse." He waited a beat. "Oh, shit," he sighed, holding his face in his hands again. "Or it could all go wrong."

OMG, please hunt again!

We need new spooky stuff!

Wtf is that behind you...?

Huck looked at the chat, frowning. "What?" Spinning around, nothing was there. "I thought I felt something earlier."

Feeling? You got a sixth sense? Lol.

No, seriously, who is standing behind you?

This time, Huck checked the camera. His heart raced as he expected to see the red eyes again. But there was nothing there. He sighed in relief.

"There's nothing, guys. Nice try." He laughed nervously.

Mark?

No, that was def Jasper! WTF, Huck?

They're gone now.

"Don't do that, guys," Huck said seriously. "It's not funny." But he couldn't help checking the live stream. On the playback, something behind him glitched before vanishing. "Holy shit," he breathed. Metal filled his mouth. "This is what I'm talking about, guys," he said. "Something happens and I taste metal and my head buzzes. Then I see shadows."

> See a doctor, weirdo.

> OMG, Huck, be careful! Don't play with dark stuff!

> They say if you go looking for it, hell will find you.

"I figure I'm already there, guys," Huck said, eyes locked onto the spot that had glitched. "The camera picked it up, but it only showed on the playback."

Leaning back in his chair, he closed his eyes. Trying to tune in to the sense, he relaxed.

> Don't do it, Huck!

> One demon possession coming right up.

He waited. The air conditioner clicked on, then right off again. It was too cold. He took a deep breath, shaking. The metallic taste filled his mouth again. The spot in his skull right behind his eyes buzzed. Opening his eyes, his vision swam. A black halo sucked his room into it, like a long dark hallway appeared. At the end loomed a black door, not unlike the ones in his house. Something told him to open it.

Reaching out, his hand actually extended forward into the freezing air. The closer he got, the more his vision blurred like oil on a window. Then a rushing scream filled his ears. The metallic pang in his mouth got so bad he wanted to puke.

Someone screamed for him to stop.

His feet went up and the next thing he knew, his vision stabilized and he flew backwards. Feet over head, he tumbled over in his chair. His head hit the ground, and his chair rolled over to the side. Looking up, he took in his ceiling fan and the glow in the stars his ten-year-old self had plastered there. His head ached. He sat up, pushing against the carpet. His head swam like he'd been holding his breath for several minutes. Getting up, he winced at the screen, the blue light blinding him.

> Nice trick.
>
> Did you see that? Holy shit!
>
> Are you ok?
>
> What happened?

"Hold on," Huck panted, grabbing the timer and skipping back a few seconds on the live stream. He watched himself sit back in the chair. Nothing happened for about fifteen seconds. Then the camera glitched, going fuzzy. When it came back into focus, something grabbed the back of his gaming chair and pulled so hard, it flipped him backwards. "That's when I came to, looking up at the ceiling."

Cool trick, someone in the chat wrote again.

Disheartened and panicking a little, Huck sat back down. "I don't believe in this stuff, guys. I never have." He glared into his own eyes on his computer screen. He couldn't believe it. If he had, he'd go mad…

The lines of chat continued to flash along with the emotes and other flare. He didn't care. He didn't read their remarks. Most of them were just comments egging him on, calling it fake. It didn't matter what they thought. What mattered was that something had been in his room with him.

Without thinking, he called out, "Jasper?"

The chat lines stopped.

Nothing. No taste of metal. No buzzing behind his eyes.

"Fine," he said out loud. "I'm doing a hunt. There's this old graveyard at the edge of town by this creep church. I'll make a post for info, so watch the website for that. I'll go..." he checked his computer's calendar, "tomorrow night. Full moon. See you then."

He shut off the live stream and breathed a sigh of relief. Shooting up from his chair, he packed everything he'd need to tempt out whatever had started to haunt him.

Chapter 11:

The Graveyard

"Are you serious?" Holly shot across the living room the next night when Huck came down with all his gear slung over his shoulder. "You're going alone? What happened to Aaron and the rest?"

Huck rolled his eyes sadly. "It was too hard to connect again with them," he mumbled, going to a drawer and rummaging for extra batteries.

"How hard did you try?" she asked, swirling a huge mug of hot tea. She lounged like this every time she got off a double. Some dating show played on the TV.

"Hard enough," Huck replied. "Any extra triple As?"

She nodded to her desk in the corner. "Drawer above the checks. I don't like you going alone. It's late already."

"Yeah," he smiled at her, searching her desk. "Have to go when it's dark out."

Holly bit her lip then took a slow sip, sighing in defeat. "Don't get abducted."

"Possessed, mom," Huck called over his shoulder as he ran out the front door. "Aliens abduct you, ghosts possess you."

She nodded. "Oh, of course, my bad."

THE FIRST THING Huck did to prepare for his first video back was turn on his head camera. He started to record and lightly commentated like he and Jasper used to do.

"Hey guys, I'm doing set up," he said out loud. He made a mental note to do a voice over, telling the future viewers the time stamp of when the actual hunt started. "I had to slide through the broken gate. The day they fix it is the day I have to find new stomping grounds. Sad day," he added with a forced smile into his hand camera.

He had never set up alone before. There was less banter and no one to ask to check angles and lighting. He got so caught up in finding places to put his tripods that he forgot he was alone.

"Hey, Jasp-," he started, digging in one of the black duffels. He froze. Jasper wasn't here. He waited, crouched in the grass for the feeling to pass.

It had gotten easier to remember they were gone. But every once in a while, it just slipped his mind. Sometimes, routine kicked in and he checked Mark's bedroom to see if he was awake or already in the shower in the morning. He'd pick up his phone and want to send a message to Jasper. He'd be halfway through the action before remembering that the person he wanted to see wasn't there.

The night bugs sung into the stillness. Turning back to the bag, he pulled out the last tripod and started in on the other tech.

He cleared his throat. "Anyway. I'm going to set up motion sensitive lights at the back of the mausoleum," he commentated. "They'll flash a picture if anything remotely solid passes them. Then of course the heat signature cams and the night vision." He grunted, lifting a few of the items and carried them farther down a row of graves. "I watched this one guy who used an old camera from a G-Box 720 to find a shadow figure in his basement. Fortunately, we have better tech."

A few minutes later, he had a good section of the grave-yard covered in various lenses and lights. He stood at the end of the row, facing the dark outline of the mausoleum at the other end. His breath rose in white clouds into the night.

"Cold for summer," he mused to his camera. Then he waited, not sure what to say. "I guess there's no harm in telling you all this," he sighed. "I miss him. I know there's doubts about what happened in Coven Wood, but I don't know how else to prove it to you guys."

He waited again. A crow cawed somewhere to his left.

"I guess I could go back," he mused softly. "Cut that. I don't want them getting any ideas."

Making up his mind, He looked down at his night vision camera in his hand. "Ok, guys, here we go." He started to walk, eyes glued to the screen. "I'm going to call out and see what happens."

He took a left before reaching the end of the row and slowly made his way down towards the trees and black fence on that side. Nothing but the crunch of dewy grass and the night bugs made the waveform on his tech dance.

"Hello?" he called out finally. "Is anyone here with me?"

The waveform spiked with his call then went almost flat again. He hummed in thought and made to turn back around when suddenly— *FLASH!*

Blinded by the sudden brightness from behind the mausoleum, Huck flinched and shut his eyes tight. He groaned and blinked rapidly to get his eyes to adjust again.

He froze in place, not daring to move. The headstones around him pulsed a green and red from the white light. At first, he listened. If it was a person, he'd have heard their steps in the long grass. But nothing came.

"Holy shit, guys, I don't hear anyone walking," he whispered.

It flashed again.

This time, Huck sprinted to the back to try to catch something—a vapor, a wisp, anything. Nothing showed on the screen. He looked up. Nothing. Just before he sighed, a clatter came from above. In a slight panic, he looked up, craning his neck. Something moved on top of the mausoleum.

"What the…?" he whispered. "How did it get up there so fast?"

A clicking, like a dog's nails on concrete, ticked from above towards the front of the structure. Taking a deep breath, Huck dashed to the front. Just as he reached it, the light behind flashed again.

"C'mon!" he shouted into the night. "Stop messing around. Show yourself."

Just as he took another breath, a long, sad sigh hissed out of the darkness behind him. He spun, shining a flashlight he pulled from his black messenger bag at his side. The beam stretched down the row to his left to a large statue of some saint near the end.

Huck screamed.

A pair of perfectly white, round eyes in a pitch-black face blinked then ducked behind the statue. His heart thudding up into his throat, Huck dashed towards the statue. As he ran, his recording equipment picked up a single word, hissing it into his headphones: *Look.*

He stopped and flashed the beam around more. "No way, no way," he panted. "You guys saw that, right?"

As he searched for the specter, a metal tang filled his mouth and his skull started to buzz again. "It's happening!" he said out loud to his camera. He quickly described the sensation. "It feels awful," he added. "Almost like—Ah!"

Something grabbed at the hem of his jeans and tugged. Just as the light swiveled to his right, something moved in the grass behind the headstone.

"Come back and face me!" he shouted into the dark. To his audience he mumbled, "I'm kidding, don't freaking come near me. I about shit myself." He laughed nervously.

It took about fifteen more minutes of calm nothing for Huck to finally decide to enter the mausoleum.

"It's not exactly locked," he mused. He'd calmed down significantly since the thing touched his leg. Most likely a rabbit. He showed the loose chains on the gates and the rusted out lock. "Jackpot," he whispered, pulling the gate open. "This was a private mausoleum. It's got a big foyer in the opening and a few halls to the side. It was built back in like the 1860s to house the prominent citizens of Boaz and descendants of the founders. There's probably three dozen crypts in here. But they eventually moved the burial ground to a new cemetery where they built a columbarium instead."

The foyer yawned at least twelve feet tall. Must have seemed huge in the 1800s. Each side had two halls of crypts with ornate decorations hanging from the stone rafters.

"It's kind of pretty, you know what I mean?" Huck said out loud. "There's an art to it. I think the chapel attached to this graveyard was built before the graveyard, but I can't the sure. I'll look it up once…"

He stopped talking. A spike on the waveform silenced him.

"That was a voice," he said softly. "Something said 'that one,' I swear." He stopped about halfway down the hall, shining the light. It shook slightly in his hands. "As you guys know, I'm not super into this stuff. I mean, I don't really believe it. If I did, I'd…" Call up Jasper? Try to reach out into the beyond to apologize to Mark? Somehow, it seemed disrespectful.

"Ok, here goes." He smiled, taking a deep breath. Holding his breath, he ran past the rest of the crypts in the walls to the end of the mausoleum where a stained glass window glowed above his head. His feet clattered in the concrete vault, echoing loudly. His gear clicked and clattered with him.

"Phew!" he called once he reached the end. It T-ed off onto either side. A bench waited at the end of each new passageway. Windows lined this area as well as a few plaques. There was a small door down the left side that looked like it led towards the chapel. "Made it past all of them," he smiled.

He fanned his light back down the hallway to see where he'd come from. It passed over something in the gateway. He didn't move the light back. Something held him stiff. He knew he'd seen something standing there, staring at him. If he passed the light back, it'd come to light and he'd see it for sure. Instead, he froze with the light splashing over the burial wall. His hand shook violently.

"Guys," he whispered, not moving his lips. "I see something." His peripherals picked it up. A tall, thin man-shaped shadow. Long, sharp fingers hung to its knees. It was so thin, he was sure it could slip through the bars of the gate. It didn't move. It didn't breathe.

The longer he waited, he bigger the thing got. Like it slid down the hall towards him, not moving its legs.

Shit, oh shit! he thought in a panic. *How is it coming towards me?*

Once it got close enough that he swore it had to be in

camera view, the thing's arm reached out to him. With a shout, Huck finally unglued his feet from the ground and dashed away. His eyes hurt so bad from the buzzing now that tears streamed down his cheeks.

As he turned to go down one of the cross sections, a specter appeared there, right in the flashlight's beam! The ghost was a man in overalls and a straw hat missing its top. He looked dirty. When Huck met its eyes, it lunged towards him, hand out stretched. Flipping on his feet, Huck dashed back the other way. There was no door on this side. Screaming in panic as faces appeared in the plaques, he turned back. The darkness with the black shadow in it didn't waver. Nothing moved. His last hope would be to rush past it, hope it didn't snag him, and make it to the little door where the old farmer ghost had vanished.

Something told him the black shadow still waited. That it called up the ghost to stop him. Forced it to appear.

Cursing wildly, he shouted and ran past the hallway. The first ghost didn't appear but something worse did as he ran towards the little door. The doors to the burials in the walls pressed out like rubber gloves. Hands fought to be loose of the walls, reaching for him. A moaning and crying accompanied the flailing limbs. One managed to grasp his shoulder and pull hard. Only terrified screams ripped from Huck's throat as he fought to not be dragged into the grave. The little wrought iron door was just mere feet away.

He dropped his camera and spun out of his hoodie, letting the ghosts take it. He slammed his body into the gate but it didn't move.

"Help me!" he screamed into the night. He slipped his hand through the gate and tried to find the latch in the dark.

One last glance over his shoulder solidified his fear. The black, tall thing made its way around the corner, floating steadily in his direction, inches above the ground. It's round, red eyes locked onto his. Now he was trapped. More specters appeared—a glaring woman, a man with a butcher's knife, a wickedly grinning little boy in modern clothes—all bearing down on him.

"Please, help me!" he cried out the gate again to anyone who might be passing. He pressed up against the iron so hard, bruises appeared on his ribs.

Just as the glaring woman reached out for him, the gate flew open from the outside. A familiar, blond mess of hair wavered in Huck's blurred vision. Recognition forced him to leap out into the confused arms of Logan. He spun around the cop, putting Logan between him and the mausoleum, eyes wide and looking back into the dark halls.

The hallway loomed cold, dark, and empty.

"What the hell, Huck?" Logan growled. His tone vibrated in rage but he pulled Huck close and marched quickly away from the haunted vault.

"You didn't see it?" Huck gasped, barely able to get words out. "There's something in there. It came at me. It attacked me!" He panted rapidly, suffocating no matter how quickly he breathed.

Logan held Huck tightly, moving in front of him to protect him from whatever he thought he saw. He looked back, tactical flash light splashing it's white light all over everything. "Nothing's in there, Huck," he said after a moment. "It's quiet."

Seeing Huck didn't calm down, eyes wild and locked onto the dark portal, Logan guided him out of the graveyard and back to his cruiser. He kept his hand firmly on Huck's shoulder. "You need to calm down," he ordered. "Breathe slower or you'll pass out."

Huck tried, taking deeper breaths.

"You could have been stuck in there for days," Logan chided him. "Good thing I was patrolling tonight." He handed Huck his fresh coffee from a diner in town. "Drink that."

Huck pressed the lid to his mouth and took a long swallow. The warmth from the dark roast cascaded down his insides, thawing him out. He didn't realize how cold it had gotten. His clammy skin glimmered in the street light.

"Thanks, Logan," he sighed, still shaken. "I was just out here filming."

The cop nodded. A voice came over his radio on his chest, but he turned it down. He bent down and picked his hat up off the ground. "Dropped it running in there," he said in good humor. "You sounded like you were dying."

"Felt like it," Huck sighed. He finally pulled his eyes away from the now fog-covered graveyard. "You believe in ghosts, Logan?"

The man smiled crookedly and looked down at him. "Kinda. Sometimes, I guess. There's this guy in Connecticut I used to know. We used to work together. Years ago now. He was into ghosts and the spirit world and all that shit. Sorry, I mean, stuff."

Huck nodded, encouraging him to go on.

"He was something of a consultant on special cases," Logan sighed. His eyes glassed over, remembering. "On *weird* cases. I knew him from college. That's a story on its own. But we became friends. He was researching cults, ritual murders—that kind of thing. But he believed there was more out there than we know."

Interested, Huck looked up at Logan. "He's right. There is. At least, I think so. What happened? He still working?"

At this, Logan winced sadly. "Yeah. He moved to Connecticut a while back. More hauntings up there. We had a falling out, though. You could look him up, I guess. He's a private paranormal investigator or something now. Look for New England Private Paranormal Society," he added when Huck opened his mouth to ask. "That's his 'firm'." He put air quotes around the last word. "Should come up if you do a quick internet search. But, Huck," he turned to face his young friend again, gently taking his shoulder in a firm grip. "Sometimes, when you call into the darkness like that, something answers back. Whether you believe in it or not. Ok?"

Warmth and security finally trickled down Huck's spine. "Thanks, Logan. And sorry I caused a ruckus."

"Any time, kiddo." Logan looked around. His eyes followed something Huck couldn't see, like a hunter stalking invisible prey. "Yeah. There's no telling what kind of things you'll see in a graveyard."

Chapter 12:

The Guy In Connecticut

Huck edited the video over the next few days. It took him forever to work up the courage to look at the footage and listen to it. The first night back from the grave-yard exploration, he didn't have any nightmares. Encouraged, he worked on the footage. As he cut out the long, boring bits filled with headstones and his breath wafting in and out of frame, he searched the corners of the frames, the dark spots—anywhere a ghost might lurk.

When he got to the bit where he knew the eyes had peeked out from behind the statue, he braced himself. The first playback, he let it run in real time. The huge, glowing, round orbs pointed at the camera. A shiver ran down his spine but he forced himself to watch. Eventually, he paused it on the ghoulish frame and stared into the thing's empty eyes. The more he looked, the more he tried to convince himself that it had been a kid playing a prank. Or an old woman visiting a grave. Maybe even a cat the way the orbs poked out of a black mass. These things always had some kind of explanation.

His eyes didn't buzz and the metallic taste didn't come

back, so he finished editing, added in the music effects and intro, and posted it on his website. Just minutes after uploading, the view counter ticked up. Normally, he, Mark, and Jasper would hang out online for an hour after uploading to reply to comments. This time, he opened a new tab and started to search for anything he could think of: how to protect yourself from ghosts, spirit repellent, why would a ghost attack, and so many more options.

This led to a rabbit hole and before he knew it, he had over twenty tabs open on warding, sigils, protective amulets and something about salt and burning. He ended up in the online newspaper archives of the county, flipping through anything that mentioned specters, ghosts, or hauntings. He laughed a little, coming across a few months back in the early 2000s where the town thought they had a coven of vampires harassing livestock. Classic, tiny midwestern town. He was about to flip the digital page when a picture caught his eye.

The image was old and whoever had uploaded it to the website did a poor job, blurring it. But he recognized the blond man-bun. A tall, dark-haired man stood next to Logan in the picture. Logan had been fresh from the academy and appeared to be on a case in the picture. Huck smiled and shook his head. Below the image it read, "New Ad Astra Ranger and Boaz County police captain Max Logan and paranormal private investigator, onetime local Max Winchester who recently relocated to Connecticut, stand in front of the burned out warehouse where a suspected vampire cult was thought to reside."

"Max Winchester?" Huck read out loud. The name was so familiar, Huck almost thought he could place a face with it. The image was too blurred for him to make out the dark-haired man. "Wait a minute," he mused, opening yet another tab.

He did a quick search. Logan had mentioned a guy in Connecticut who worked on paranormal stuff. This must have been him. A few searches returned the guy's website. Huck had to crawl over half the website before he believed it was a private paranormal investigator's website: it looked like a page for a doctor's office: clean, white, and teal.

A few blog posts talked about what this Max Winchester did, but it was all phrased as if he tried to hide the paranormal side. Most of them rehashed mysterious murders, disappearances, livestock deaths. There were very few pictures. A gallery linked from the blog, but a warning across the top said, "Most items depicted here were cursed or haunted. Look at them with caution."

The page had only nine pictures on it, all lined up nicely. The objects were dishearteningly regular. One was even a baby's toy phone from the sixties. Maybe evil ghosts and spirits couldn't pick what they haunted?

"The spirit world isn't in to fashion, that's for sure," Huck mused, clicking on the bio. It mentioned this guy grew up in Kansas, discovered his gift for "seeing into the dark" and how he struggled with skeptics but eventually made his living. Didn't mention a wife or kids. Nothing too personal. "Max Winchester," he said again. "Why do I know that name?"

Shaking his head, he eventually left the site, printed off a few simple warding tricks and checked the comments under his video.

Desperate hoax, one commenter said. *Way worse than his old vids. You can see the mechanics, people. Fake.*

"Fake," Huck mumbled out loud. His spirit fell. "The one time something actually happened." He picked up his phone and opened the front facing camera. Stretching out his neck, he inspected the vanishing bruise there. He should have photographed it that night while it was fresh.

Want my view? one commenter said. *Do a seance or something and reach out to Jasper. Get him back on the show lol.*

Huck scoffed in disgust. They would never know how disrespectful they sounded. Leaning forward, Huck turned off the monitor to block out the site for a minute and collapsed, putting his face into his hands. He moaned out loud.

Then it happened. He froze, eyes buzzing. The slightest taste of metal slid down the back of his throat. Slowly, he parted his fingers, looking down at the desk. Just behind him, a cold spot started to blossom out. It touched his back, and he shivered. Holding his breath, a chilling sweat broke out onto his skin. He spread his fingers and slowly looked up. The black face of the monitor gave a featureless reflection in its matte screen.

At first, he saw nothing. It was dark around the outline of his head. Then a shape stepped out behind him and off the side. Huck screamed and spun around, sending his keyboard and mouse crashing to the floor. In the moment he spun around, the faint, white outline of a person vanished.

"Shit," he gasped, eyes locked onto the space. The buzzing in his skull subsided. His breath rattled in his chest. "Why?" he cried out. "What do you want from me?"

"Huck?"

Holly stood in the doorway, staring wild-eyed at him, toweling off her freshly washed braids. Her brown eyes flitted from her terrified son to the spot on the ground he gaped at.

"Baby?" she asked again. She took in the keyboard on the floor. "What happened?" She knelt down and picked up the few keys that popped off on impact.

Dropping his pale face into his palms, Huck let out a quiet

sob and shook his head. "I'm sorry. Something made me jump."

She tossed her tower onto his bed and picked up the keyboard. "This one was a one-off gift. You break it, you're buying the next one."

"Sorry, mom," he sighed, leaning heavily against the desk. He sniffed and crossed his arms. The cold lingered. "What do you think happens after you die?"

She tilted her head and sat down on his bed, going back to her towel. She crunched it into her hair, thinking. "Well, people have a lot of theories."

That wasn't really what he wanted to know. The words of the manic cult people rang in his head, telling him he'd killed. He was a foul soul. Never could he tell Holly he was responsible for Mark's death. For Jasper's. He had more blood on his hands than anyone in town.

"Never mind," he sighed.

Holly smiled sadly at him. Then, her eyes went to the paperwork on the foot of the bed. "Boaz State University?" she asked, picking up the letter.

"Oh, yeah, about that," Huck started.

"You got in?" she shouted, leaping up. "Huck, why didn't you tell me!" She squealed and lunged at him, crushing his bruised ribs in a hug with the mysterious strength only mothers possess. "This is great, this is great," she crowed. "We'll pack and I can help move you in. What's your major? Did you apply for scholarships? It's ok if you didn't, we'll find a way. Are you going to live on campus or live off? Do they require freshmen to live on campus for the first year? I thought it was too late to get in and was only hoping we could get you in! Oh, Huck—"

"Mom, holy shit!" Huck couldn't stop the smile that broke his face. He grabbed her arms and pried her off him, sitting her down on his bed and joining her. "Yes, I have to live on campus the first year."

"I won't move you in if it will embarrass you," she promised. With a gleeful grunt, she leaned over and kissed his cheek excitedly. Then she paused and placed her hands on either side of his face. "I don't know what I'll do without you. I'm too young to be an empty nester. I'll have to join a bingo club. Eat lunch at 11am with grandmas at the hospital."

When her face fell, Huck's heart broke for her a little. Her eyes turned dark, and she absently gazed at the floor. He knew she thought about Mark.

"Don't get too lonely," she said, her voice suddenly thick. "You should have had each other." Her eyes glowed with tears. "I know this will be harder on you. You have to be strong."

He heard her avoiding what she really meant to say: "You'll be alone." He bit the inside of his cheek. "I won't be alone, mom. I swear I'll try to make friends."

"And you won't be far," she said, more to herself than Huck. "BSU is just two hours away." She stopped. Her eyes lit up. "BS University." She chuckled.

Huck joined her, nodding. "Oh, yeah, I plan to make as many jokes as I can."

"Oh," she sighed, pulling him in to a hug again. "You'll do great. But seriously, take this opportunity to find some friends. Make connections."

The reason it would be so hard was simple: he'd never had to make friends. He'd been born with Mark and they'd never had spats like normal brothers. Jasper naturally came into his life. He thought about it: He had Jasper. Mark had never really had another friend.

"I think the loneliness got to him," Huck chanced. "Mark never had a friend like I did."

Holly nodded, pushing back from him and wiping a tear. "I think so. He was a lonely boy."

They sat in silence for a bit. Holly started to make comments about what to pack and what to leave. She promised to not turn his room into a home gym while he was gone.

"I'd never use it anyway," she laughed. "I'm too tired when I come home from the hospital."

"Hey, mom," Huck cut in softly. "That letter you got from my biological mother?"

She sucked her lips in and nodded. "What about it?"

"Did you reply?"

Holly took a few steps away and fidgeted with the corner of a big piece of art hanging on Huck's wall. "You know, you don't draw like this anymore. Maybe take an art class at BSU?"

"Mom," Huck cut in. "The bio parents?"

Sighing in defeat, she crossed her arms and leaned against the wall. "Marion called." She said the name like a curse. "She and Max are in town—"

"Max!" Huck shot up.

Mom jumped in fright.

"I remember now," Huck shouted. "Max Winchester!"

Mom nodded. "What's wrong, hun?"

"Nothing." Huck went back to his computer and turned on the monitor. He opened up the paranormal private investigator's website again. Yes, it did say Max Winchester. But no mention of a Marion.

He quickly searched for Marion Winchester in Connecticut and found her. Unlike Max, she splashed her image all over. He didn't read much to find out what she did, but it must have paid well. Marion was a lean, blonde woman who held her head high. She wore pearls in almost every picture and high heels. She even had two men in suits and sunglasses flanking her in most of them. He found she did charity work, owned a few recycling plants, and got involved in small business dispute a lot. Nowhere did it say she was married.

"Oh, wow," Holly breathed, looking over his shoulder. "Swanky." She sounded a little bitter. She pushed away and sighed, grabbing up her towel. "Now's not the time to meet them, Huck baby. Maybe we can contact them again after your first semester."

He stared at the woman on the screen. Not one image had her and this mysterious Max in it. But he worked in the paranormal. Was Max like him? Could he have some answers? Did Logan know Max was Huck and Mark's biological father?

No, Huck thought. *Logan would have told me last night.* The Winchesters were extremely secretive.

But… they didn't want him. Or Mark. Huck had been in the system his entire life. Not once had they reached out before. They didn't want him.

"You're right," he replied as Mom left. If they never wanted him before, why now?

Chapter 13:
Gravedigger

That weekend, Huck went back to the cemetery in broad daylight to gather his bearings. He stood outside the sharp, black pickets and looked in. He held one small camera in his hand, scanning the still, empty yard.

"Silent as it should be," he said out loud. He panned over to the mausoleum. "I wonder…" Traipsing around the perimeter of the graveyard, he kept his camera focused on it and made his way around back. "Ok, just checking."

He zoomed in on the little back gate to the structure. It hung at an angle, viciously ripped open. The inside still loomed dark.

"I thought maybe I dreamed it," he sighed. "But, as you can see, the thing is pulled open." He frowned, looking at the screen, which showed the lock in more detail. The padlock hung on the gate, still locked. The concrete wall, where it would have attached, had three round holes where it looked like someone ripped the screws straight from the concrete.

"Must have been old," he mused. "Logan just tore that thing off." He smiled. "He's great."

Huck finished his lap of the yard on the outside and came

back around the front. When he did, he froze. A fresh grave he hadn't noticed before yawned open a few rows in. The unmistakable clank and hiss of a shovel thudded up from the grave in a dull rhythm. Panicking, he ducked down behind the taller grass and angled his camera up to take in the scene. Unsure if this was a specter or a human, he waited.

When nothing happened, he gulped and stood up. Carefully slipping in through the bend in the fence, he approached the open grave. A water bottle and a small bluetooth speaker sat near the opening. Some kind of lyrical orchestra piece softly drifted from the speaker. Taking one more cautious step, Huck peeked over the edge. A tall guy in a cut-off white t-shirt, jeans, baseball cap, and sunglasses attacked the ground furiously with a shovel. The muscles on his back contracted into sharp knots when he hit the resistant ground. The gravedigger stopped, seeing Huck's shadow on the earth. He snapped his head up.

"Hey," he called up in a friendly tone, smiling. He stood up and leaned against his shovel, wiping sweat away. "Funeral's not till Monday."

"Uh, I was just…" Huck stumbled as the guy in the grave tossed the shovel aside.

He jumped, grabbed the top of the grave, and pulled himself out easily. Huck stepped back, shocked at his raw strength. He couldn't even do one chin-up.

"Wow, that was impressive," Huck offered, dropping the camera down to his side. "You're tall."

The man smiled, white teeth glinting in a tanned face. "And you're small. Sorry," he said quickly, still grinning. He reached down to his water bottle and took a long drink. "Personal jibes aren't good among strangers." He held his hand out. "Arkin. I work for my grandpa sometimes. He's the funeral director on Main Street."

Huck took his hand and shook it, squinting up at the taller boy. "I didn't know this graveyard was still operational. I was filming," he offered, letting Arkin know he hadn't been doing anything nefarious. "I can delete it if you want."

"Nah," Arkin sighed. He reached down and picked up his speaker, turning it off. "I'm finished anyway and could use a drink." He looked over at Huck. "I'm not from Boaz. Want to take me into town and find something to eat?"

At first, Huck was instinctually going to say no. Then, Holly's words about finding friends, hanging out, helping alleviate the burden on his mind, came up. The struggled pinched his brows, and he looked away from Arkin.

"Hey, if you don't want to," Arkin said, raising his hands.

"No, wait." Huck closed the camera screen. "It'd be good for me."

Arkin smiled, curious. "Sure. Good for you."

They walked away from the fresh grave together. Arkin veered off to a shady spot where he grabbed up a duffle bag.

"So what's your name?" he asked. He quickly flipped his sweaty shirt off.

Huck started and turned towards the gate to avoid looking at Arkin's impressive chest. He never understood how some guys could just walk around shirtless. The guy was jacked, so that probably helped. "Uh, Huck. My name's Huck."

"As in Finn?" Arkin asked.

"Yeah," he laughed. "My biological parents were weird, I guess. My brother's name is Marcella, but we called him Mark."

Arkin laughed. "Damn, they didn't give you two a chance. So, car?" He stepped around into Huck's view.

Huck nodded. "I have an old, black Chevy Corvette. My friend Logan found it for me and we worked on it together last summer."

The other guy's eyes lit up. He smiled and pulled a clean shirt out of his duffle, slipping it on. "Please, let me see it."

HUCK BEAMED INWARDLY as Arkin admired his car. "It's old and costs a ton to maintain, but I love it," he offered as Arkin circled the car.

"You fixed this up yourself?" Arkin asked, running his hand over the sleek, black paint. "This looks professional."

"Well," Huck shrugged, following him around. "Logan did most of it. He got the car from a scrap yard and seemed really into it. I've never seen him cry before and he almost did when we finished fixing her up. 'It's art, I don't care what anyone else says!' he said." Huck tried to mimic Logan's smooth voice but it just sounded stupid. He winced and shrugged it off.

Arkin half nodded, impressed, and stepped back to admire it one last time. "Sounds sentimental, but I get it."

They got into the car and Huck drove them into town. There was a myriad of small, local restaurants to choose from. Huck offered several, but Arkin just wanted burgers and a milkshake. The day warmed up, so after they ordered their food, they sat at one of the red picnic tables in the restaurant's outdoor seating area under an equally red umbrella. They chewed in silence for just two minutes before Arkin spoke again.

"So, filming in the graveyard?" he said around a mouthful of burger.

Huck nodded. He carefully told Arkin about his web series and the ghost hunts. As he spoke, he felt more and more at ease, like Arkin's presence calmed him. Arkin listened, making eye contact, nodding, and not interrupting.

At first, it felt strange to Huck to have someone so invested. It reminded him of Jasper. So, he told Arkin about Jasper.

"I heard about that disappearance all the way up north," Arkin confirmed. "Damn, I'm sorry, Huck. North High, my high school, we were supposed to play you guys that Friday. But they canceled."

Huck took a sip of his milkshake. "So, what are you doing in town?"

Arkin smiled and flexed his chiseled arm. A neon green bandaid practically glowed in the sunlight on his perfect skin. "Giving blood. I supply my gramps since I'm a universal donor. He says it makes him feel young again."

A light laugh eased the tension on Huck's face.

"They say that when you donate, sometimes people pick up traits of the donor. Just for a bit. Poor gramps needs a boost."

"Is that true?" Huck sputtered.

"Picking up traits of a blood donor?" The other boy shrugged. "Makes sense I guess. If it were, I'd hope Superman would donate." He playfully flexed, then laughed it off.

"I gave blood to my brother," Huck said. He measured his words, wondering if this could be true. "He got into a bad car accident. They thought he'd die before he got to the hospital from all the blood he lost. It was an emergency. They basically made me give blood."

"You didn't want to?"

The implied accusation stung. "I wasn't exactly a selfless person. But after, that's when things got wild. Mark said he was seeing things. Voices spoke to him."

Arkin frowned, listening. "How could that have anything to do with you?"

Huck looked up. A crushing sadness overtook him. It had

been nice knowing Arkin. He'd leave after what Huck was about to say. "Sometimes I see things. Ghosts, maybe. Maybe Mark had that after I gave him my blood."

"Does he still see things?"

Huck stopped mid slurp on his milkshake. He shook his head. "No…" His throat closed up so tightly it hurt. He swallowed. "He died six month's ago."

"Shit," Arkin sighed. "You have not had an easy year. What happened?"

To others, he'd tell them he didn't want to talk about it. But Arkin made it not hurt. Like he actually cared. The way his bright, gem-like eyes stayed steady on Huck's face promised he actually listened. Listening and not asking to be in his videos, not asking to hangout at the mall, not asking for anything. The comfort lured Huck in.

"I must have given him my trait." Huck thought about how he'd been reacting to seeing things. "It's horrifying," he said out loud, knowing Arkin wouldn't understand. "Maybe he was scared. He couldn't handle it." He thought back to the other night. If Logan hadn't been there to pull him out, what would've happened? "I should have been there for him." Emotion choked him. "He was alone in the end. He must have been so scared. We could have faced this together."

Embarrassed, hot tears pricking his eyes, Huck buried his face in his hands and over-long hoodie sleeves.

"Whoa, hey," Arkin said softly. He bracingly shook Huck by his shoulder. "You can't blame yourself for his death."

"But it was my fault," Huck moaned. "I ignored him. I didn't care about him. I told him so."

Arkin didn't retract his hand and waited for Huck to calm down.

"Sorry," Huck sighed, lifting his now tear-stained face. "I

do that a lot these days. Eighteen years, not a single tear. Not now."

"No worries," Arkin said, leaning back. "You have a lot to work through. I can't imagine." He took a sip of his milkshake. "We could hang out if it helps. I'm in town for the rest of the weekend. I have digging to do, but that's only a few hours every day."

Huck sighed, wiping his nose. "I thought they used machines for graves these days."

Arkin sighed sarcastically. "If only. The bigger cities might. The graves in modern cemeteries are spaced out more for the big machines. Sometimes urns will just be buried by hand. But in these old places, it's all man-power. Graves are too close together."

"Oh," Huck mused, intrigued. He was about to agree to hanging out with Arkin but then remembered that BSU's move-in day was the next week. He groaned sadly. "I have to pack for university. Moving in on Monday."

"Right," Arkin nodded. "Well, here." He reached into his pocket and pulled out his phone. He gave Huck his number. "People are friends all the time over the internet. We can do that too."

"Really?" Huck asked, cautious of the friendly guy he'd found in an open grave.

"Sure." Arkin smiled. "If you have a sec this weekend, hit me up. Or find me online. You game?"

"Yeah."

For the first time in almost a year, a spark of joy ignited inside Huck. "I like PVP games, FPS, MMOs—all that stuff."

Arkin opened his mouth to reply, but winced instead. "Sports games?"

"Oh." Huck nodded. Before, he would have scoffed and told Arkin to forget it. Real gamers didn't play that repetitive, yearly release crap. But he could give it a shot. "I've never played one of those."

"I've done a few battle arena games," Arkin offered in reply. "Hey! I'll teach you how to play football on the G-Box and you teach me how to throw fireballs and no-scope and all that stuff."

The spark came back. "Deal," Huck grinned. A long distance friend was ideal. But if he knew that at the end of the day, Arkin waited online, he'd have something to look forward to. Someone to talk to.

"I'm HOME!" Huck called, kicking his shoes off by the front door. "I met the coolest guy…" He stopped in the kitchen door. "Mom?"

Holly leaned over the sink, head down, a wineglass in her hand.

"Rough day at work?" Huck asked, slinging his backpack onto the table.

"I wish," Holly sighed in good humor. She threw back the rest of the wine. "The bios showed up. Right when I got home. Almost like they knew my schedule."

The warm, sunny feeling that came with Arkin's smile slowly froze over inside Huck. "The bios were here?" He looked around, expecting them to pop out of the pantry.

Holly nodded again. "They want to see you tomorrow. Want to meet."

"Holy crap," Huck sighed. They had emailed. Called. Sent letters. Came by the house. What did they want? "Mom, I—"

"I love you," Holly interrupted. "So much." She sniffled

and looked out the window over the sink. "If you want to see them, you can. I'd never stop you."

"It's not that." Huck took her hand in his. "Do you want me to?"

She smiled at him. "I want you to do whatever you want when it comes to them." She searched his mismatched eyes. "Do you want to meet them?"

His father, Max Winchester, was a paranormal investigator. Huck had been seeing more and more horrors. Maybe they knew? Maybe they'd help him. Maybe Max was the same as him. They could have answers.

Huck took a deep breath and nodded. "I want to meet them."

Chapter 14:

The Bios

Huck eyed the restaurant through the rain dripping down the passenger side window. One light in the sign had gone out, making it flicker ominously.

"Oh, good lord, I bet that's their car." Holly flicked her head to the right.

A white Mercedes with gold rims glittered in the gray sunlight.

"They, uh, well off?" Huck asked softly.

Holly sighed heavily, pressing her lips together to keep a biting, childish comment to herself. "You don't have to meet them, hun." She reached over and gently pet his hair at the nape of his neck. Whenever she grasped it between her finger and thumb, it meant she didn't want him to go. "Maybe we should have given you a haircut."

"No," he whispered, his chest tight, not allowing him to take a calming breath. "I want to meet them. I need to know…" The words choked him. "If they're like me."

"Baby, no one is like you." She gripped his shoulder tight. "Don't be disappointed if they're not who you imagined.

When I first met them, they were nice people. They just weren't ready for kids."

"I don't hate them, mom," he finally managed to say. "I just need to know. And they deserve to know about Mark."

"Huck," Holly breathed, pulling him around to meet her eyes.

He read the argument in her face. She stopped herself; her face fell.

"Don't lead with that." She pulled him to her, hugging him tight. "I love you so much."

She gripped him like she would never release him. Unsure what she feared, he hugged her back.

"I'll be at the mall," she said as he climbed out. "Call me if anything happens. I'll be back in a flash."

"I'm fine," he shouted through the door as he shut it.

He flipped his black hood over his head and shrugged against the wind and the rain, running into the steak house. The inside glittered with finery he'd never imagined. Dim lights from crystal chandeliers made the place glow warm and soft. The tinkling of silver and glass was quieter than any restaurant he'd ever been in. The outside with its dead, flickering light had misled him. This had to be the one fancy restaurant in town.

"Do you have a reservation?" a woman in a white button-down shirt and black vest asked him, raising a brow.

"Uh." He took his hands out of his hoodie pockets and looked around. "I don't know. I'm meeting a couple."

"Name?"

"Huck."

She looked up through her brows, glaring. "The last name of the people you are meeting?"

Embarrassed, his neck heating, he quickly said, "Winchester."

"Oh!" The girl perked up at this. She smoothed her black vest and primped her hair with her twiggy fingers. "The Winchesters are indeed here. They said they were waiting for their sons." Her eyes unabashedly roved over his body, lingering on his large belt buckle in the shape of a cartoon ghost and his old hoodie. "This way."

Wishing he could vanish into the shadows or melt into the too-fluffy carpet, Huck followed her to a round table near the back. The white tablecloths and red walls starkly contrasted with each other, but looked rich. He scanned the tables, wondering which couple were his biological parents. Every set of man and woman sitting at the glitzy tables were out of his league. Images of coming here as a child with his biological parents filled his mind. Would he have been well-behaved? Would he and Mark have grown up with everything handed to them?

Would Mark still be alive?

He smoothed his tasseled hair as best he could. The raindrops helped.

"Your guest?" the hostess announced, motioning to a table.

Huck met the eyes of the woman who gave birth to him and his brother. He'd longed to see her face for almost eighteen years. Dreamt of it.

The woman's smooth, gracefully aging face was framed by deep, golden hair run over too many times with a straightener, forced to shine by a thick layer of products. She wore golden jewelry and a white cardigan with just the top buttoned, the sleeves empty on her shoulders.

He met her eyes. They were both brown. They didn't smile when her pale pink lips did.

"Are you Marcella or Huckleberry?" she cooed, reaching both hands up to clasp his. Her fingers were cold.

"We go by Mark and Huck," he corrected her, pulling his sleeves over his hands when she let go.

She didn't look amused at him botching the names she no doubt picked out. No one else but this woman would name boys Marcella and Huckleberry.

Awkwardly defending himself, he stammered, "I'm Huck. Huckleberry Derringer was too embarrassing to put on my website."

"Derringer?" She recoiled ever so slightly and turned to her husband.

Huck looked at his biological father for the first time. He didn't need a doctor to tell him this man fathered him: he had the same porcelain skin, blackest hair, long and shaggy onto his shoulders, the sharp jaw and alabaster nose. But his eyes were a striking, sapphire blue. Both of them. Seeing this, half the reason for wanting to meet his parents died, leaving his heart empty. Somewhere inside, he felt like they let him down.

He sat down, facing them both on one side of the table. "Yeah, Derringer is mom's last name. Er, it's Holly's last name," he corrected. "My dad's—her husband's last name. We took it when we were thirteen—I took it when I was thirteen. Right before she tried to adopt us officially. She said it made fate decide we belonged together." He stopped talking, the stumbling exhausting him. His face burned and his chest tightened. He wished he could summon up the self-confident asshole he used to be.

It hadn't gotten any easier to say I. He'd promised himself to try, but it was harder than he thought.

"The courts let you change your name?" the woman asked, her shoulders tightening. "Before they surrendered you for adoption?"

"Placed," Huck corrected her. "They say you're supposed to say 'placed for adoption'."

For some reason, her question made him feel like he'd done something wrong. Or that he didn't know what he was talking about.

"It was hard fought," he went on hopefully. "Holly and Richard pulled hard for us. It was something we wanted to do. We made the choice ourselves, Mrs. Winchester," he added when the woman shifted. He looked at the man for support.

"Hell, Marion, let's introduce ourselves to the kid before we grill him." The man smiled charmingly across the table, quirking just the one side of his mouth like Huck did. He held his hand out. "Sorry, Huck. You can call me Max. Maxwell Winchester is what my clients call me, but I prefer Max."

Huck took his birth father's hand and shook it over the flickering candle. "Yeah, I actually found you online," he said timidly. He wanted to sink into the carpet and slide out the doors. His shoulders came up to his ears as he tried to hide in his hood. "Logan kind of sounded like he knew you."

Max frowned lightly, and Marion looked away, sipping from her water.

"Logan?" Max asked. A weird glint passed in his eyes.

Huck nodded. "Well, his name is Max too, but we call him Logan. Logan Savage. He's the sheriff of our town and a ranger in the Ad Astra."

Even Marion turned back to face Huck. Her too-thin brows flickered into a confused frown. "He's dead. You said —" She turned to her husband, but he laughed it off, taking her hand.

"Could be anyone out there with the same name," Max offered.

The smiling mask looked grotesque to Huck. He knew

that mask too well. He'd practiced it in the mirror ever since Mark died.

An uncomfortable silenced followed as the waitress brought out wine glasses.

"I don't drink," Huck said quickly when the waitress looked at the adults questioningly.

"Good man," Max smiled. "You're eighteen now or close? Finished school?"

Marion drummed her fingers with sharp thuds on the white tablecloth. She fixed her eyes just over his right shoulder.

"I got my GED." He cleared his throat. "May 25th was commencement. At the high school. I didn't go."

"GED?" Marion quipped, disdain sagging her pretty face.

"College?" Max cut in.

Huck nodded. His face paled and his guts froze. "There's a university that offers the program I want."

Genuinely intrigued, Max sat up. "What do you want to study?"

"Parapsychology." He braced himself, but it wasn't enough.

"Oh, my god," Marion moaned, turning away.

"With a minor in marketing," he added quickly. "For my business." His gut dropped at her disappointment. "What is it you guys do?"

Max opened his mouth, holding his response as he glanced over at Marion.

"I don't work," she snapped softly. "People work *for* me."

"I freelance," Max offered more politely. "Consultation services."

Marion fixed her eyes over his shoulder again, glaring.

"I wanted to meet you," Huck offered hopefully. "I was

curious about you guys. Wanted to see if you had my eye mutation."

Max smiled, not saying anything.

Unable to hold herself together any longer, Marion burst, "Where is Marcella? Is he coming?" Her fingers flexed like talons, digging into the white cloth.

Huck's heart froze. "No, he's not. Mom—or anyone— didn't tell you?"

At this, Max's eyes dropped, and his bright face dimmed. "Ah," he sighed heavily, as if Huck confirmed something he suspected.

"What happened?" Marion clutched her gold necklace.

This was the last conversation he wanted to have with complete strangers. Strangers who had birthed him and his brother. They had been expecting both their boys to show up to this long-awaited meeting. On top of that, she wanted Mark. That much was obvious. And they were stuck with him: the weird one. He'd already disappointed Marion once. It would be better to paint a good picture first.

"Mark was awesome," Huck started. Marion gulped at the past tense. "But he had a lot of demons."

Max ran his hand through his hair. "You don't have to talk about it. We just expected to see you both."

Marion hissed to her husband, "I wanted to see Mark. We needed *him*."

"*I'm* here," Huck begged. "We were identical."

"Were you?" Max asked. "Matching eyes?"

Huck shook his head. "Not until after the accident. I gave him blood. It was weird. But he wasn't like me." He measured his tone carefully, speaking each word with a brief pause in the middle. How could he bring up the ghosts and specters? He eyed the wine jealously.

"Mark wasn't like me. We… saw the world differently

and I think that drove us apart." He picked up the silky napkin and fiddled mercilessly with the corner. "We all went out one night. He had a girlfriend. We got into a wreck. It made the papers and everything, lit a field on fire."

Marion gasped, gripping the stem of her glass.

Huck remembered the night vividly. "He needed blood, and I donated. A few days after his surgery, his eyes matched mine. That's when the demons came out."

He meant it literally, but the adults didn't seem to understand that. Of course, he'd never seen a demon. But if Mark was seeing for the first time what Huck saw most of his life, it would have seemed like he was going mad. If only Huck had known. Been less of an asshole.

"I'm to blame," he went on, his hand shook now so he hid them under the table. "He was going through a really rough time and I kept him at bay. He never understood me. We were close and this should have brought us closer, but I was angry that he didn't experience what I did." He looked up.

Marion glared at him, no tears in her red eyes. "You went through some kind of emotional," she flailed her hand in his direction, "goth phase and shut him out because he wouldn't join you?"

"No," Huck shouted back, indignant. "I blame myself, ok?" The emotion choked him, making his voice crack.

He'd wept a million times since losing Mark. He'd never shed tears as a child, and now they all came out.

He'd hoped his biological parents would understand, want to know, were people he could talk to about his gift. Mark never let his experiences out into the open and they consumed him. Drove him into the worst solitude. Huck was terrified that'd be him. Who could live seeing what he did?

Marion groaned, slapping her thigh in a final gesture. "This was a waste of time."

"What?" Huck placed his hands on the table, wanting to hold them back if they decided to leave. "I'm a waste? Because we're not both here?" His eyes watered. Why could he not keep his tears to himself anymore? "What's wrong with me?"

Crossing her arms, Marion glared at him through narrowed eyes.

"Hell, Marion," Max moaned, rubbing his eyes. "Huck, we gave you two up because we were too young. We weren't ready to have kids."

"*You* weren't," Marion snapped.

Huck flicked his drying eyes to her. "No offense, Mrs. Winchester, but I don't get a warm, cozy feeling from you." Definitely not a "mother" vibe.

Max leaned onto the table, throwing back the last of his wine and signaling the waitress for more. "Look, your mother —Marion—is ten years older than I am. She was ready to start a family and I wasn't. I had stuff to work out in my own life. But accidents happen."

"I'm an accident?" The question came out before Huck could stop it, high and desperate.

"No," Max said with conviction. "There was a lot of tension in our relationship. I… may have wanted to break things off."

"So I made him stay," Marion said with a smug smirk.

Not sure he understood, Huck nodded slowly. "But then?"

Marion took a drink now. "Things got worse after you two were born. You wouldn't understand. It was just best that we start over. Wait. Try again."

The last statement hit him like a hot bullet. Try again? So there *was* something wrong with him.

"Did you?"

Marion pulled a gold chain out from her sweater front.

She opened the locket on the end and turned it toward Huck. "Your sister, Celeste."

The girl in the photo smiled up bashfully at him. She had her mother's dark eyes and golden hair. Her genuine smile showed her braces.

"Full sister?"

Max nodded, smiling. "She's almost thirteen. A real spitfire."

"She will be again." Marion pulled the image away from Huck. "She is why we reached out to you."

Confused, Huck asked, "Why?" He met Max's eyes. The man cast his down, avoiding the look.

"There are some things money can't buy," Marion said quickly, picking up her wineglass. "She needs a kidney. Max and I are not a match. She's a rare type and needs a universal donor." She eyed him.

So she remembered Huck was a universal donor, but couldn't be bothered to write him a birthday card once a year?

"We were hoping Mark would give one to her," she went on. "Celeste has already lost one and is very ill and needs another."

Huck had felt let down before, but not like this. His chest sank, he even felt himself sink into the chair harder. He couldn't hide the hurt on his face.

"You only came to find me for my organs?"

"Not only," Max whispered quickly, half-heartedly reaching over the table for his hand. He stopped himself. "We wanted to be part of your life, too."

"Really sounds like it," Huck snapped. The wretched tears of rage filled his eyes again.

"We wanted Marcella," Marion moaned pointedly, pouring herself more wine.

Huck threw the napkin from his lap onto the table. "I'm out of here."

"What about your sister!" Marion shouted, standing up and seizing his arm. She pulled him back with a strength he didn't see coming. He tripped, falling back into the chair. She pinned him there with her talons. "Are you going to let her die after losing Mark?"

The hot tears burned his cheeks as they fled his rage-filled eyes. "That's not fair! You have no idea what that was like." His jaw ached from how hard he clenched. "You weren't there for us. For him! He couldn't handle it."

"Huck, I get it," Max whispered as eyes turned towards them. "Don't get loud."

"Let go of me," Huck shouted, trying to pull away from Marion. The woman's harpy-like talons dug into him harder. "You're hurting me!"

"Marion, stop!" Max stood up and grabbed his wife, releasing Huck. "I'm so sorry, Huck. Here." He handed Huck his business card. "Call me later, ok?"

Snatching the black, matte card, Huck dashed away, running into the worried hostess who came rushing to see what the commotion was about. He pulled his phone out and called Holly.

Like the superhero she was, she appeared outside in a matter of seconds. She didn't ask what happened. Seeing him cry into his palms, sleeves pulled over them, she wrapped him in her arms. She didn't pull his hood off, letting him hide inside, and petted him over it instead.

"Oh, baby, I'm so sorry," she whispered. "I should have known this wouldn't end well. I knew my first impression was the right one."

He sighed shakily, pulling away. Gaining control over his emotions, he said, "They wanted my kidney."

Holly blanched. "What?"

"They called me an accident. Said they made a mistake."

"Oh, shit." She touched his chin gently. "They're jerks, Huck. They made me and your dad do supervised visits for six months with an agent after you two were born before they decided we could foster you two for the first time."

"Really?"

She nodded. "We fought hard for you two your whole lives." Standing on her toes, she gave him a quick peck on his tear-soaked cheek. "Because we loved you two so much. Right from the start."

He rubbed the last of the tears away with his over-long sleeves. "Love you too, mom."

Sighing, he looked back, wondering if they'd come out and see him. "I have a sister."

"Oh?"

He nodded, scoffing through his clogged nose. "She's dying, of course. Needs a new kidney. They found me just to ask for it. But they wanted Mark. Not me. They didn't want to know me. Marion might have pulled me into a white van and left me in a bathtub of ice if Max didn't stop her."

At this, Holly shook, her lips going thin. "Let's go home. You need to rest."

Chapter 15:

Room 666

Sunday went by in a fast, surreal blur. Huck had to pack, process the gory, vehement request of his biological parents, and reassure his mom that he'd be fine several hours away at the university.

"Promise me you won't go into off-limits places for filming," she said, handing him yet another black hoodie, folded like only she could.

Huck smiled at her knowingly. "Mom, no one wants to watch me investigate a packed supermarket for ghosts. But don't worry, I'm… putting that on hold for a bit."

"Good boy," she beamed. "Because you want to make the Dean's List in your first semester."

"I think *you* want me to make the dean's List," he corrected. His phone buzzed. Picking it up, he saw the university finally emailed him his room assignment. The hall director and assistant both sent him emails, apologizing for the late reply. He scoffed darkly. "They had a hard time finding a roommate for me," he told Holly. "They are apologizing in advance. Good grief, what does that mean?"

"I know they tried to find you a single room," she offered,

checking to make sure he had tooth paste. "But they said they probably wouldn't. But that's good. And if this person sucks, you can always move rooms next semester."

He nodded. "Yeah, I guess."

She came up beside him, hugging him tight. "Oh, I love you! I wish you could just stay here forever." She rapidly kissed the top of his head several times. "Try to make friends, ok?"

"We have a deal," Huck gasped around her iron embrace. "Mom, I can't breathe."

"Oh, sorry." She let go and sighed again. "It's not too late to drop out."

"Mom!" Huck laughed with forced annoyance behind his broad grin. "Stop worrying. Nothing bad is going to happen."

HUCK LOOKED at his dorm room assignment sheet for the seventh time to make sure he was in the right place. Why did the dorms look like a badly rendered prison hall? Gray, metal doors lined the white linoleum floor. Above them, a light in the center of the hall flickered. Despite this, noise vibrated all around him. Fellow students ran back and forth carrying boxes, crying, and hugging helicopter parents. Seniors stood in doorways, eyeing the freshmen with disdain and some kind of jealousy.

Once again, he checked the assignment sheet. Yes, he'd read it right: Room 666. Room mate: Clint R. The sixth floor, the sixty-sixth room. End of the hall. Looking up, he ducked to dodge a flying stuffed gorilla being chucked by another student. There it was. Partly ajar, perfectly nestled between the halls, stood a gray door so dented it gaped at the top. The number 666 hung in rusted letters in the center.

The two rooms half-facing his dorm door were locked with padlocks on the outside. Signs hung off the two adjacent doors, saying those rooms were vacant and being renovated. They looked like they'd hung there for a while: faded, water warped, and torn. At least it might be quiet, with two empty rooms on either side.

Not expecting the anxiety that came with being around loud people, Huck pulled his shoulders up to his ears to hide and squeeze down the long hallway. No one seemed to notice him, but he imagined their eyes on him, judging him.

Taking a breath, Huck pushed the ajar door fully open. The dorm was huge compared to what he'd imagined. A tiny living room sprawled out before him to a large, floor to ceiling window on the far wall. To his left and right were doors leading into bedrooms. The one on the left was closed, but the right stood open. Inside, the sound of classic rock and a voice singing over it snaked out. Curiosity overcoming his social anxiety, he pushed open the bedroom door with his free hand and peeked in.

A boy his age with bright blond hair cut into a sweeping more-on-top hairdo pulled clothes out of a suitcase with lithe, muscled arms. He wore his blue t-shirt with the sleeves rolled up a fraction of an inch to show off the tight muscles that flexed with every tiny movement. Huck swallowed hard as his heart fell. He scanned the inside and saw a desk right up next to the door. A school ID laying face up had the boy's face on it. The glare from the windows blocked the face out, but the ID read Clint Remington. His heart sank as he realized he had to spend the next three months around this loud guy. His organs cringed as a new fear of social interaction took him over he was not accustomed to.

"Hey!"

Huck nearly swallowed his tongue in fright as the athletic

guy reached over and flung the bedroom door open. Huck stammered an apology for spying that changed into a lie about being in the wrong room while his ears filled with pressure. His face burned red with embarrassment.

The guy smiled coquettishly. "Hey, I know you!" He flipped the music off and faced Huck again. That's when it hit Huck.

"Arkin?" he blurted, blinking rapidly. "But it says I'm rooming with someone named Clint."

Arkin beamed a dazzling smile that rivaled the sun. "And my form said Huckleberry Derringer." He arched a manicured brow. "Believe it or not, I actually forgot that was your name."

"I'm glad," Huck chuckled nervously. "There's a long story behind that name."

"I know," Arkin smiled. "I've read Mark Twain. Super long."

Confused, and now a little concerned, Huck tilted his head. "Don't get me wrong, I'm glad. You never said you were going to BSU."

"Yeah, yeah, sorry," Arkin said, pulling Huck inside. He took Huck's backpack and set it on the desk. "I used to go by Clint. Arkin Clint Remington. I *hated* the name Arkin. But when I started high school and called myself Clint, they called me clit."

At last, a small smile sneaked its way onto Huck's face. "That's unfortunate," he mused, wincing.

"Well, I thought Arkin was weird, and I'd get teased," he went on, shrugging. "Damn, was I wrong. Clit was way worse. So around junior year, I blew up the football team with my impressive skills and I finally got everyone to call me Arkin."

Huck awkwardly clasped his hands. Without his backpack

to keep his hands occupied, he felt exposed. He cast around quickly with his eyes for something—anything—to say. A bright black and red football jersey and helmet sat on Arkin's bed. "Uh, football?" he asked.

"Hell, yeah!" Arkin smiled, raising his hand halfway above his shoulder.

Unsure what to do, Huck held his hand out to shake.

"No, like this." Arkin took Huck's hand, raised it like his, then brought it down for a high five.

Embarrassment scorched Huck's ears. How many times had he done that exact gesture? He needed to calm down and reengage his brain. This new, scared version of himself annoyed him.

Arkin caught it and shook his head. "Hey, no worries. I like guys like you. You're different from me. I hang out with a lot of versions of me."

"Right." Huck half-heartedly pointed to the helmet. "Football?"

"Kicker," Arkin supplied. "Not near as glamorous as a quarterback or anything. My job's a lot easier."

"Figured you'd have a good arm," Huck said. Feeling came back to his brain, and he internally felt good about being able to make conversation. "With all the digging."

"Good arm, bad aim," Arkin joked. "Sorry I didn't mention university. I came down here from up north to come to ol' BSU. Stopped by to help my gramps on the way. He likes to see me. He gets lonely, like old folks do."

Huck nodded again. Arkin's bright cheeriness almost blinded him. He wasn't sure how to reply to the energetic guy. But that didn't seem to matter. Arkin quickly filled the silence.

"So, Huckleberry, I read the dorm rules. We're not allowed to have a hot plate or candles. But microwaves and a mini fridge are fine. I brought both. Feel free to use them."

Huck nodded, eyeing his backpack.

Arkin went on. "I have weights first thing in the morning. I don't care if you stay up late, just keep it quiet after eleven so I can sleep." He motioned to the middle section and then to Huck's room. "Separate rooms because this is the old section of the dorm. But—"

"Oh heck, football boy, keep it down!" A playful, female voice said from the wall.

Huck froze, wondering if he was the only one who could hear the disembodied voice. "Did you hear that?" he asked, going pale. Now was not the time to learn his dorm was haunted.

"Yeah," Arkin smiled crookedly. "It's Lilia. Come here." He pulled Huck over to the desk. Pressing his hand against the wall, Arkin slid aside a little metal plate on a screw that blended into the wall.

"Whoa," Huck breathed. "Secret tunnel."

"Secret air vent!" Arkin and the girl's voice said together.

"I'm Lilia," the girl said through the wall. "I'm a room away from you."

"Wait," Huck started. "The rooms next to ours are empty. I saw the signs."

"Once removed," Lilia giggled through the vent. "The old air ducts fell down in the room between ours, but are still attached to the wall. Come into the hallway."

Huck hesitated. He only had the energy to meet so many new people in one day. "You go," he said to Arkin. "I want to unpack."

"No, no," Arkin said, grabbing Huck by his arm and dragging him toward the dorm door. "Don't worry, I got you. She's great."

Sighing in defeat, Huck let Arkin pull him back out into the raging dorm hall. The doors slammed open and closed continuously, voices shouted across the hall, and panicked parents hurried back and forth. He cringed from the chaos, falling behind Arkin. He'd have to apologize later for being a stupid shrinking flower.

"Hey!" the girl's voice hissed from their left.

A pretty girl with a small nose ring, long, wavy blue hair, and a skull t-shirt stuck her head out the door. She winked. "In here."

Arkin went in first, letting Huck use him as a shield.

"Welcome to the thunderdome!" The girl, Lilia, hopped and threw her arms up high, showing off her room. She was just a bit shorter than Huck, with elegant features. Her blue hair came down to her waist. She wore too-big Doc Martins and had black nails. The room was entirely covered in intricate Gothic decor and neon lights. She smiled at Huck. "I'm Lilia. I'm a forensics major with a minor in art."

Lost for words and overstimulated, Huck nodded. "I'm in one art class. For an elective." Her dorm was one room with a set of two bunks in the tiny bedroom. Three roommates. Huck shivered.

Lilia went to the bedroom wall, crawled onto her bunk where a pair of pink, fuzzy cuffs clinked on the bedpost, and flipped a matching metal lid on her wall. "This goes all the way across the empty room into yours. Isn't it cool?"

"Yeah," Huck managed to say. "I'm sorry you have three roommates."

"Nah," Lilia sighed, still smiling broadly. "I love being around people. Gives me energy." She scanned Huck up and down. "He's cute, Arkin, I don't know why you didn't tell me."

"Slipped my mind," the other guy said easily.

The room, with its spider webs and skulls, closed in on Huck. His breath hitched in his chest and a light sweat beaded on his temples. "I have to go," he said over the ruckus of her music and the noise in the hall. "Nice to meet you."

He caught her hurt look at Arkin as he turned and dashed back to his dorm. Once in the safety of his own room, he grabbed his bags from Arkin's room and went into his own. Closing the door, he sighed, leaning against it.

A LITTLE MORE THAN an hour passed in a semi-silence. Huck unpacked his few things, set up his meager belongings, and connected to the internet. He made a few posts on his various platforms about Arkin and the dorm and his plans for investigating the older town the university rested in. Boaz City was old, naming the county it sat in, and had more than enough haunts to keep him busy for the next four years.

He just sat down to do some research when a gentle knock sounded at his door. Sighing, Huck called, "Come in, Arkin."

The door pushed open to reveal Lilia, Arkin behind her. "Hey," she said softly, moving slowly. "Sorry I came on strong and loud. I'm bad at adjusting to people. Arkin told me you've had a rough year. So I'm going to…" She mimicked letting out a huge breath and closed her eyes.

Huck glared up at his roommate.

Arkin raised his brows. "Hey, she needed to know that you're not normally like that."

How did he know? They'd only met a couple of days ago. Arkin must have seen the look in Huck's eyes because he came in and sat next to him. Lilia followed, holding something in her hand. She held it out to Huck.

"Chocolate milk?" she offered, smiling hopefully.

They were trying to be nice, Huck knew that. And he did like Arkin. He used to be the chatty one in front of the camera. But having someone else do the talking quickly appealed to Huck now. "Thanks," he said. "I'm sorry. I got freaked out." He stopped. Would Lilia make fun of him? Call him weird? A liar?

"Like Arkin said, things have not been great recently," he offered. He accepted the chocolate milk and took a drink. It was oddly good.

"I make it with real coco," Lilia offered. "If you're willing to give me a try again, I think we could be great friends."

Something about her reminded Huck of his old friends. Flighty, shallow. But he'd promised Holly. "Ok," he said at length.

She smiled. "Oh, ghost hunting, huh?" She pointed to his laptop's screen.

"I told you," Arkin said.

She nodded. "Do you watch *The Absolver*?"

Huck shook his head.

"It's *so* good," Lilia said, smiling. "This guy is the only one outside the Catholic church who is sanctioned to do exorcisms."

"Lie," Arkin sighed. "The dude is a hoax."

Lilia glared at Arkin. "Here, look him up. He's so cute."

"I knew there was a reason for your vehement defense of him," Arkin moaned.

Curious, Huck typed the name of the show into his search bar. The name Valon Gabriel came up. "Oh," he gasped, sitting up. "I know about this guy. People have said he's phony. What makes you think he's real?"

Lilia shrugged. "I guess I just like that kind of thing. He's had lawsuits brought against him for bad seances. People try to debunk him. All the usual. But I have this intuition about him. You can buy his merch too." She reached over, clicked on his website, and scrolled down Valon's online store. "I bought a bottle of holy water before coming here."

Arkin scoffed, and Huck had to agree. The packaging of the silver crosses, the holy water, and other paraphernalia was cool, but looked kitschy. The holy water came in a round, clear bottle with a cork, sealed with red wax. A big, black and silver cross splashed across the front. There was also a vial of salt for sale. All of it bore the cross and chains logo of the show.

Huck took a quick drink of the chocolate milk. "Looks a little weird, but I wouldn't mind watching his show." What looked fake to the rest of the world just might be real. Huck had seen things these two could never understand.

He clicked on Valon's bio and froze. The man looking back at him out of the too-dark website was good-looking with his long, brown hair, and priestly getup complete with a white collar. But his eyes stuck out. One bright blue, one vivid green. He hadn't noticed before in the website's trailer.

"Yeah," Huck mumbled. "We should for sure catch his show when we can."

Chapter 16:

The Absolver

As far as college classes went, Huck felt challenged by all of them. He'd thought with his web series he had self-discipline and motivation. For years, he'd uploaded on time, never missed a day, and was good at setting time aside for editing. Maybe high school just hadn't been that hard? At BSU, time flew by before he could grab it. It left little to no room for being awkward.

"Did you grab the laundry?" Arkin asked one Thursday deep into the semester. "My jersey is missing."

Huck had been designated laundry and Arkin filled the fridge and bought things like detergent and cleaning products. Huck was in the middle of homework for the art class he shared with Lilia. He glared at his cheap paper, half thinking about his history assignment.

"Yes, but it still stank, so I put it in for a second round," he answered his room mate.

"Like we have the money for two rounds of washes," Arkin joked, half serious. "Please tell me it's in the dryer. I need it for practice in fifteen minutes."

Huck nodded. He eyed his charcoal drawing, then looked

back at his phone. He'd taken a screenshot of the eyes peaking out from behind the obelisk in the graveyard and tried to draw it. The more he looked at it, the less frightening it became. It helped calm his nerves.

His watch beeped, reminding him to get to class.

"Huck?" Arkin shot from his side of the dorm. "Jersey?"

"Dryer number four," he called, grabbing his collapsible easel and running out the door.

THE ART TEACHER, Elora Ember, walked around the studio to inspect the homework. Huck made it just in time and set up his easel. He flipped to the creepy picture on the over-sized pad and set it up. Anxiously, he listened to Elora (she insisted the students call her by her first name) give critique to Lilia.

Elora nodded, turned her head, and then pressed her chin into her hand. "It's a little derivative," she said to Lilia.

Lilia's face fell. "I was trying to mimic a few artists in the lines and lighting. And the way this part of the image inter-acts with the edges—"

"I get it," Elora cut in, smiling. "It's just not working, Lilia. It's trite. Rather than mimic other artists, this is the time to find your own style."

Despite the teacher's smile, Huck felt the words. She swept over to him, her long, red hair catching the early morning sunlight. She smiled at him. She held his eye for just one second too long, making him squirm.

"Now what is this?" she asked, pointing to the charcoal drawing.

Huck swallowed and cleared his throat. "Just a ghost in a graveyard."

He caught Lilia smirking, crossing her arms. She mouthed

"trite" to him and rolled her eyes. He shrugged, but Elora put her hand on his shoulder. He looked over at her.

"Is this something you've seen or are you drawing from imagination?" she asked. Her hand didn't flinch from where she touched him.

Huck's throat went dry. "Um," he croaked. "Sometimes I'm not sure what I see. I thought drawing it might help. I don't know…" he trailed off.

"Brilliant!" Elora mused with a coquettish smile.

"Hu?" Lilia shot, coming around to look at the drawing. "How is this not derivative?"

Elora clasped her hands in front of her and shook her head. "Learn to see, Lilia, and you'll know." She smiled again at Huck. "I never noticed your eyes."

Awkwardly, Huck bit the inside of his cheek and shoved his hands deep into his hoodie pockets. Lilia's mouth fell open a bit, and she narrowed her eyes.

"Moving on," Elora announced.

As she moved away, Lilia mouthed to Huck, "What the hell was that?"

Huck shrugged. Elora gave him the shivers, but he didn't care so long as he passed the class.

The rest of the class marched on in studious silence. The huge concrete room filled with the scratching of charcoal and other drawing utensils for the next three hours as the students worked on larger projects. Lilia joined him behind his easel.

"You know I'm not really mad, right?" she said playfully as he shaved down a piece of charcoal.

"Yeah," he replied. "This is your thing, so I get it."

She looked at his new project. "Who's this? She's pretty."

"My mom," he said, holding up his phone so she could see the picture he used for reference.

"Oh, wow," Lilia breathed.

"Yeah," Huck agreed. "She's great. And, yes, I'm adopted. Everyone always asks when they see her."

Lilia shrugged. "That's cool. So did you look up Valon Gabriel again? Are you going to do a hunt soon?"

He sighed, but smiled. "Probably. I need to keep the content up if I want to stay monetized. And, yes, you can come," he added when she clasped her hands together and hopped on the balls of her feet. "Arkin wants to come too."

"Yay!" she whispered, grinning. "But seriously, check him out. He's local."

At this, Huck looked up. "He is?"

She nodded. "His studio is downtown. Only about fifteen blocks from here. He's something of a local celebrity. He's super cool about meeting fans."

Lilia didn't know, but that meant more to Huck than just the fame. He'd have to be careful, but finding out if the guy was like him could be worth a trip to a hokey exorcism studio. With all the encounters he'd been having, someone around him who understood might help.

Making up his mind, he pulled out his phone and started an email to the address at the bottom of Valon Gabriel's website.

Dear Mr. Gabriel,

I found your site recently and would like to meet you. I don't know if you meet people in the field, but I too have a web series...

He then linked his website, signed it, and sent it.

"Did you just...?" Lilia gaped at him. "OMG, can I come if he says you can visit?"

He'd be happy for the company, but there was the whole "I see ghosts" aspect. "You'll think I'm crazy," he said in reply.

Lilia shrugged, smiling. "I don't care. I'm going to meet Valon Gabriel!"

HUCK WANTED to wait for a time when Arkin could go with them. Boaz State University got a sound beating from a rival university that Saturday, so the following day, the three of them walked downtown to cheer Arkin up. Huck fought all day in his head how to tell the other two. The stress made him anxious and short tempered, so he ended up just not saying anything.

Lilia led them down the street to a tall building that housed several business properties. All were empty accept Valon Gabriel's, which loomed overhead on the third floor. He didn't reply to Huck's email, but Lilia insisted he was cool with meeting fans.

Despite there only being one business in the building, there was a security guard behind a desk watching over the elevators. He looked bored and watched them walk all the way from the glass door to his desk.

"You here to audition for the ghost show?" he asked, eyes never blinking.

"OMG, yes!" Lilia cut in over the boys.

The security guard nodded to his left, where the elevator was. "Floor three. His secretary will meet you."

"You lied," Huck hissed as the three of them ascended. "I thought you said he was cool with meeting people."

"Duh," Lilia smiled. "But why not audition too? Maybe this will be my big break."

"Audition?" Arkin asked as the elevator slowed. "Why do they need to audition for a reality show? I thought this was supposed to be real."

"Maybe he just needs to hear their cases before he agrees to a whole production," Lilia offered.

Arkin nodded sarcastically. "Oh, sure. Do I want to do a seance for a vampire or a run-of-the-mill exorcism?"

Huck laughed at this, and Arkin smiled down at him.

"That's not funny," Lilia huffed, leading them towards the receptionist's desk.

The waiting room for the studio looked just how Huck used to imagine his own when he and Jasper first started out. Red carpets, ornate, dark wood walls. A black chandelier with fake flickering candles lit the area dimly. Old paintings in thick, golden frames lined the walls. A few marble busts of famous exorcists, ghost hunters, and even Sir Arthur Conan Doyle dotted the perimeter.

"This must be what Chris Angels' bedroom looks like," Arkin said wickedly.

"Shut up," Lilia snapped.

"Can I help you?" the receptionist called from her faux antique roll-top desk. "If you're here to audition, I need you to sign in and sign this non-disclosure agreement."

Giggling with glee, Lilia ran to the desk and started to fill out the paper.

"Actually," Huck said shyly, "I emailed Mr. Gabriel a few days ago to meet him."

The receptionist looked up over her rainbow-framed glasses. Her eyes bored into Huck's, flicking back and forth between them. "Oh, I see," she mused. "I remember. I haven't gotten around to telling him."

Huck's shoulders slumped.

"But," she said, staring up. "He's about ready for a break from auditions. Let me see if he'd be willing to chat."

She shoved another piece of paper on a black, glossy clipboard across to Huck. "Sign," she ordered.

Curious, Huck glanced over the form. It read "Nondisclosure Agreement" across the top. "An NDA?" Huck asked, failing at keeping the disbelief out of his voice.

The women raised her right brow condescendingly. "You wouldn't expect Mr. Gabriel to let his secrets out, would you?"

"Sounds like a magician," Arkin mumbled, snickering. "A faker."

"You can stay out here." The woman pointed hard at Arkin.

"No," Huck cut in, signing the NDA, then handing it to Arkin. "They come with me."

She glared at the three of them. Huck knew he couldn't exactly bargain. They wanted to see Valon Gabriel, not the other way around. The receptionist narrowed her eyes into Huck's and something behind her stoney face caved.

"All right," she sighed, waving them along. "If this doesn't go well, I'm going to get in trouble."

She led them down a dark, gray hallway to a door marked as Studio One. She cracked the door open and peeked in before whispering, "Valon, there's a boy here who'd like to meet you."

A mumbled reply came from inside. "Not like that," the receptionist said. "A witness."

Another one-word answer. She nodded her head.

Before she could step aside, the door flung open. A tall, lean man in a perfectly fitting black clerical robe opened the door. His long brown hair was half pulled back into a ponytail. He wore the white collar of a priest and a big, silver cross on his chest. Lilia squeaked in glee.

Valon Gabriel's eyes, one electric blue and the other neon green, locked onto Huck. "God be praised," the man whispered. He stood aside and opened the door all the way. "Please, come in. See the studio."

His voice came soft and warm from deep in his throat.

"Are you serious?" Lilia gasped. She pushed past Huck and Arkin.

Huck took in the studio before speaking. All the walls were painted black. Several racks of lighting lined the ceiling, along with aerial rigging and other contraptions. A sound board stood several yards back. Wires and cables snaked out from the station and slithered under a rug in view of the camera. Boom mics and other equipment waited off to the side in what Huck assumed would be off camera.

"This is legit," he breathed. "A dream studio."

"Yes, yes, thank you," Valon replied, his hands together. "Gisele didn't mention you saying anything about your gift in your email."

"Oh," Huck stammered. "I didn't."

Arkin frowned at Huck. "Gift?"

Valon smiled, holding a hand out towards Huck. "Yes. A rare gift. I've been looking for someone with your talent."

Huck swallowed. "I wanted to talk about that, actually. Are you…?" He motioned stiffly to his own eyes. "That is, can you…?"

"See the other world?" Valon asked softly. He nodded, smiling. "You call it the DarkFront, correct? Gisele showed me your website when you first reached out. Do you see that other world?"

"What the hell?" Arkin asked, blinking.

Something in Huck galloped into excitement. He ignored Arkin's question. Finally, he'd found someone he could talk to. Maybe even ask questions. "Yeah, I do! I have so much I want to ask," Huck started, all nervousness forgotten.

"I'm sure you do." Valon's voice was so soothing. He spoke slowly, not in a hurry. "And I'd love to. But first, I have to ask: would you be willing to help me on a case? So I can test your connection to the DarkFront?"

Now he hesitated. "Like how?" Huck asked.

"What the hell is he on about?" Arkin cut in.

Valon glanced at Arkin. "You don't know?" To Huck, he asked, "You didn't tell your friends?"

Fear sprouted up again in his gut. Huck shook his head mutely.

"What a burden to bear alone," Valon mumbled sadly. He took Huck by his shoulder and motioned to his studio. "I can't do this alone often. A lot of what you see on the channel is enhanced."

"What?" Lilia gasped from where she stood, inspecting a table set up for a seance.

"Shocker," Arkin groaned.

Valon smiled graciously at Arkin. "I understand your sarcasm, my young friend. But you," he looked at Huck again. "You could be just what I need. Where two or more gather, as they say."

All he wanted was to talk with this guy. See if there could possibly be someone else in the world who knew and understood what he was going through. Huck didn't want to end up on a TV like some sideshow amusement.

"I'd be willing to mentor you," Valon offered when Huck didn't reply right away. "We could help each other."

Huck hesitated again. Something didn't feel quite right, but he couldn't put his finger on it. Did it matter when—in return—he'd have someone to help him understand the things he saw? Maybe find a way to control it? Or better yet, turn it off.

"Ok," he whispered, still unsure. "What do I need to do?"

"What the hell?" Arkin shouted.

Chapter 17:

Haunted

Throughout the next week, Huck tried to find a good time to tell Arkin about his experiences. Every time he thought he found the right words, they choked him, getting stuck in his throat. His chest would tighten and fear silenced him. He thought about emailing Valon again, calling the number his father gave him, maybe even reaching out to Logan. He wanted to tell someone, needed help to bear the burden.

Friday, late evening, he sat on his bed, holding his phone. He stared at Jasper's name on the contact list. The instinctual urge to send him a message or a picture had not lessened in the months since his death. Even worse, the desire to tell someone about the guilt he carried not just for Jasper but for Mark pulled at him. He wanted to call Jasper and tell him. The sensation of being trapped, with no one to talk to, pressed down on Huck the more he wanted to let Arkin in.

In the room across the common area, Arkin played loud music, psyching himself up for the game the next day. The last game loomed just behind the BSU Ravens. Huck knew

Arkin would be in a volatile state, but he had to say something before the words exploded out of him.

Huck knocked on the partially opened door and poked his head in before Arkin replied. His roommate tossed a shirt on, grabbed a huge duffle bursting with football gear and marched towards the door. His head shoved down like he might ram the door with invisible bull horns.

"Look out, man," Arkin huffed, shaking his hair out of his eyes as he pushed past Huck.

"Do you have a second?" Huck asked, following him out the door and down the hall.

"Can we walk and talk?" Arkin asked. "I have practice in five minutes at the big stadium."

Huck took one and a half power-walking steps to keep up with Arkin. "I'm terrible at saying things, so I'm sorry in advance," he started. "But I feel like I need to come clean to you."

Arkin smiled and laughed. "So it has been you using up my toothpaste?"

"No," Huck replied sheepishly. "It's still Lilia who uses it up and squeezes the tube like that. Sorry. But remember all the stuff we talked about when we met Valon Gabriel?"

Arkin nodded, concentrating on the stadium walls ahead. He broke left, heading to the locker room.

"That night, you asked if I've ever seen a ghost and I said sometimes?" He jumped up the curb with Arkin. "It's true, and I just need someone to know that."

Arkin stopped, hand on the locker room door, half pushed open. "What?" he clarified, finally looking Huck in the eye.

Huck froze. "Yeah. I see things. All the time. Ghosts and some things I'm not sure what they are."

With a sigh, his roommate rolled his eyes and marched

down the hall. The locker room smelled of musky deodorant and sweaty boys at the same time.

"Arkin, wait!" He ran after him, following him into the underground space of the stadium.

Their voices and footfalls echoed in here. A few lights flickered and the rowdy ruckus of the rest of the team and the coaches shouting at the boys overcame Huck's please.

"Why are you telling me this now?" Arkin hissed, ducking into the locker room.

Just one second of hesitation stilled Huck before he shoved his way through. Inside, steam came from the showers where some of the team horsed around. Loud shouts followed a few footballs being tossed across the way. Locker doors slamming, locks banging against metal, and calls almost drowned Huck out.

"Because…" Huck hesitated, averting his eyes as a guy in just a jockstrap jogged past. "I like you a lot and I need someone to talk to."

This had been the wrong place and the wrong time to say the wrong words. Half the mouths flapping around them stopped and eyed Huck with raised brows. A few immediately laughed and elbowed their neighbor, pointing to Arkin with evil grins.

Arkin stopped and snapped around to face Huck. He mouthed a curse, face reddening.

The ground wouldn't swallow Huck up out of mercy. He ducked his head down but mumbled, "I just need someone to help me figure this out. I'm afraid at some point I'll see… I'm afraid I'll see Jasper or Mark."

"Holy shit, Huck," Arkin hissed, bearing down on him. He marched back, glaring hard at him. "Get out of here. This is not the time."

He spun on his heel and vanished into the labyrinth of

lockers and concrete walls, awful jokes and jibes following him. A few of the footballers looked back at Huck and snickered rudely, making obscene gestures with their hands. Huck wanted to die.

"Well, screw you!" Huck shouted after Arkin, voice cracking and face going infernal. He yanked his hood over his head. He ducked down and sprinted out of the locker room. It was only three in the afternoon, but he had no other classes. Good thing too. He'd rather die than show his face somewhere right at this moment.

The jog back to his dorm allowed him to cool down a little, but also to fester on the interaction. He couldn't figure Arkin out. He thought they'd broken the ice by this point. Maybe he'd done something wrong. How did someone their age make new friends? Maybe that wasn't an option anymore. Perhaps he'd have to be alone for the rest of his life.

Back in his dorm, he tortured himself with thoughts of what else he should have said. He went over and over other scenarios where he told Arkin sooner. If he weren't such a selfish coward, he could have had a better conversation over lunch or waited until the weekend. He needed to unload. He *had* to speak to someone. The fear and guilt would consume him all too soon. He flopped onto his bed and his eyes caught the black matte card on his bedside table. He eyed it for ten minutes before picking it up and dialing the number.

"Connecticut Private Paranormal Investigations," the low, soft voice of his biological father replied.

"Um," Huck breathed into the phone. Of all the scenes to play out in his head, this was not one of them.

"Huck?" Max asked, his voice rising.

"Yeah," he sighed.

Max took over the conversation. Thank goodness. "Are

you back in town? I'm in Boaz City for research and was hoping maybe you'd be here for the weekend."

Relief flooded him. "I can be," he said. "Mom—er, Holly I mean—would love that."

"Great." A smile lifted Max's voice. "Meet me at that sports bar on Main Street. Text me when you're in town."

THE BLACK, 1990s Chevy Corvette rumbled slowly down Main Street. Huck kept his eyes peeled for the white Porsche he was pretty sure belonged to his biological parents. Instead, he saw a lime green Ferrari. That had to be his father's car. Maybe his love of cars was biological? He parked on the street and crossed over to the sports bar. As expected, Holly had been thrilled he'd be coming home for the weekend, but reminded him to be careful when meeting with Max.

This meeting place was far more Huck's speed. No glitzy tables or waiters with their shirts tucked in. He found Max sitting at a raised table for two near the back wall, away from the flickering TVs showing various sports channels. This time, he wore a blue plaid shirt and jeans. He waved Huck over.

A little nervous, Huck hoisted himself up onto the barstool. Max took a drink of his beer.

"Order anything," he said. "I've got you covered."

"Thanks," Huck replied shyly. He clasped his hands in his lap and entwined his fingers hard.

Max's eyes finally left his phone. They studied Huck carefully. "What's on your mind?" Max asked. "I can tell from your posturing something's eating at you. Go on. I can wait."

If he wanted to know, Huck would let him know.

"There's… a lot I want to say," he began. "I want to talk about Mark and Jasper. And…"

"You see specters." Max took another drink from his beer, his eyes never leaving Huck's.

Huck's mouth fell open. "You know?"

Nodding, Max pointed to Huck's eyes. "The sign of a witness. I've seen it during my investigations. It's rare unless you work in the field."

In his chest, Huck's heart pounded like he'd just run a five-mile dash. "Yeah. I've seen it twice in less than a year." He gulped.

"Listen, Huck." Max leaned back. "I'll save you some agony. I've read up on you. I read about your friend Jasper in that off-the-map location up north. I wanted you to know that I'm looking into it."

"Really?" Huck burst. "No one believes me. I haven't been able to figure out what happened. I—" He stammered and babbled, unsure how to proceed. Finally, someone would listen to him.

Or so he thought.

"I saw your channel, too." Max smiled, cutting him off. "Not bad. Runs in the family, I guess."

"But you don't…" Huck motioned to his own eyes.

"Ah." Max ran his hand up and down the neck of his beer bottle. "I did. I had a run in with a coven of…" He chewed his bottom lip, trying to find the right word to use. "Thing is, the operation went bad. Way bad. Logan was there."

Huck nodded. "He mentioned he knew you. He didn't say you thought he was dead. He also doesn't know you had kids."

The jibe didn't pass Max's face gracefully. "I thought they lost him during that job," he said honestly. "I'm here to kind of followup. In a way. Thing is, I got hurt during that investigation, had an operation and got a donated eye." He leaned onto his elbows on the table. "I still have it, though. I know exactly what you're going through. I was afraid this would happen. It was one of the reasons I didn't want to have kids. Didn't want to pass it on."

"Yeah, well it did," Huck snapped. "Mark didn't have it, though." He choked on a lump in his throat. "But then he did. After I donated blood to save him. He never talked about it. I have no one to talk to about it now. I'm afraid if I don't…"

"That you'll end up doing what he did?" Max asked softly.

Huck nodded. "And that's why I can't give my kidney to Celeste." Honesty like he'd never felt before raged up inside him. "She'll be like me. Maybe forever. I can't do that to someone else."

Max shook his head. "No, she'll have me. We can work on it together. If it happens. We don't know that it will."

And what about him? Who did Huck have? Like a cold water balloon burst over his head, the chilling truth trickled into Huck. Max wasn't here to help him. To mentor him. Max wanted something from Huck. He really was alone.

"Uh," Huck started again. "I'm working with this guy named Valon Gabriel."

With a violent scoff, Max leaned back and shook his head. "He's a charlatan, Huck."

Well, he's going to help me, he thought bitterly.

"He wants my help with this séance," he went on. "I was wondering if you had any advice."

Max rubbed his brown stubble, considering the boy before him. "You sure you want to throw your lot in with him?"

Huck shrugged. How was he supposed to know? He was

desperate for anyone who might help him figure this out. Anyone he could talk to. Anyone who cared.

"Well, I can't stop you." Max reached down to his antique leather messenger bag. He pulled out a large, thick book. It was black with gold lettering on the spine. He handed it over to Huck. "Check up on this whenever you can."

The spine read: *Specters and Other Spirits*. Huck flipped it open and let the pages flop back down.

"Authored by some of the best paranormal investigators in the states," Max explained. "Should help you stay safe, at the very least. But," he lowered his tone, "don't go looking for trouble. Don't try to find a way into this place you call the DarkFront."

Something in Max's voice made him look up from the sketches of shadow people and pagan sigils. Max's brow furrowed.

"Seriously," his father went on. "Getting there is easy. Can happen by accident. Getting out is a whole other issue."

"Getting in?" Huck felt compelled to whisper the question. "*In* to what?"

Max's phone went off and he stood up. "I have to go. Marion doesn't know we met. Just watch out, Huck. You could witness some terrible things if you poke at the DarkFront."

"Max, wait!" Huck called. "Is this all you wanted to say to me?"

But the man retreated out the door and vanished into the darkness.

Chapter 18:

First Contact

Huck got back to his dorm late Sunday night with a stack of containers of food from Holly. The trip hadn't really made him feel any better. He'd hoped Arkin would have said something over the weekend. There had just been one text from Arkin while he was away for the weekend.

> Where you at? You didn't come home last night.

He didn't reply. If Arkin actually cared where he was, he'd wait up. The bitterness followed Huck inside. Before he entered the dorm, he noticed through the windows how dark the building was. No lights lingered on in the stairwells. Usually, the hallway's lights remained on all the time. He stood for a minute in the dark stairwell, looking up. An eerie silence floated down to him. No humming of machinery, no voices even whispered.

Did the power go out? he wondered to himself.

Unconcerned, he hopped up the stairs to the sixth floor.

He waited a second at the end of the dark hall to catch his breath.

That's when he felt it.

More than hearing it, the odd, ragged clicking moved into his ears and down his neck, more like a sensation than a sound. It reminded him of a car trying to start, but softer, more deliberate. And breathy. He couldn't explain it, but he *knew* the breathing came from the center of the spiraling square stairwell. Like something hung suspended there.

The urge to run snapped through him, but he didn't. If he ran, the presence would chase. He had to pretend he didn't know it was there. Like a stalker in the streets or a grocery store. Just walk calmly. When he made it about halfway down the hall, the presence finished ascending and for sure hovered right at the top of the stairs.

Quickly, Huck picked up the pace, cold sweat making his black hair stick to his neck. He throttled the urge to turn and look. Something told him he'd not see the thing, but the thing would see him turn. Quickly, he shoved his dorm key into the lock and turned it. Right when he got inside and shut the door, the presence zipped down the hall, as if trying to slip inside before he closed the door. With a soft cry, he shut it and pressed his hands against it.

Nothing ran into the door. No hard slam. The tingling in his eyes dissipated.

He fixed his eyes on the door for nearly ten minutes before satisfied the thing had vanished. Looking around, the room was dark too, the only light coming in the street-facing window. To his left, Arkin's door was shut. No light came from underneath. He must be asleep.

"I see you are real concerned," Huck growled, going to his room.

Not sure what he expected from Arkin, he sat down at his

desk and flipped on the little desk light. Maybe he wanted Arkin to fill a void in his life. Maybe he just wanted someone to care about him. Sure, Holly did. But he needed someone to share with. Someone who wouldn't lock him in a safe-house underground for his own safety once he told them about the things he saw. He missed being able to pick up his phone and send stupid jokes to someone. Just texting someone that he'd had a bad day seemed like something of the distant past.

The loneliness creeping in, Huck opened the book Max gave him and flipped through the pages. The fright from the presence vanished in the light of the lamp. The book was thicker than his British Literature text book with textured, old pages. It didn't look ancient, but more like something from the late 1800s. It smelled musty and a little like sulfur. One section crackled as he opened it, cinder fingerprints on the edges and bits of sand-like charcoal near the spine. Huck ran his finger over the blackened prints, wondering whose they were. Tiny bits of salt came away on his skin. He'd read something about salt before.

Hours went by as he absentmindedly scanned a few more chapters. Everything he could think of was listed in the pages: ghosts, poltergeists, witches, cults, a whole host of other kinds of spirits, vampires even, and demons.

One drawing in the demonology section stood out to him. All the demons looked like a more vicious form of shadow people (which he found out were not actually ghosts) but in different shapes. Some had goat's legs and horns. But then he saw a familiar one. Tall, thin, with long arms down to its knees and many-jointed deadly sharp fingers. It was a little formless beyond that.

He read out loud: "Called the beacon. It is drawn to those already in the interim of its world—a witness." Huck stopped right after the first sentence. Valon Gabriel had used that word. So had his father. Reaching over to a sticky note pad, he wrote the word down to remember to look it up.

"It often hungers for those who can sustain it," he read on. "It feeds on all the regular desires of its kind: fear, hate, lust, and others. But the beacon is primarily drawn to those who harbor guilt. Often consumed by this darkness, the victim, especially a witness, is like a shining beacon, hailing the spirit towards it."

The shiver that rocked him actually made his chair squeak against the floor. Huck looked up to scan the page again, trying to find this thing's name. Somewhere in the first paragraph, he found it.

"Gormalech," he whispered. He forced himself to glare at the image. Just a year ago, he never would have believed any of this. Not now.

His mouth filled with the taste of metal, and his eyes stung. He blinked. Just before he looked up, he saw one final sentence: "Like the nickname, Gormalech the beacon is drawn like a beacon to those who utter his name."

The door to the hallway yawned open. Huck turned to stone where he sat, eyes boring into the too-dark doorway. He hadn't heard it open. The glaring halo from his desk light made it hard to see into the hall. But if he turned it off...

His eyes buzzed so badly as an oily perimeter encroached on his eyesight. The room inside this peripheral changed. It turned into a dark, blue, hazy light. Something black moved there. But he couldn't look at it. He had to focus on the emptiness in the open door. Something stood there. It watched him.

It made eye contact.

Huck screamed, leaping up from his desk, not sure what to do. The entire building creaked, groaning with the weight of whatever hunted him. With that movement, the presence shot into his room. Huck made a dash for the mini fridge where a small container of salt stood for Arkin to over-salt everything he heated up in the microwave. But the thing preemptively rushed him.

At first, this thing had just been a sensation. Huck felt it now. Something hot, covered in bristles, slammed into him. He tumbled backward, landing hard on his stomach, eyes at floor level. That's when he saw its feet. They entered the oily waver as it stepped towards him. Three-toed, scaly, and melting the floor with each infernal step.

"Oh, shit!" Huck screamed, pushing himself up.

He couldn't get far. The thing grabbed his ankle with a hot, sharp hand. It burned his flesh, filling the room with the stink of sulfur and of melting skin. He screamed in pain and fear. Then, it dragged him towards the dark door.

"Arkin!" Huck screamed at the top of his lungs. His nails exploded into instant pain as he dug them onto the linoleum floor. One broke off, his blood drawing a red line as the thing pulled him towards the darkness. "Help! Arkin!"

Like a hero in an action film, Arkin appeared from the darkness of his room and leapt over his jumble of football gear just inside his doorway. He dove for Huck, landing hard on his ribs. His hands found Huck's flailing ones and gripped his wrists hard. Suddenly, a deadly tug-of-war started. Huck groaned in pain as the thing pulled his legs and Arkin pulled his arms. His sides split and something ruptured in his ankle. All the lights vanished as the oily overlay consumed almost all of Huck's vision. The world he saw looked spectral. A white glow emanated from his face in this world, almost blinding him.

Suddenly, with a tremendous tug from the thing, Huck came back to reality. Pain tore through him and he couldn't stop the sobbing screams.

"Fuck off!" Arkin screeched into the nothingness.

In an instant, both boys shot backwards. The thing let go of Huck's ankles. Huck flew into Arkin's chest, hitting him hard. Then Arkin tumbled over the furniture and landed hit the wall, slamming his head against the windowsill. In a tangle of limbs and gasping, both boys waited a moment. The lights came on in a flickering buzz.

Huck sobbed, his hands clamped over his own eyes, bawling into his palms. Arkin's arms clenched around Huck's shoulders, clamping him into a vice-like embrace. Huck could hear his roommate's shuddering breaths over his own. Everything else was quiet.

"Do you still see it?" Arkin asked, trying to sound strong. "Huck!" he shouted when Huck didn't raise his head.

Parting his fingers just enough and craning around, Huck looked out the door. "No," he gasped. He shook his head. "It's gone."

"You sure?" Arkin drew his knees up on either side of Huck, ready to spring into a fight should he need to.

Huck nodded. Arkin stood up, dragging Huck up with him. He shoved Huck behind him and glared down the hall. Every door down the long hallway had opened now. Most stared in annoyance at the pair. Some laughed, snickering at how they held each other. A few catcalls, whistles, and other rude comments came through the door.

"Screw you," Arkin shouted at them, slamming the door shut. He leaned against it, taking a deep breath, eyes wild. "Holy shit," he gasped. "Are you ok?"

Making himself as small as he could, Huck turned against the old radiator. He pulled his hood over his head and drew his knees up, shaking. The smell still lingered in his nostrils and the images of that other place burned into his retinas. Tears streamed down his nose and dripped onto his jeans.

Arkin knelt next to him, firmly placing his hand on Huck's head. "It's gone," he sighed, finally bringing his heart rate down. "You said it's gone. It's ok."

Huck couldn't bring himself to speak. His throat had closed anyway. No way any words would get out. Arkin stood up and went into Huck's room to inspect the open book on his desk.

"You got a book?" Arkin said from inside Huck's room. "You can't be messing with this stuff, man."

He had to. Arkin didn't understand.

"You need to leave this alone," he went on, coming back to where Huck cowered against the floor. "Don't even go see that guy and his lame-ass show. Leave this crap alone."

He understood, but Arkin didn't. With a shaking hand, he pulled up the leg of his jeans. A blistering, purple bruise in the shape of a long-fingered hand showed there.

"I have to," he said. "More than ever, I need answers. This thing has been following me since Mark. I know it. I've felt it for almost a year. Maybe even longer. It won't leave me alone. I know it won't!" Hysterics rose in his tone.

Arkin came back to him, crouching down and sitting next to him. He frowned in thought, grabbing at his blond hair as he did battle inside. "Ok, look. I'm sorry I snapped at you."

"Wait, Arkin," Huck cut in. He dropped the hem of his pants to hide the wound. Finally, he raised his head and dropped his knees. "That fight was my fault. I should have come to you at a better time. I never think of others. I just get so wrapped up in myself." He buried his face in his palms. "I'm so sorry I embarrassed you in front of the team. And this," he motioned around the room, "none of this is your burden to bear. I tried to force it on you."

The taller boy pressed his lips together and frowned in thought. "You are kind of a jerk. But I'm tough. I can take it."

Huck looked up at him, hopeful.

"I liked you from the moment you freaked out, seeing me in the grave." Arkin smiled. "I don't believe it was luck that paired us together here. I'm strong, right?" Arkin flexed jokingly. "Maybe I could be your ghost-hunting Van Helsing."

Huck allowed himself a little laugh at this. He nodded. "Sure. So does that mean we're friends?"

Arkin frowned, a little confused. "Duh," he quipped. "And we need to text Lilia. She was worried when you didn't come home."

At last, a small drop of comfort rippled out in Huck. Lilia had been worried and Arkin said they were friends. Maybe he didn't have to be alone after all.

Chapter 19:
Guest Apperance

Lilia skipped ahead of Arkin and Huck. The three of them left campus earlier that afternoon and hung out at a coffee shop near the studio. Huck had too much of the jitters to sit in his dorm and do homework that Saturday morning, so Arkin forced him to leave earlier. Lilia was excited to watch the show live and see her celebrity crush in action.

"It's mostly faked," Huck said as they rode the elevator up. He said it more to relieve himself than to harp at Lilia.

"Yeah, yeah," she sighed. "Doesn't mean it's not cool or touch on reality."

Before, Arkin would have laughed or made a joke. Now he stood stoically by Huck, his face stoney. "I swear, if anything looks even slightly off," he said seriously, "I am pulling any plug I can find and shutting that shit down."

Lilia smirked. "Is the big football scholarship boy getting a little spooked?" She playfully punched him in the arm.

When they disembarked, the receptionist took them around a different way than before to a set of dressing rooms. She stopped before letting them in. "Remember, while we enhance our show for drama, you have signed non-disclosure agreements. We trust you will keep the integrity of the show at the forefront of your mind during the shoot." She smiled, slightly pleading. "Also, we do take the paranormal seriously. While the show is for entertainment purposes only, the clients today are very real. A seance like this often comforts victims of loss. Please keep them in mind."

Lilia bounced on the balls of her feet, quietly clapping her hands together as the receptionist opened the door to let them in.

Already inside, Valon Gabriel stood talking softly with a young couple. He had his hands clasped in front of him, his face showing great sympathy. He gently placed his hand on the woman's shoulder and said, "Don't worry. Soon, we will have answers." He motioned for them to go out the back door.

Turning to the three of them, he smiled broadly at Huck. "My guest star!" he beamed, coming to them. "I am excited to have a witness like yourself among us today. Your abilities will shine like a beacon and make the seance today so much stronger."

"Thanks for helping me," Huck replied.

Valon nodded. "We help each other. After the show today, I am more than willing to discuss things with you."

"How much of this is real?" Arkin asked, cutting in.

Valon smiled at the snippy tone. "Most of it, I am afraid."

"Are you just saying that to psych us out?" Arkin asked.

"Cut it out," Lilia hissed. "Can I go into the studio?"

The older man nodded. "Of course. We need five for the seance. I assume you will not be joining us?" he said to Arkin.

Arkin raised a brow. "Nah, I'll man the phones in case I need to call the Ghostbusters."

Valon laughed gently. "How marvelous. This way, then."

Soon enough, Valon, Huck, Lilia, and the couple sat around a wooden table with an inlaid golden pentagram and other golden circles and symbols on it. The studio was dark except for a few candles, some red mood lighting from off camera, and the soft glow of the monitors behind the tech. A director from behind all the tech called, "And we are live in three, two," he mouthed, "one," and pointed to Valon.

"Greetings and blessings be upon you, believers," Valon said to the camera. Above his head, a viewer count instantly ticked up so he knew how many eyes were on him. "Today, we have a very special show for you. I am joined by Sarah and Jacob, who came to me some time ago, asking for closure for their small child, Jessie. Jessie, as you know, was kidnapped and went missing long ago and was recently found dead." He paused for dramatic effect. "The case went cold, and they came to me to reach out to the beyond for answers. Or should I say, the DarkFront." He smiled towards Huck. "Joining me on my right is Huck Derringer from the web series The Dark Front." He looked back at the camera. "That's what he calls the place we are about to open. Huck is very special. He has a gift just like me. So if you see something today out of the ordinary, know we expect to. With so many spirit-sensitive people gathered here, I cannot say what might happen."

Huck caught Arkin rolling his eyes in disgust behind the director. He smiled at his friend, who shook his head.

Valon held out his hands, palms up. "Let us join hands. For where five of us gather, may the circle not be broke."

Excitedly, Lilia gripped the hands of Jacob and Sarah.

Their faces pinched in fear and a bit of morbid curiosity. Valon implored them to tell their story to the viewers. Sarah couldn't, tears filling her eyes. So Jacob took over. He explained how two years ago, their daughter Jessie went missing. They looked for months and months. Everyone gave up. Then, one day, about eight months ago, they found her remains.

"I swore that if I found out who took her," Jacob went on, "that they'd pay." His hands shook. "I had a feeling about our neighbor, John." He nodded, pressing his lips together to avoid his voice cracking. "I should have said something sooner. Gotten him looked into."

"Guilt often follows those of us who have seen death," Valon said soothingly. He closed his eyes. "I sense something is coming."

Huck didn't feel anything or taste metal in his mouth. But the table shook. It jerked up, then down just enough to make Sarah gasp loudly.

"Friend or foe," Valon called into the room, which quickly filled with mist from the effects team off camera. "Reveal yourself to me."

"Seriously?" Arkin sighed from Huck's left.

He felt it, too. Sudden embarrassment made him cringe. He caught the floor boards kicking up from a motor underneath to make the table move. The mist was stupid and campy. And not in a good way. His heart sank, feeling bad for the couple.

"Shut up!" Lilia hissed to Arkin. "I can feel something, too."

"What is it?" Sarah sobbed softly.

"Silence!" Valon whispered harshly. "I am opening the door."

No sooner had he said this, then Huck felt something. His

eyes buzzed in his skull, making that ghostly peripheral show up again. He swallowed and the tang of metal filled his mouth. He couldn't hear or understand what went on around him as sound got muffled out. In the corner of his eye, he saw what looked like a hallway appear. Something black and shadowy passed by it. He jumped. His hand held still, gripped by Valon. Somewhere to his side, he heard Valon's voice.

"This is it! He sees something! Huck, tell us what you see."

He tried. His mouth opened slowly. "I'm not sure. It looks like—"

A hand, large and rough, gripped his neck from behind. Just like before in the graveyard, an unbearable chill ran down his body from where the thing grabbed him. He cried out but couldn't move.

A horrible, deep, grating voice behind him said, *Tell them you see Jessie.*

Huck's eyes went so wide they watered. He couldn't get a good breath in. His body shook from fear and the penetrating cold now engulfing him.

"It—it," he stammered. "It wants—"

No! the demonic voice roared in his ear.

Suddenly, Huck felt the thing press its cold face into the back of his head. He squirmed under its grip but couldn't move. The thing pressed harder until the icy presence no longer touched his skin but penetrated below the surface.

No, don't! Huck thought he screamed it, but only he could hear his words. *Get out of me!*

Soon, every organ, muscle, and vein froze from the ghostly cold. The thing had gotten inside him. His body tensed and then moved against his will.

Shit! He screamed in his head. He couldn't so much as see the ghost that possessed him as feel it. He knew it was that John man they talked about. In a moment, he saw John's death.

He'd been running from the law, keeping a low profile. Yes, he'd killed Jessie. After doing terrible things to her... for months. He kept her locked away. The feeling that she was meant to be a kind of sacrifice crept in, but never fully formed. This wasn't some sick, personal fulfillment. He needed Jessie. She was valuable to... to someone.

"I see Jessie," Huck's mouth said.

Don't make me lie to them! he screamed in his head to the ghost. The room swam in the white and blue oily overlay before his eyes. He saw the room slowly disappearing into the darkness. The DarkFront was opening. The place of ghosts and specters.

"You do?" Sarah sobbed.

"Don't break the circle!" Valon interjected.

"She wants me to let her speak," Huck said.

No! It's John. It's not Jessie! Huck thrashed against his ghostly captor. He couldn't throw it off. He sensed John liked his struggle and felt the ghost's pleasure at his fight.

To Huck, the ghost said, *Am I John?*

Then, as the thing made Huck tell the grieving parents that all was well, she was happy in a new place, and a myriad of other lies, he felt it reach inside him towards his heart. Almost like a cold snake slithered inside his chest. It wanted something...

"Why'd you let me leave alone that day?" Huck asked the parents, forced by the ghost.

"What?" Jacob asked, tears streaming down his red and puffy face. "Jessie, what do you mean?"

Huck tilted his head. "You let me leave. I was eight, daddy. You let me walk home alone. Didn't you love me?"

Stop it, please! Huck screamed. The movement of the thing inside him finally hurt. His entire body heated in pain.

Just then, his hand jerked of his own will, ripping itself out of Jacob's hand. The group went into an uproar then, Lilia and Valon calling to not break the circle. Excited by his tiny victory, Huck tried again.

Let me go! he roared to the thing.

How? the ghost gasped, its voice turning more demonic by the second. *He comes. I was to hold you until he comes!*

Oh, hell no, Huck thought violently. He bucked and kicked against the possession, screaming and shouting until his own voice ripped from his throat into the physical world. He knew he must have actually cried out because somewhere Valon shouted for Arkin to get back. Really, having Arkin come and grab him might help, he thought. But no one came.

The more he fought, the weaker the ghost became. Finally, Huck leaned forward and then threw his head back with a shout. As he did, the cold, evil presence shot from his body. It almost instantly dissipated. But the DarkFront, laying over his vision like a thin film, hadn't vanished yet. Shadow shapes rushed before him. Behind him, a door banged open.

Huck hopped around and caught a familiar, tall, thin form at the end of a long hallway. "Oh, shit!" he cried and lunged to run.

As he did, he hit the table in the physical world and tripped. The DarkFront vanished with the pain that shot through his arm. He came fully conscious just as his forehead smacked against the concrete ground.

"Should we cut the feed?" the director shouted.

"Yes!" Arkin called at the same time Valon said, "No, keep going! We need your prayers now, believers."

Huck gasped, drinking in the warm air of the studio. Cold sweat beaded on his skin and blood ran down from his scalp and nose. He must have hit his face on the ground. He rolled over onto his back and tried to sit up but was too weak. Lilia and Arkin ran to his sides. Around the table, Sarah sobbed into Jacob's shoulder.

"What happened?" he gasped, choking on his own blood.

Arkin flipped his hoodie off and held it to Huck's bleeding scalp. "You freaking leapt like a cheetah over the table and face-dived the concrete," he said. His tone came ridged with anger, but his hands were gentle as they held the cloth to his head wound.

Valon rushed around the table and knelt down, motioning a mobile camera to follow him. "Tell us what you saw," he asked excitedly.

Huck met Valon's mismatched eyes. He too, had a slight sheen of sweat and his skin was pale. "I-I saw," he stuttered again. He looked around. All shadows and ghosts were gone. "I don't know. I'm sorry."

A little let down, Valon nodded. He stood up and spoke to the camera. As he did, Arkin hauled Huck to his feet.

"We're going to the hospital."

Pain surged through Huck's left arm. "I think I broke my arm," he winced.

"I'll get the car," Lilia called, leaping over the wires and out of the studio.

A FEW MINUTES LATER, they sat in a hospital room, Huck cradling his swelling arm, Arkin's hoodie still wrapped around his head like a turban.

"That was *freaky*," Lilia offered as they waited. "Was that real? I *know* that was real. Holy crap."

Arkin crossed his arms over his chest and glared down at Huck.

"Don't look at me like that," Huck sighed, laying down on the crinkly paper. "You're not my guardian."

"Sorry I care," Arkin growled. "Why'd you let that happen?"

"Let?" Huck shot up. His head instantly spun and his arm throbbed. His stomach turned queasy. "That thing came into me without my permission."

Lilia's face slackened in fright. "Wait, you really did something?"

Huck nodded. "Totally real." He relayed to them everything, sparing no details. By the end, Lilia sat next to him, holding his arm with her head on his shoulder.

"I'm so sorry," she whispered with a tiny sniff. "That must have been so scary."

Arkin leaned against the wall. "It's frustrating."

"Yeah, must suck for you," Huck said casually.

"No." Arkin glared at his friend. "It's annoying because I can't fight that. I can't help. I'm useless."

A small appreciation for his friend warmed Huck's insides. "Actually, there was a moment I wished Valon would have let you come onto the set. I felt like it might help. Not sure how."

A tiny, almost invisible smile eased Arkin's face. Then the door opened. An old doctor in a white coat with a too-manicured beard came in.

The older man looked at Huck a little too long before introducing himself. "I'm Dr. Regis Nachtnebel, but everyone calls me Dr. Regis. It's just easier." He smiled at the teens before him. "So, broke your arm?"

"I think," Huck offered as the doctor picked it up gingerly. He hissed in pain and winced.

"Let me see this as well." Dr. Nachtnebel unwound Huck's head to another cringe of pain. "Stitches, I think," he mumbled. "And this isn't broken, but fractured. We'll get it wrapped all the same. Look here." He held up his finger and looked Huck in the eyes. He stopped upon taking them in.

"What is it?" Huck asked. "Concussion?"

"No, nothing like that," the doctor said, smiling suddenly. "Let's get you taken care of. I'll have my staff get you stitched and wrapped. I'll see you around, Mr. Derringer." He winked at Huck and exited the room.

"Creep," Arkin mumbled.

Chapter 20:

Mother Dearest

The stitches weren't bad. Even the wrapped arm wasn't bad. What was bad, was Holly calling Huck on their way back to campus to scream at him for hurting himself. Of course, the hospital called her for the insurance information and now she was livid. Shouting ensued the rest of the way home as Arkin bellowed how he said it was a bad idea but Huck wanted to do it anyway.

"This is the point of friends!" Holly's voice came so loud it crackled the speaker phone. "Listen to him next time, will you?"

Arkin gave Huck a cheeky grin in the car's darkness.

"Eyes on the road," Huck snapped. "I didn't spend two summers mowing lawns and winters shoveling snow to fix this baby so you could crash it being a jerk."

"Huck, baby," Holly sighed. He could practically hear her rubbing her temples. "*Please*. Be careful." No warning made her voice hard, just honest begging. "Can you just focus on school?"

He nodded. "I will, mom."

"I love you."

"Love you, too."

"Aww," Lilia cooed from the back seat. "Not to be a mood buster, but what about the game this weekend?"

Arkin looked sideways at Huck. "You don't *have* to come. I know it's a long drive to Missouri. Away games suck."

"We should support him abroad," Lilia offered. "I've got my art final almost done, so I'm good to go."

Huck looked down at his neon-green-wrapped arm. "If it's all the same, I'd rather stay at the dorm. I need to do research for another video, anyway. I haven't uploaded in a while."

Giving as ever, Arkin nodded. "That's ok."

The tension in his roommate's voice was palpable. It was an away game, a rematch against their biggest rival. Surely he could give up one weekend. *This should be an easy decision,* Huck thought to himself. But he had to keep uploading. The anniversary of Jasper's death was coming up. He needed to keep the view flow coming and have something planned for the terrible event in Coven Wood.

Maybe it was time to think about going back…

"Sorry, Ark," he finally said.

Lilia sighed sadly. "Damn, I wanted to road trip."

"We will," Huck promised. "I was thinking we could all go to some haunted place together and do a big event. Like an overnighter."

"Oh!" Lilia clasped her hands together. "Sounds like you have an idea."

Huck nodded. "I think I do."

THE WEEK WENT by with little to no events. He and Lilia now had the top grades in their shared art class, and Elora used their work as examples. His other classes were boring. He couldn't take any parapsychology classes until the next semester. The school had a rule about freshmen taking those classes and he had to work on general education the first semester. So instead of furthering his paranormal study, he learned algebra and U.S. history for the fifth time in his life.

By the time the weekend rolled around, he almost wanted to ditch everything and go with Lilia and Arkin. Lilia came to their door early Saturday morning. She had divided her blue hair and dyed half of it black and the other half red for the BSU Ravens. She wore red and black and even painted the Raven on her face.

"You know the game isn't until tonight, right?" Arkin laughed, grabbing his duffle bag.

"I'm just being supportive," she smiled. She snatched Arkin's backpack and skipped down the hall.

Arkin stopped in the doorway. "You sure you don't want to come?"

Huck couldn't exactly explain. Putting Arkin first over Jasper felt like cheating on his best friend. "I have to do something. I'll be anxious until I look into it. I'd be no fun. I'm sorry."

With a nod, Arkin left, closing the door.

Opening his laptop, Huck typed in the same search terms he'd used over and over for the last ten months. Coven Wood. Cults in Kansas. Reports of human sacrifice. Missing people. Jasper Wessen. This last one brought up his obituary. Huck glossed over it until a line at the end caught his eye. "Jasper Wessen leaves behind his father Carlisle Wessen who oversaw the burial, and a mother and older brother who reside in Norman, Oklahoma."

A crushing weight pressed down on Huck. He knew Jasper lived with his dad and stepmom, but did not know he had an older brother. How self-absorbed had he been? A few searches later, he found someone named Aiden Wessen in Norman. Maybe Jasper and Aiden didn't get along? Or did Jasper's dad cut off contact? It only took him a second to decide not to reach out to Aiden. He went back to the other searches.

Nothing every time.

Annoyed, he started another search for something haunted close by. Something he, Arkin, and Lilia could do with an interesting enough past to entice viewers. The usuals popped up: the gates of hell in Douglas County, some house in Jackson County, the Elms Hotel, and a place claiming to be a cursed castle. Most things were a few hours drive away. His eyes drifted to the matte black card still on his desk. Maybe Max would have a good idea. He should call him anyway and tell him about the event on Valon's show. If he hadn't watched it already. If he had, wouldn't he reach out?

He picked up his phone and saw an alert for a voice mail. He must have missed it ringing. Curious, he checked recent calls and was surprised to find Valon had called him.

"Wonder what he wants," Huck mused out loud. Checking the clock, he saw it was almost midnight. He stood up from his chair and opened his bedroom door. He exited to walk tiny circles around the common area between the bedrooms and listen to the voicemail when something caught his eye.

The door to his dorm stood open. He froze, looking down the hall. All the other doors were closed, and the hall stretched on, more quiet than usual. Most people must have been at the game. Or gone home for the weekend. He focused in on the end of the hall, holding his breath and narrowing his eyes.

His phone buzzed again in his pocket, making him jump. Pulling it out, he looked down. The screen read: Caller hidden. He let it ring two more times, wondering who it might be before curiosity made him answer.

"I thought you wouldn't pick up," a deep, feminine voice mused. It was Marion. She sounded annoyed.

"What?" Huck snapped, pacing down the dorm hall to release the tension.

"I'm in town. Come down. I need to talk to you," she quipped.

"Over my dead body," Huck laughed dryly in reply.

"I hope not," Marion sighed. "If you don't come down, I'll send my men up."

His mouth popped open in amused shock. "My friend is in my dorm. He'll be waiting for me." Why did he feel the need to add a layer of safety? Why did Marion give him the creeps?

"I'm sure," she mumbled. "We're parked out front."

Huck stopped the call and jogged down the three flights of stairs to the glass doors that looked out on the street. The white Rolls idled near the pavement. The windows were so black, he couldn't even see a silhouette of her inside. When he stopped to inspect the car in the streetlights, the window cracked a bit.

"Come here, Huckleberry," Marion quipped from the inside.

Cautiously, he approached. Bending over, he peered into the tiny slit between the window and the door. The inside was so dark he couldn't see anything. Her blonde hair and diamond jewelry twinkled gently.

"Driver side," she ordered.

Giving a quick glance to the front seats, wondering if she really had bodyguards, he slowly made his way around the back of the Rolls. When he reached for the handle, the door popped open. Sure enough, a huge man in a black suit, red tie, nearly opaque glasses stepped out and reached for his arm. Huck stumbled back, but the man caught him and pulled him towards the car. Aggravated, Huck let himself be pulled in. He slid across the seat to land right next to the bedazzled woman. Marion's piercing eyes bore into him, making him feel like he was about to be chided.

"What do you want?" he asked, aggressively shrugging.

Marion didn't answer. She rested her elbow on the door and put her chin in her palm, looking away. Just as Huck was about to insist she speak, the big man got in quickly. Before he closed the door, the driver peeled out, speeding down the street.

"Oh, hell no!" Huck shouted. Diving over the man's legs, he reached for the door. He imagined hitting the pavement and rolling, but the huge man grabbed him. With one hand, he pinned Huck to the seat. "What the hell, Marion?" he spit.

The smell of powdered gloves and chemicals suddenly filled the air. He snapped his head around to the man. A white cloth was pushed against Huck's face. Gasping, trying to scream for help, Huck tried to shove the man off and punch him at the same time. His fractured arm cracked in agony when the man grabbed it and pinned it down.

"Stop struggling, Huckleberry!" Marion screeched.

"Relax," the big man cooed into his ear.

Huck couldn't stop his body going limp. His brain fogged over. "Don't... please..." he managed. Marion's eyes fixed out the window, refusing to look into his face.

HUCK COULDN'T FEEL ANYTHING. His eyes opened but only halfway for what felt like hours. He thought he wanted to shiver but couldn't make his body do it. His toes hurt like the time he ran around in the snow barefoot as a child. His head spun, so he spent several minutes taking deep breaths. Something on his side hurt. Like a searing pain.

Finally, he got his eyes open all the way. Looking around, he took in a dilapidated bathroom. A toilet sat to his right, just at eye-level. An envelope waited on the closed lid, propped up. It had his name on it. His bare arm hung lip and pale over the side of the bathtub. That's when he realized he lay horizontal in an old tub.

"What the hell?" he managed to say. His voice cracked from thirst and cold. A window on the opposite wall lit up the room enough. The sun just peeked over the horizon. How long had he been out?

He tried to sit up but couldn't. Partially melted ice clung to his almost naked body; only his boxers covered him. The freezing water from the melted ice was tinged pink.

"Oh, shit," Huck gasped, pulling himself up with great effort. He'd heard about this. Seen it in movies. With a cry of cold pain, he finally hauled himself into a sitting position. The water turned a little more red with his movement. He continued his string of panicked curses. His legs had very little feeling, so he used his one good arm to pull himself up onto the edge of the tub. The bathroom mirror lay on the floor in four pieces.

Careful to not hurt himself, he flopped onto the broken tile and sat up against the wall. Panting, he looked around. He didn't recognize the bathroom. Out the door waited an empty living room of what had to be an abandoned house. Out the window, he recognized the sound of the nearby city but red and yellow leaves shivered in a light breeze.

Now that he left the ice and water, his body heated enough to make him shiver. He still couldn't feel his legs so he'd have to wait a few more minutes to walk out, find his phone, and call for help. He didn't want to shout here, exposed, and vulnerable. And what if the man or Marion waited in the next room? What did she want? What had happened?

Eyeing the envelope, he reached for it, grunting in the effort. His blue fingers shook, hooking into the sealing and tearing it. To his surprise, a prepaid card fell out. A thick piece of paper waited inside. Pulling it out, he read:

Dear Huckleberry,

This could have been much easier. I didn't want to hurt you, but you forced my hand. I recently visited your sister in Florida (she lives with my parents on the coast) and she has gotten worse. We could not wait.

I know you may panic when you see what I've done, but know that you'll be fine. Truly, you will. When you wake up, call someone to take you to the hospital downtown. We charged your phone in case you sleep longer than expected. There, you will meet Dr. Regis Nachtnebel.

He stopped again. Yeah, he'd met him. He had gotten bad vibes from him then.

He's the one who performed the surgery to remove one of your kidneys. He has to get it to us quickly, so he will not be able to take care of you once he removes it. He's a miracle worker and assured me you'd be fine until you made it to him after you wake. I must warn you: do not go to the authorities. You and your adopted mother do not stand a chance. I have more authorities in my pocket than you could hope to meet in your lifetime. Also, please consider Celeste. She deserves a chance to live. Don't you want to give her that chance? This is your opportunity to save a life, Huckleberry. Do the right thing.

The card is for you. It will cover all your expenses, including your recovery. Regis told me he'd leave the address of where he deposited you so you may call for assistance. Consider this a favor.

Thank you, my son, for saving your sister's life.

Huck shook so bad, he dropped the letter. Reaching over, he grabbed up a shard of the broken mirror and held it to his side so he could see. A long, red incision met his frightened gaze. It looked infected. A few stitches pulled his flesh together. Realizing what had happened, he screamed and dropped the mirror. A faintness came over him again, spurring him to get up.

With great effort, he got to his feet and stumbled into the living room. His phone sat on an end table near a dust-covered chair. He fell once or twice, bruising his back and ripping a couple stitches before he finally got to his phone. Curses at his biological mother streamed from his mouth. Sweat beaded on his entire body now. Once he had his phone, he collapsed onto his floor. Pain heated every limb. He dialed Arkin's number.

Arkin picked up on the second ring. "Hey, man, we're at the ice cream joint down the street. Got back into town super early this morning thanks to Lilia's definitely-not-dangerous driving."

"Arkin…" Huck panted. Words seemed impossible to get out. "Hel…help me."

Arkin's panicked tones filled his aching head as he went to the notes on his phone. Dr. Nachtnebel had put the address in. Gasping and feeling more faint by the second, Huck repeated the address mindlessly until Arkin stopped chattering in panic.

"Stay awake, stay on the phone!" Arkin shouted. "We're coming."

But he couldn't. Unable to even hold his arm up, he dropped the phone. His head lolled to the left. The front door waited there, closed but cracked enough to let golden sunlight in. He watched the dust orbs slowly drift around.

His head spun. He didn't know how much time passed before Lilia and Arkin burst through the door. Arkin fell to his knees, shaking Huck.

"Call an ambulance" Arkin snapped to Lilia. Behind him, Lilia screamed when she saw Huck.

Huck waved his hand weakly. Marion said to just go. Don't call. Had she threatened Holly? What would happen if he didn't follow her instructions?

"Just… hospital," Huck wheezed.

Crying and cursing, Lilia ran to help Arkin lift Huck up. "Shouldn't we get him some clothes?" she sobbed.

Arkin pulled his hoodie off and tossed it over Huck's head. "We don't have time," he growled. "He's freezing and bleeding out."

Getting to his car went by in a blur for Huck. His body hurt so much he couldn't stop the moans of pain. Lilia wept and kept checking his temperature, hugging him tightly. Arkin drove like a madman the few blocks to the hospital. Huck vaguely saw the emergency room entrance and the panicking nurse at the front desk. She stood up when he came in and vanished to find someone.

A few blackouts later, Huck opened his eyes to a too bright light above him and a masked man in white to his right. His eyes went wide as he recognized Dr. Nachtnebel. He tried to sit up, unsure what this monster under his mother's pay would do to him.

"Lay back, Huck," the doctor said in a soothing, deep voice. He lifted the hoodie to inspect his side and clicked his tongue. "This is not how I left you. My stitches have been ruined. I told Marion I should have stayed, but she insisted I leave quickly. I couldn't very well transport you here myself."

The doctor turned around and picked up a mask with a long tube coming out of it. "Time to go back to sleep so I can patch you up."

"No," Huck moaned feebly. He cast around for Lilia and Arkin. Was he alone? He tried to call for help but the weak attempt made the doctor smile condescendingly. "Please, don't," he begged, his voice cracking.

"Don't save you?" the doctor asked sarcastically. "That's all I'm doing. You are free to walk out later."

The doctor slipped the mask over Huck's face. When Huck tried to push it off, the doctor grabbed his hands like he scolded a petulant child.

"None of that, Mr. Derringer." He held Huck's wrists down hard. "Just breathe nice and easy. You're in excellent hands." He stopped, looking away to smirk. "Actually, my excellent hands were *in* you."

A tear fell from Huck's eye down his temple. He whipped his head around, trying to throw off the mask. Through the thin window in the hospital room door, he caught sight of a familiar uniform.

"Lo-Logan!" he croaked through the gas.

Dr. Nachtnebel blanched. "Yes, your stupid little friend called him before I could stop him. Remember what your mother said: no police." He smiled down at Huck, eyes going heavy. "That's it. Breathe it in. Go to sleep, little Huckleberry. I'll take care of you."

Huck passed out before more tears could leave his eyes.

Chapter 21:

Trapped

The pressure on his finger woke Huck. At last having feeling return to his entire body, he took in the soft sheets and comfortable pillow under his head. The hospital stink filled his nostrils. But so did the warm, salty aroma of a burger and fries. He opened his eyes, praying he woke up alone or with someone not after his organs. A pair of black boots rested on the side of his bed.

Logan sat slouched in a chair, eyes closed, with his feet up on Huck's bed. His ranger uniform lay on another chair against the wall. He wore a simple plaid shirt and jeans. A cup and bag from a familiar fast food place sat on the floor next to him.

Thirst consumed Huck the moment he thought about the beverage. A rolling desk waited next to him with a pitcher and plastic cup. He reached for it, but it was out of his arm's length. His movement woke Logan.

"Hey, kiddo." Logan jumped into action the moment he saw Huck awake. "You don't want hospital water. Here." He picked up the cup on the floor and handed it to him. "Got your favorite."

The fizzy, sweet liquid stung his throat but also never tasted so good. He gulped down half of it before Logan took it away.

"Ok, don't make yourself sick." He handed him the bag.

Huck tore into the food. He hadn't eaten since the morning before he'd woken up with his kidney stolen. "What time is it?" he asked through a mouthful of burger.

"Monday night," a voice said.

Logan and Huck snapped their heads around to look at the doctor who came in the door. Dr. Nachtnebel smiled. "Captain," he said pointedly to Logan. "I expected you to be gone by now." He checked his watch. "You're off ranger duty, yes?"

"Yeah," Logan growled. "Huck's a friend of mine, though."

"Don't worry," Dr. Nachtnebel cut in. "Everything has been taken care for little Huckleberry here." He smiled again. "You will miss a few classes, but don't worry. You have a doctor's note." He laughed at some joke Huck didn't get. "Sunrise soon, captain. Don't linger."

The doctor left, chuckling darkly to himself.

"What the hell happened?" Logan hissed, crossing his arms and glaring down at Huck. "I got a call from your phone from some guy named Arkin at six in the morning."

"My roommate," Huck said, shoving a fistful of fries into his mouth.

Logan nodded. "He thought you got organ harvested." He shrugged, shaking his head in disbelief. "What the hell? Do I need to call Holly?"

"No!" Huck choked on the food. "Don't call mom. I don't know what Marion will do if I tell her. It's pretty obvious she's not afraid of anything."

"Marion?" Logan dropped his hands. He glanced away,

thinking, before looking back at Huck. "They did this to you?"

Huck nodded, but said, "No. She did. I have this weird feeling Max has nothing to do with it." He swallowed hard.

"You knew my dad?"

Logan stammered for a bit before he replied. "I didn't know he was your dad. That's wild." His eyes unfocused and he went still.

"She wanted me to donate to Celeste, but I wouldn't," Huck said.

Logan gripped his long hair hard and paced angrily on the spot. "Press charges, Huck," he spat. "Bring her to court. This is insane!"

"It won't do anything, Logan." Emotion rose in Huck's throat again. Tears pricked his eyes.

"It will!" Logan shouted, coming to his bedside. "That's how the law works."

Huck licked his lips and pressed them together to stop the rising sob. "It's not that, Logan. It won't matter. It won't fix what she's done."

He couldn't explain it to Logan without telling him about everything that had happened to him in the last several years. The visions, the feelings, the specters—even the darker entity that seemed to be haunting him. He'd sound crazy. Maybe if he had told Marion and Max, they wouldn't have done this to him. To Celeste.

"It's worse than just cutting me open and leaving me in a tub of ice," he finally said.

"Like what?" Logan asked. The honest, openness of his face almost made Huck tell him. "Huck, I'll believe you."

Just then, an alarm went off on Logan's phone. He turned to look out the window. "Shit. I have to go." He grabbed his uniform but stopped halfway to the door. "Huck, you can tell me anything." He glanced at the rising sun and then the door and then Huck again. "I wish I could stay. I took your friends home already."

Huck frowned. "What about my car? I remember them driving me here in it."

Logan rubbed his chin, checking the window again. "They couldn't find it. I'll see if it's been towed or something." He gripped Huck's shoulder tight. "I'm so sorry I have to go. Call me. Seriously. Anytime."

Huck nodded. "Have fun stopping crime, captain."

Logan rushed out.

Alone again, Huck finished the food. If anything, he wanted to eat, rest, and leave. Being alone in the hospital—knowing some man who worked here had gutted him—freaked him out. More than anything, he wanted to heal and forget it had ever happened. Yes, his heart hurt for Celeste and the horrors she'd have to face now. But there was nothing he could do about it.

He wanted to go back home. Forget the rest of this semester. If anything warranted taking time off from school, illegal organ harvesting from a psycho bio mom did.

A FEW TENSE DAYS LATER, Huck stood in the parking lot of the hospital with Lilia. Arkin and her took a rideshare to come get him and look for his car. Huck scanned the lot, holding his phone with Arkin on the other end.

"I swear I didn't park it somewhere it would get towed," Arkin said. "I remember thinking how pissed you'd be."

"You were right," Huck offered. He couldn't spot his old Corvette anywhere. "I don't see it."

Lilia put in, "I *know* we parked in lot D24. It's gone,

guys." She sighed. "I'll check the front desk and see if someone turned in a card for a tow company."

Huck waited for Arkin to come back before trailing Lilia inside. Arkin apologized over and over for the missing car, swearing he'd find it. Lilia was on her way out before they reached the front.

"The front desk lady has nothing," she sighed, digging her own phone out. "I'll call back the driver to pick us up. Or we could walk?" She eyed Huck.

"I'd rather not," he replied, wrapping his hand around his middle to gingerly poke at the healing wound. "Thanks for skipping class to come get me, by the way."

"Always a pleasure to skip class," Arkin smiled.

Lilia nodded, ordering the ride. "The art teacher was really concerned about you. She asked if you were ok. Oh, and I sent a picture of your doctor's note to the rest of your professors like you asked."

"Thanks." Huck glanced up at the hospital windows. He somehow felt like Dr. Nachtnebel might be watching him. Of course, nothing peeked out from the windows. He shook his head. He was being paranoid.

As they waited, Arkin and Lilia brought up some of the talking points Logan had.

"Seriously, you can sue her ass," Arkin offered. "You'd win, pretty sure."

"We can be witnesses," Lilia piped up.

Huck sighed heavily at this. "Guys, that's not the issue. I don't even really care about that. Besides," he held up the credit card Marion gave him before pocketing it again, "this wasn't capped as far as I know from the hospital bills."

Lilia grimaced. "You're going to keep using it? That seems... gross."

"No reason not to," Huck replied. "I want my worth."

Both Arkin and Lilia pulled looks of disgust. "I suppose if that's how you want to cope," Lilia said.

The rideshare driver appeared, and they got in for the short ride back to campus.

Huck went on. "This is what happened with Mark, I'm sure. He got some of my blood and started to share in my ability. The damage will be done when Celeste gets that kidney. With Mark, it might have faded. But not with her."

"Are you going to let her suffer alone?" Lilia asked sadly.

This was the question he'd been pondering. "I don't' know," he said slowly. "I can't control this. I certainly can't tell someone else how to. And I don't know how bad it can get. After the seance..." He stopped, shivering at the memory. "This is so *real*. I think the only way to figure out..." He trailed off, catching sight of something ahead. "Wait!" he shouted to the driver. "Can you pull over?"

Confused, looking at his clients in the rearview mirror, the driver acquiesced and pulled over.

Arkin and Lilia looked ahead, catching what Huck saw. "Oh, shit," Arkin whispered.

Huck leapt from the car and ran a few yards towards the wreckage on the road ahead. A familiar black Corvette leaned dangerously on the shoulder, plowed into a metal barrier. The hood crunched on the left where it gave way, caving in to most of the front engine. His heart broke the closer he got and the more damage he saw. The front window had been bashed in. The windshield cracked, half caving in.

"Huck, I'm so sorry," Arkin started. "I swear I locked it."

"It wasn't you," Huck cut in.

He reached a hand out and touched the paint Logan had helped him put on. They'd worked over a year on that car. He mowed lawns and shoveled snow to make enough money to buy the parts. Logan gave him and Mark matching cars on their 16th birthday. It was their project and brought them together. Holly had sold Mark's.

"How did this happen?" Lilia asked, hands over her mouth.

"Marion," Huck said darkly. "Trying to keep me from traveling. I'm… far from Mom here. Far from Logan except when he's on a rout. Far from anything that can help me."

"Bitch," Arkin spat.

At this remark, Huck nodded. She could torture him. Cut him open, take his organs, curse her own daughter. But what had the Corvette ever done to her?

"Uh, is that your car, man?" the driver behind them asked. "I can call a tow."

Huck took Marion's credit card out from his pocket. "Thanks."

It turned out, Marion was aware of what Huck might do with the card. Once the Corvette was shackled up onto the tow and Huck tried to use the plastic to pay, it got declined. They had to fill out paperwork for later billing and with a heavy heart, Huck watched his car pulled down the highway.

"She's really mean," Lilia offered regarding Marion.

"I would have used different verbiage," Arkin added.

They got into the rideshare car and had him finish taking them back to campus.

"You can have a job over break at my friend's store," Lilia offered. "It's like a retro store, but they pay good. They have a location here and one the city of Boaz. You could work over the summer."

"Thanks, Lilia," Huck said honestly. He knew Mom wouldn't fight him on it. Yes, fixing the car would be more expensive than just buying a new one, but that wasn't the point.

"So," Lilia said gently. "What now?"

"What do you mean?" Arkin quickly shot. "Nothing. Right, Huck?"

Huck shook his head. "I have to figure this out. I can't let what happened to Mark happen to Celeste." This was his chance to try to do the right thing.

Arkin gaped. "You serious?"

Huck couldn't stop the meaningful, sad look he gave his friend. "Yeah. I have to."

After a beat, Arkin leaned back. "Where do we start?"

A few ideas waited in Huck's mind: either he'd have to go to Max for help or he'd have to go back to Valon. At least Valon was close, despite his hokey demeanor. His show was fake—or at least that was the impression Huck got—but he had called Huck a witness. And Valon had the same heterochromia. Just like him and Max. Did Valon experience the same visions? Either way, he had to figure something out and it wouldn't be easy.

Chapter 22:

Halloween

Taking a deep breath, Huck listened to the ringing on his phone. He stood in the common area of his and Arkin's dorm. The time to move his Corvette from the tow yard had come. The place called him the night before and said it'd been a few weeks and either he needed to come and get it, or they'd strip it for the cost of the tow and boarding. Being stuck at school, he'd not called Holly yet. He had to come up with a good story. He didn't have one.

"Huck baby!" Holly said joyfully over the phone. "Are you coming home for Halloween this weekend?"

He met Arkin's eyes across the room. Arkin waited on the floor opposite their TV, holding a controller in his hand. He shook his head as if to say he had no help to offer in this situation. Huck pulled up his shirt and looked at the scar on his side in the mirror hanging on their door. It had healed nicely.

"Uh, actually no." He sighed. "I can't. And I need a favor…"

"Sure, hun," Holly chirped. "I'm in a super good mood. I got the weekend off and me and some girlfriends are going out." She made a happy, squealing noise. "It's been ages since I've done that!"

Huck rubbed his temples. "Then this is really going to bring you down."

"Are you ok?" Holly asked.

I mean, I'm alive, he thought. "Yeah, yeah," he said to her. "Someone…"

"Vandalized!" Arkin hiss-shouted suddenly, starting a round on the console, tired of waiting. He bit his lower lip, concentrating on making his character run for cover.

"Yeah, someone vandalized my car. Real bad," Huck said. The anxiety in his chest lessened a little. "I had it towed all the way home. I was wondering if you'd be ok with parking it in the shed again? I want to fix it up."

Holly clicked her tongue, and Huck could just imagine her shaking her head. "I knew the big city was a bad idea."

"It's not that big," he said, relief flooding his tone. "It's pretty banged up, but I'm going to ask Logan to help me again. Maybe over winter break."

"Shouldn't be a problem," Holly said casually. She waited a beat. The way she left the sentence told Huck she was about to ask another question.

"What's up?" he encouraged her.

"Umm," her voice quivered. "I was wondering if you wanted to… come home for your birthday?"

November 11th. His birthday. Mark's birthday. The day he took his life. Just weeks before Jasper died. What a terrible month.

"Uh, yeah, mom. I might try to do that. I… I don't know. With class and all." It was a lie, but what should he say? He didn't know how he was supposed to handle this. "I will if you want me to."

Silence stretched on before she said, "It's up to you, babe.

I know that was a rough month last year with Jasper, too. I just don't want you to feel alone. Or like you have to bear anything by yourself. Ok?"

He nodded, even though she couldn't see it. "Thanks, mom. And thanks for picking up the car."

Stopping the call, he stared down at his phone.

"Hey," Arkin said, cutting into his thoughts from across the room. "You good?"

Huck nodded. He joined his roommate on the floor and entered the game halfway through. They played in silence for a while, slowly getting into the game, jeering at each other, poking fun at the other team, and letting the simplicity of playing video games relax them. They lost a few rounds and won a couple before Arkin took the conversation back.

"So what's in November?" he asked.

Huck looked sideways at him, then locked his eyes onto the screen. "Birthday. And one year since Mark and Jasper."

With enough said, Arkin didn't bring it up again. "We should do something for Halloween," he offered once the silence went on too long. "Lilia and some other girls are throwing a party in the alley."

The alley was a street of housing downtown that had been taken over by university students. Private residencies, it was close to campus and the landlords almost exclusively rented to the students. It was the place to go for drinking and loud parties not allowed on campus.

It could be fun to go out. Socialize. Huck had never been a drinker, but that's what college was about, right? Besides classes and learned anxiety, the parties were part of the experience.

"Maybe have some shots and flirt with girls?" Arkin offered.

Now that he mentioned it, Huck hadn't thought about

girls in a long time. To avoid *that* conversation, he tilted his head, inclining it towards his room mate.

"You're a football scholarship guy," he smiled slyly. "How come I've never seen you flirting with girls?"

Arkin shrugged. "Been too focused, I guess. Trying to end with a strong first semester."

Through the secret tunnel, Lilia's squeals of glee pierced their ears. A ruckus of more feminine cries went up as well. The door next to theirs burst open, and the cries entered the hallway.

The sound of students enjoying themselves darkened Huck's mind. Could he do a whole night of shouting students, dressed up, flirting, drinking, and dancing? People in costume tended to be more liberated than they were without the mask.

"You go," Huck said. "It's more your scene."

Arkin dropped the controller. "Don't make me go alone. We can go together. I had this idea where we dress up as—"

Huck's phone went off. Jumping at the sudden vibration, he pulled it out of his pocket. It was Max. "What does he want?" Huck mused out loud.

He got up and walked into his room, answering the phone. "What?" he snapped. "I have nothing else to give you guys. I've got even less for you to take."

"Calm down, Huck," Max said steadily. "You're alive, aren't you?"

"Are you serious?" he shouted back. Arkin appeared in his doorway, glaring. "You had some guy literally kidnap me, gut me, and leave me in a tub of ice!"

"That was all Marion," Max cut in. "I swear. I had no idea. I'm so sorry. It must have been terrifying."

"A little bit," Huck shot back. "Then, she threatened me and mom."

"Yeah, don't do that," Max offered. "People have tried

before. It's not worth it with her, her connections, and family."

Huck frowned. "What do you mean?"

"Nothing. Never mind." Max waited a beat. "Look, I know you're wound up about that and you have no reason to trust me, but I was wondering…" He took a deep breath. "I was wondering if you wanted to come downtown. I'm here on a job."

"Again?" he asked.

Max clicked his tongue and hummed a reply. "I'm looking into some older cases. While I was here, something kind of attached to my initial investigation came up. I thought you might like to see what I do. Maybe try some things out. Covertly, of course, as I do work with the cops and they're not super into what I do."

A light flickered on in Huck. Maybe this was his chance to figure this out. But Max didn't have his gift. Did he?

"Uh, I need to tell you something," Huck started.

Max cut him off. "No. You don't." He sighed heavily. "In fact, I need to tell you something. A lot of somethings. Will you come downtown?"

Huck met Arkin's eyes. Arkin frowned, tilting his head questioningly. What better time than Halloween weekend? Especially with the anniversary coming up. This could be the start to getting answers, getting control.

"Yeah," he said, his voice heavy. "I'll get a ride downtown. Tell me where to meet you."

ARKIN BEGGED Huck not to go as he filled his backpack with a night's supplies and clothes.

"The man literally doesn't care that his wife stole your

guts," Arkin shouted, following Huck around the dorm as he packed. "And you're going to go and spend the night alone with him? No way. I'm coming too."

"Arkin, come on," Huck begged. "I have to go. He's my father. What if he's like me, has had experiences? This is what he does for a living—he can help me."

Of course his roommate didn't understand. He'd probably never once seen a ghost, been stalked by a shadow or entity he couldn't explain.

"This could be dangerous," Arkin begged.

"Yeah," Huck agreed. "But I have to face it. I have to figure this out."

Defeated, Arkin handed him the black hoodie he always wore. "Text me every hour. I'm serious. Or I'm coming down to drag you back to campus."

Huck rolled his eyes. "Calm down. I'm pretty sure the worst has already happened."

TWENTY MINUTES LATER, Huck sat in the back of a rideshare car and headed deeper into the city. Max gave him the address of the hotel he was staying at and the room number. Since it was Halloween night, the city blazed with orange light and clamored with the sounds of parties and shouts of people celebrating. Party-goers packed the parking lot of the hotel so Huck got out on the curb. He didn't have time to double check the room number before someone shouted his name through the crowd. He turned to see Max jogging towards him with a pack on his back.

"Quick," Max whispered. "The press are on their way."

Huck didn't have time to argue before Max hauled him into a black sedan and shifted into gear.

"Where are we going?" he asked.

Max pointed a few blocks down. Red and blue lights flashed down an alley. "Crime scene." He smiled like it was Christmas. "A lady I know called me in. Fortunately for her, I was in town. I almost never get to look at a fresh scene. Always have to do the research later." Max's shoulder-length brown hair was stringy and unwashed.

"How long have you been in town working this other case?" Huck asked.

Max scrunched his face, thinking. "I've been between here and Boaz a lot in the last week. I'm tracking something."

Curiosity exploded inside Huck. Was this what it would look like once he had a hold of this awful thing? Would it be far less scary, more controlled, and—dare he hope—useful?

Stopping the car in a no-parking zone, Max came to a sudden halt. He smiled over at Huck. "Time to work."

Excited, Huck slung his backpack into the back seat and followed Max out. Together, they weaved through the cop cars and yellow tape. A few cruisers lined the alley and the red and blue lights splashed over the brick. Everyone gathered at one particular spot, looking down.

"How old are you?" Max asked. "I just don't want to show you something too gruesome."

Huck swallowed. "Almost nineteen."

"Great." Max ducked under the tape and moved towards a short, female deputy with reddish blonde hair. "Hey, Sal," Max said to her.

The deputy turned. Her badge glinted in the red and blue lights. "Ah, you," she said. Huck noted that half her tone was sarcasm, the other was happy to see him.

"You call, I come," Max said slyly.

"Uh-huh," Sal replied glumly. "Normally, I wouldn't call

in a crook like you, but you have a rep with the Rangers. They seem to think you'd bring good news."

Max grabbed Huck's upper arm and pulled him along. "This is Huck. He's going to be helping me."

Sal's brows twitched into a slight frown. "Have we met?" she asked. "That name sounds familiar."

Huck shrugged.

"Anyway," Sal sighed, leading them deeper into the alley. "We're trying to get this cleaned up before holiday pranksters figure out we're here." She eyed Huck. "You ok with blood?"

"I think so," Huck offered.

Sal nodded. She led them to a dumpster and walked up on some debris and crates she'd piled in order to flip up the lid completely. She put on some powdered gloves and handed a pair to Max and Huck each. "My boss will kill me once she finds out I called in a paranormal investigator," she said as a warning. "But..."

With a grunt, Sal hauled the dumpster lid open and shined her flashlight in. Huck stood on his toes, gripping the side to look in. Max stood a good head taller and looked over the top of Huck's head. Inside lay a dead body, gray, with its cheek bones protruding sharply. At first, Huck thought maybe the person was just really skinny. But the more he looked, the more he saw bones all over underneath thin, bloodless flesh. Like something, or someone, had drained the body of all its warm, red blood. Across its drained body, sigils and symbols danced, cut clean through the flesh.

Chapter 23:

Bump In The Night

Sal put her hand on her hip and looked up at Max and Huck. "You can see why I called you in."

"This isn't that," Max cut in quickly. He quickly snapped his head up, looking into the dark tops of the buildings beyond the heads of the streetlights.

"What?" Huck asked. A little fire lit under him. Yes, it was disgusting, but something about being on the scene—the warm night air, and the flashing lights—invigorated him.

When Max didn't explain, Sal did. "About eighteen years ago, when I was just fresh out of the academy, there was some major cult movement in Boaz."

"No way!" Huck didn't mean to smile and sound as enthusiastic as he did. "Do you mind?" He pulled out his phone. "I just want to record the audio. This would make a great episode."

Sal winced and shook her head. "Not yet, kiddo. But for sure, hit me up once we get this thing underway. I'd be glad to give you an exclusive."

Huck expected Max to protest. He was Huck's father, after all. But the man continued to inspect the body. Letting them chat, Max leapt into the dumpster and bent down to examine the corpse with his phone light. Huck watched as Sal went on in her Minnesota accent.

"Well, everyone thought it was one kind of cult then another as these murders cropped up," she explained, watching Max turn the head of the corpse using two pens so he didn't touch it. "Then the popular theory was a coven of witches."

"Witches?" Huck breathed. To Max he asked, "Are they real?"

"Oh, bless you," Sal smiled, lightly smacking Huck's shoulder. "The coven may be real. And the members, but obviously that voodoo isn't going to hurt a soul. Outside the murders."

"It's not voodoo," Max mumbled, lifting the victim's gums to look at his teeth. "There's a difference, Sal, between voodoo and what went down all those years ago."

Sal smiled. "Oh, of course, Max. That was vampires."

"Vampires?" Huck gasped. His head spun. He came with Max to find out about his visions, not get a whole bestiary of existing spooks summarized for him.

"Yeah, they start out as creepy little teens," Sal explained. "Then they find somewhere on the internet that drinking blood is cool and they do it under the bridges at night."

Huck laughed nervously in relief. "Oh, so not *actual* vampires."

"Not to the small mind," Max sighed. He stood up and pocketed his pens.

Sal giggled kindly and shook her head. "Good ol' Max Winchester. This is why we call you in. I will get in trouble if you hang around too long, though," she added, glancing over her shoulder at the sheriff.

"Hey, Sal," Max asked, hopping out of the dumpster. "When was Sheriff Savage last on duty in this area?"

"Logan?" Huck asked, struck.

The deputy looked between Huck and Max. "Oh, yeah, boyo. Savage and Winchester. Back in the day, we called them Maximum Overdrive. It was confusing as they're both named Max, so Savage went by Logan."

"You thought he was dead," Huck remembered. "Logan had no idea you were my father. But why'd you think he was dead?"

Sal raised her brows and scanned Max. "You've been out of Boaz too long, Winchester. But it seems your misunderstanding was cleared up by your question." She pressed her lips to the side, thinking. "Sheriff Savage is a Ranger, so he drives all over the place. He was in town not long ago, but on personal business."

Yeah, seeing me, Huck thought. *In the hospital.* He couldn't help glaring at Max, remembering what his wife did.

Suddenly, Max slapped his hands together like he was dusting them off. "Well, you got this, deputy. You are for sure correct. This was a cult killing. An initiation."

"Oh!" Sal looked up at Max. "You sure?"

He nodded, looking up beyond the streets lights again. "Blood was drained through the neck. You can see the incision behind the ears. The symbols are a dead giveaway, too. Also, large chunks of hair were burned off on the back of the head. You might want to check with Sheriff Savage. See if you can find out what he was doing around the time of death."

Sal's brows pinched. "What are you saying, Winchester?"

Huck's mouth dropped open. Was Max suspicious of Logan?

"He was here is all," Max said casually. "Maybe he saw

something. Look into the cult, Sal. Might find symbols or something around town. Like gang signs."

The deputy rested her hand on her firearm and watched Max walk back down the alley. "Whatever you say, Winchester." Her tone hung like a question in the air.

THEY DROVE BACK to the hotel in silence. Huck couldn't shake the feeling that Max had lied to Sal. He didn't know what the lie was, but he heard it in Max's tone. He didn't have the guts to ask his biological father about it until the pizza they ordered arrived. Max spent a few hours on his laptop, looking things up and reading, mumbling and taking notes. Huck texted Arkin that they were safe in the hotel.

Finally, Huck spoke up. "So, is this what you do? Your website is pretty barebones. I wasn't sure from looking at it."

Max looked up, now wearing black-rimmed glasses with the screen reflecting so Huck couldn't see his eyes. He took them off and rubbed his eyes. "It's getting late. We should sleep. I need to go out early tomorrow morning."

Huck scooted forward on the bed to get closer to the desk where Max sat. "Is Marion cool with the paranormal thing?"

A bitter laugh cut the air. "It wouldn't matter if she wasn't," Max replied. "I respect her line of work and she leaves me alone."

The harsh tone shocked Huck. "You guys do seem different. How'd you end up together?"

Max reached down to his worn, leather pack and pulled out an old, thick journal. He flicked through it while he answered. "By accident, really. She needed someone... how can I put this? She needed an ornament for her arm. I was good looking, a showman, an entertainer. Weird."

Huck nodded. "I know the type." He noted again how his father and he had almost the same face. Except for the eyes. "Did you love her?"

This elicited a dark chuckle from Max. "I did. I really did."

The past tense couldn't go unnoticed.

"Max," Huck started, holding his breath. "You said you know I see visions. Things."

"Specters," Max offered.

Huck nodded again. "Do you think it has something to do with," he motioned to his eyes, "this?"

"Yeah." Max found what he searched for in the journal and typed on his computer again. "I used to have it."

"Really?" Huck couldn't contain his joy. "Did it fade away? Or did you find a way to make it stop?" Max had two blue eyes.

With a heavy, labored sigh, Max looked up. "No, Huck. I lost my green eye." He met Huck's eyes and saw him waiting. "I was working a case with Logan."

Huck smiled lightly at the mention of the sheriff. The man who'd helped him and Mark through some of the roughest nights of his life.

"I thought it went away?"

Max shook his head. "We ran into some, well, more physical specters than usual. We quarreled about how to proceed. That's when we fell out, I suppose. But we both ended up in the lair of the creatures. Got pretty hurt. I lost my eye to a wound, and I thought I lost Logan. I left."

Huck swallowed. "You left him?"

Max nodded. "I got a donor eye. Lost some of my powers with it."

A little of the fresh hope dwindled in Huck. "Do you still see specters?"

Max half nodded with a shrug. "I'm not as strong as I once was. It's harder for me."

"Why don't you just let it go?" Huck asked. "I…" He shivered. "I hate it."

Tilting his head, Max asked, "Why?"

A dry scoff cut Huck's throat. "Because it's awful. These things see me, they attack me."

"Yeah," Max nodded. "That's why you can't stop. Even if you can't see them, you are a witness. They can see you. They want you. Better to see it coming." He leaned back and put one knee on the desk. "You don't have to fear them."

Aghast, Huck's mouth dropped open. "I can't stop them. Of course I fear them. I was hoping you'd tell me how to stop it."

Finally, a genuine emotion passed over Max's face. "You run from them? They attack you?" He rubbed his chin.

"Yeah," Huck replied.

"I didn't expect that." Max stood up.

Feeling like he somehow let his father down, Huck watched Max pace. "I'm sorry," he said flatly. Why did he feel bad?

"We can work on that tomorrow," Max said, still distracted. "Right now, I need to think about this vampire case."

Huck shot up. "Vampires?" he shouted. "You told Sal it was a cult. People. *Humans*."

Max shrugged, annoyed. "It might be, but I doubt it."

Huck got the weird feeling Max *wanted* it to be vampires. Not that it actually was. He was ignoring the signs he himself had pointed out.

"I needed her out of the way," Max finished. "I like to work alone."

A million scenarios played through Huck's mind.

Vampires. Ghosts. Specters. What else lurked in the darkness? What otherworldly dangers waited just behind the shadow of a partially closed door?

"She's looking into this," Huck said suddenly. "She's thinking she's going to track down some psycho witches. Is she going to find a nest of vampires instead?"

"Probably," Max mused with a dark chuckle.

Shaken, Huck gaped at his father. "Don't you care? You have to tell her!"

Max shook his head. "She'll be fine. But I'm going to go out at sunrise." He checked his watch. "You need to get some sleep. Huck," he met his son's eyes. "Trust me. It's fine."

THE SOUND of the door opening and closing roughly woke Huck the next morning. Max tossed his bag down and went into the bathroom. Huck swore he saw red covering the front of Max's shirt.

"What's going on?" Huck called across the room. The tap turned on loudly in the bathroom. "Max?"

"I have to shower, Huck," the man shouted, slamming the door to the bathroom.

The loud crack made Huck jump. A trail of dirt tracked over the floor where Max had walked. Outside, the sun had fully risen behind a thin veil of gray clouds. Curious, Huck got out of bed and looked for Max's bag. Unable to find it, he realized it was in the bathroom with Max.

Huck texted Arkin again without reading the long string of novel-length replies. He said he was ok, alive, and safe. He waited a minute until he was sure Max had turned on the shower and was under the water before going for the laptop. A password waited to be typed in. It was an older computer and had a password hint button right underneath. Clicking it, the phrase, "revenge is mine" popped up.

"Weird," Huck whispered. He started to try a few words and phrases. Nothing worked. He listened for any sounds coming from the bathroom. Max was mumbling to himself. "Umm," Huck mused, trying to think of any revenge stories he knew from classic literature or something a rich Connecticut man might use.

Nothing coming to mind, he tried his own name. Then Mark's. Then Celeste. That's when it hit him.

"Logan Savage," he mumbled as he typed it.

The computer unlocked.

Not sparing a moment to be confused by the password, his eyes quickly scanned the open webpage. A news website with annoying scrolling banners and too many pop-ups shined back at him.

"Boaz County Deputy Sally Silverman found dead at suspected cult sight early this morning," the headline read.

Arms heavy, Huck fell back against the chair. He stared in shock at the short, journalistic piece. It ended with "story in development."

Sal had gone on investigating throughout the night. She'd walked right into danger. Danger Max could have told her about.

Huck got so wrapped up in re-reading the report he didn't hear Max come out of the bathroom. His father stood, dripping wet, with a towel around his waist. He glared at Huck, and Huck glared back.

"She died," Huck whispered.

"Yeah," Max nodded. "But so is the one who did it."

"You sound pleased about it," Huck noted.

"I didn't find what I was looking for." Max grabbed a t-shirt and pulled it over his tasseled hair.

"You were looking for something specific?" Huck asked. "And you just let her die?"

Max sighed, annoyed. "I told you, I work best alone. She should have backed off. Huck, you can't just tell people things like 'Don't go in there, there's a cult that sacrifices humans.' You'll figure it out soon enough."

Despite the douche bag move, Huck understood a little. He'd hesitated about telling Lilia and Arkin. And they liked him. He couldn't imagine trying to explain—especially quickly—to someone he wasn't friends with. Still, Max's cavalier attitude put him on edge.

"So tonight," Max started over, "I am taking you to St. Vincent's Cemetery."

A tiny trickle of fear slid down Huck's spine, chilling him. "Why?"

Max smiled. "You want to get ahold of your visions, right? I have an idea."

Chapter 24:

Buried Alive

Huck gripped his hands tightly in one another as Max drove him far out of town towards the state line.

"How far away is this place?" he asked. "I tried to look it up and couldn't find it."

Max leaned easily back in the seat of his expensive car, one hand on the wheel. "That's because they shut it down in 1914. Locals thought it was cursed. Had a lot of activity."

"Why?" Huck knew every haunting had a legend, lore, or history that explained at least some of the mystery. Learning all that had been his job when planning a video. Made it easier to regurgitate for the camera since he was the front man.

"Lots of things," Max said. His tone dropped, sounding bored. "Native burial grounds, mine caves ins, some witches cursed it—take your pick. It's old."

"And what are we going to do?" he asked. He felt oddly compelled to add, "I have class tomorrow morning. And my roommate is bugging me to know when I'll be home." Why did he feel the need to warn Max people would look for him?

This guy was his father. He wouldn't do anything to hurt him. Would he?

Max's lack of an answer didn't put Huck at ease. His sharp blue eyes flicked back and forth over the horizon. "Ah, here we are," he mused, a small, dark smile pulling a wrinkle onto his cheek. "That's the graveyard up there." He pointed to where his high beams cut through overly tall grass and unkept shrubs.

"Cemetery," Huck mumbled in reply, eyeing it through the darkness.

"What's that?" Max asked, turning the car off and getting out.

Huck followed him. "Cemetery. Graveyards are attached to churches. This one is alone. It's a cemetery."

Very alone. The night crushed in on all sides, spreading out into darkness he couldn't see into. A wrought-iron fence leaning in all directions crawled out on its spidery legs into the tall grass. A dilapidated gate hung on rusted hinges, locked in the center. It didn't matter as someone had pried the center open so many times it now gaped wide.

The maintenance had long vanished from the cemetery. The foliage grew so tall, Huck almost tripped over headstones and crosses hidden in the long grass. Trees lined it, hanging over as if to look into the graves. A cold, October wind cut right through his hoodie and kissed his sensitive skin. He brought his shoulders up, but it did little to cover him from the cold. This cold reached deeper into his bones.

"You have protection against... things?" Huck asked. He'd not so much as carried his talisman or looked up warding in a while now. If he was going to go digging into the darkness, he should have been more prepared.

"Not tonight," Max said. He led him through the pitfalls and tripping hazards easily.

"Why?" Huck asked, his heart starting to race.

Max stopped and faced Huck. In the moonlight, he could hardly make out his father's face. "It just takes one time." Max said it like a promise. "That's all. It'll be ok."

His feet rooted to the spot as Max moved deeper in. "I don't like this," he called. "What are you talking about? Max!"

When his father didn't stop, he had to chase after him.

"Look, I've been stuck in a graveyard before."

"Good."

"No, not good! It was seriously scary. These things came after me, like they wanted me."

"They do," Max said gravely.

Huck froze.

They approached a huge mausoleum with a long hall. Max went to the hanging door and pried it open.

"No," Huck said firmly. "I am not going in there."

Max went in any way, taking a tire iron out of his bag as he did so. "Yes, you are. Huck, trust me. It just takes one time." He turned back to Huck. "You wanted my help. This is it. Trust me." He laid so much emphasis on the words that Huck felt slightly compelled.

How was he supposed to explain what happened without sounding like a complete scaredy cat? "What are you planning?" he asked instead.

Max waved him in.

With a heavy sigh, holding his breath, Huck stepped over the threshold into the long, old structure. The walls were lined with crumbling doors that led into the above ground graves. Each one had variations of symbols and wards chiseled into them. They all mentioned death dates back in the 1890s. Looking down the hall, Huck saw it split off like the last one, but there was no second exit. There was only one door in and out.

He was inspecting a large family of grave doors when a sudden crash made him jump. Max had swung the tire iron into one of the markers, shattering it. The white marble crumbled under the force, opening up to the cavernous grave.

"Don't break the graves! Those belong to someone," Huck shouted. But Max didn't stop, smashing open four or five.

"Not here they don't," he grunted. "This place is old, abandoned. It belongs only to them. They will come from deep inside. You'll have to go deep."

"Deep? What do you mean?"

"The DarkFront, as you call it, is like a globe. It's not a world within our world. It's more metaphysical than that. Supernatural. You can't just walk into it like a door. Your body stays here. It's not a mind game either. Your spirit physically goes there. Leaves your body."

"Astral projection?"

"Something like that." Max shoved the tire iron back into his bag and reached in, fishing for something else. "Come here," he ordered Huck. He looked around for something on the walls. "When I was about fourteen, I had my first encounter. The visions normally appear with maturity, but I suppose it's different for everyone."

Intrigued, Huck followed him deeper into the mausoleum. "I guess I always knew I had it," he started. "It didn't manifest strongly until… Jasper."

"Just a year ago?" Max asked. When Huck nodded, he hesitated for a fraction of a second.

"But for Mark, it was almost instant," Huck offered. He fidgeted with the sleeve of his hoodie. "It must have been intense. He couldn't take it."

Max stopped in front of a decorative spire coming off the mausoleum wall. "Which is why you have to learn fast. The more you expose yourself to it, the stronger you'll be and the more you can control it. Then, the deeper you can go."

Huck leaned close to Max to see what clinked in his hands. "You keep saying deeper. What does that—"

With speed Huck had never seen, his father grabbed his wrist and cuffed him to the spire. Max quickly jumped back, backing away, looking around.

"What the hell?" Huck screamed at his retreating father. "Don't do this. Max, please!" Understanding filled him with terror. His eyes went to the freshly broken grave doors. "They'll come. You've destroyed them, disturbed their resting place."

"Yes," Max nodded, eyes wide. "Even I feel them coming." He grabbed up his pack and hurried towards the exit. "The spirits are very active. Who knows what else they will bring out with them."

"Max" Huck shouted, his voice cracking. "What do I do?"

He stopped, listening. "They aren't caged any more, Huck. This place is old. They have a long way to go before they leave the DarkFront. The longer they're dead, the deeper they are. Find a way into the DarkFront. Control your vision."

"How?" He pulled on the cuff but only succeeded in bruising his wrist.

"If you can open it," Max went on, panting now as his eyes flashed between invisible horrors Huck couldn't see yet, "they will go back in. They will follow you in."

At last, one appeared. A translucent, white, glowing monster without a head. It crawled out of the grave a few yards from Huck, moving like bad stop-animation.

"I see one!" he screamed. When he did, the thing turned its headless body towards him. "Oh, shit, it sees me?"

Max let out a triumphant cry. "Good! That means you are opening up to the DarkFront. You are witnessing. Push harder, Huck. Open the Front and send them back before they get to you."

Behind him, Max slipped out the door, but Huck couldn't focus on his fleeing father. The thing slid out of the grave, plopping onto the floor. Huck's skull buzzed and his mouth filled with the taste of metal. The headless ghost crawled toward him. He felt rather than heard its desire: it wanted to crawl inside him. Wanted his physical body. He screamed and pulled against the cuffs, but they wouldn't give. The thing grabbed his ankle.

"It can't get inside you while you're still here," Max shouted.

"Why can I feel it then?" Huck cried. The thing gripped him harder, enraged that it could not possess the body before it. He swore it would crush his bones to dust before he shook it off.

"Go into the Front!" Max shouted. "The more it hurts and the more you feel means the closer you are."

Fine, Huck thought, and he leaned into the pain. The visions in his peripherals came back. The oily, dancing white and blue world started to solidify. As he focused on it, trying to bring it into focus, the headless ghoul pulled hard. Huck's feet went out from under him. His head smacked against the stone wall and for a second, pain cracked through his skull. Then, the blue visions took over.

The mausoleum vanished, replaced by a huge, vacant place glowing in dead, green light. Huck froze. The shackles were gone. The ghost was gone. Looking down, he took in the black floor. Every slight movement made a green, glowing ripple pulse out from where he stood. A fading, cold light came from everywhere at once, but so dim he couldn't see four feet in front of him.

"Max?" he called. His voice, amplified to ten times its normal frequency, echoed out in all directions. He covered his mouth, gasping. He turned to look around, and something clinked. Looking down again, this time, he spotted two chains: one around each ankle. He followed them with his eyes. They trailed along the black ground and into the darkness. "What the hell?" he mused.

Turning, he followed the chains. Every step clinked and clattered loudly.

Huck! a voice behind him cried. It was Max. Turning, he spotted a hazy opening in the darkness. He couldn't make out anything beyond. Was that the way back? What was happening to his body while he journeyed here?

He looked back at the chains. They were long enough for him to get back.

Wake up! Max's voice screamed from beyond the hazy entry point.

Something was happening. Scared, he bolted back toward the opening. He'd only gotten two, chain-clinking steps in before the chains went tight, jerking his feet out from under him. With a cry, he fell onto his stomach. Behind him, the chains flew up into the darkness. He gripped one and pulled hard, but it didn't budge. The sound of his fall echoed deeper and deeper into the darkness, fading away. Then it turned quiet.

To his left, watery, dripping sounds alerted him to a presence. He snapped his head back. A girl stood before him. Her feet did not cause ripples in the black ground. She was maybe fifteen, wearing jeans and a pink hoodie. She had the hood up and her hands shoved deep into the pockets. Dark, murky water dripped off her. Her skin was pale and slightly bloated, like she had drowned.

"You need to go," she said sullenly. "He's coming. He can hear me speak to you."

His eyes went to her feet. "Why don't you have a chain?" he asked. "Can you hear me?"

She didn't so much as blink. "He can hear you." She pointed to the ripples his every tiny movement made. "They know you're here. I'd take you but, you're occupied."

"What?" Huck snapped his head back to the hazy portal. "Is…" His heart stopped. "Is that ghost in me?"

She nodded. "I saw him dive in. "You need to close that door, get him back inside. He doesn't understand. Been too long."

Huck stood up. He'd hardly expected a specter to be nice. Or so young. And modern. "Are you…dead?" he asked.

She nodded sadly. "Watch out for the mines under the cemetery." She pointed back. "Nasty falls have nasty ends."

Then he heard it. A low rumbling finally registered in his ears. The smell made him notice it, though. Something like burnt toast mixed with sulfur. A fiery, hot, disgusting scent.

"He's here," the drowned girl said. "He can't hurt me. But you? He wants you. He likes the ones who make the ripples."

Deep in the darkness, black smoke wafted out. A dark red glow appeared in a shadowy mass with long, sharp fingers. Huck recognized it. That thing had been haunting him for months now.

"Shit!" he gasped, turning to the opening. The chains went tight again, holding him in place. "Help me!" he shouted to the girl.

She shrugged, shaking her head. "Can't. Close the door."

"But I'm in here," he tried.

"It's your door," she said.

Not sure what that meant, Huck pulled hard on the chains, begging them to loosen. In his panic, he wondered briefly about Jasper. And Mark. Max said this was the DarkFront— what he called the place ghosts inhabited. Would they be in this place? Max said the old dead ones were deep inside. Maybe, somewhere close, Jasper and Mark lingered. Would it be wrong to want to see them? Talk to them? Tell them how sorry he was…

The chains released, and Huck flew forward, pitching through the portal. He slammed onto his back, coughing and hacking. For just one second, everything went dark.

When he came too, his fingers were wet with blood. He lay on his back outside the mausoleum. Max loomed over him, calling his name. Huck tried to sit up, but his head split. He blinked, something sticky making his lashes cling to his cheeks. Pulling his hand away from his throbbing head, he saw his hands were covered with blood.

"What happened?" he gasped.

"The specter," Max panted, sitting back into the grass, sighing in relief. "He got inside you. You cannot let others inside you while your spirit leaves your body and goes into the DarkFront."

"How the hell was I supposed to know?" Huck shot back. His entire body ached. Lifting his shirt, he found bruises blossoming all over his torso. "What happened?"

Max ran his hand through his hair. "It didn't know what to do once it got inside you. It bashed your head against the floor, screamed, contorted *Exorcist* style and just went to town."

"On me!" Huck roared. He pushed Max away and rolled away to get up, but his head spun too much. Scratches covered his arms like the thing had tried to claw its way out of his fleshy prison.

"I'm disappointed," Max said, standing up like he was about to leave.

"Ex-freaking-scuse me?" Huck shot back. He couldn't stop his body from shaking; left over fear. "I literally got pushed from my body into an astral world, got possessed and beat by a malevolent ghost and you're disappointed?"

The man shook his head and turned to leave. "Yeah. I thought you could get a grip on this."

Thunderstruck, scared something lurked in the shadows—wondering if that shadow creature was just behind him—Huck pulled his knees up to his chest. "No." His voice shook. His wide eyes stung from the blood on his face. "This freaks me out, Max. I came to you for help. I wanted you to teach me."

"Yeah." Max's voice dropped so low, Huck could hardly hear it. "I thought you were... better than that. That was disappointing. You're not strong, Huck."

Stung, Huck looked up at his father. Tears welled in his eyes. "What?" His voice went up an embarrassing octave. Was he weak?

Max reached into his wallet and tossed a bill to Huck. "Get a ride home. Call me in a year or so when you're useful."

His heart broke. Voice shaking, he called after him, "You just wanted to use me to get in there because you can't anymore, is that it?"

Max didn't stop, fading into the night.

"Am I useless to you?" He crawled up onto his knees, trying to stand up again. "Max! Teach me to figure this out."

Not even stopping, Max called back, "I work better alone anyway."

The crunching of long grass faded as his father left him. Huck shivered now from the cold. With shaking, bloody hands, he picked up his phone and called a rideshare. He had to send his location to the driver because—just like before—nothing showed up on the map.

He gave the driver the hundred Max had tossed at him to help him not ask questions and take him all the way back to campus. Crushed, bruised, and devastated, Huck wanted nothing more than to see Arkin and Lilia and have a hot shower.

Chapter 25:
The Chains

In the middle of the week, the campus took a turn. Halfway through November, everything—students, faculty, even the buildings—seemed ready to be done. BSU's football team got ejected from the rest of the season for a long losing streak and didn't qualify to continue. This put Arkin in a sour mood, which made him quiet. After the incident with Max, Huck tried to talk through what to do next, but Arkin's aloof attitude made it difficult.

The boys sat in their gaming chairs on the floor, blasting their way through a group of enemies, but Huck didn't really see the screen before him. He replayed the brief, yet horrifying, trip to the DarkFront over and over in his head. The dead, green light, the chains that swept back into the darkness. And that shadow with the red eyes and sharp fingers that followed him everywhere. His body still bore the bruises from when Max locked him in the mausoleum, trying to force him to control the visions. He wasn't sure what Max wanted him to do. Max said go deeper, open the door, close the door, blah, blah, blah. Huck had fewer answers than before.

"Huck," Arkin barked, shaking him back to reality.

Huck jumped and blinked, refocusing on the screen. "Sorry, what happened?"

Arkin dropped the controller and buried his face in his hands. "You shot me. Don't look over here." He jabbed his hand back at the screen. "Look there. Shit, we're going to lose. *Again*."

"Can't win them all," Huck sighed.

"We haven't won once." Arkin tilted his head back and swallowed before closing his eyes.

Wondering if now was a good opportunity to bring it up, Huck guided his character into the enemy base to steal the flag. "Sorry," he started. "I was thinking about calling Valon again."

Arkin groaned audibly but didn't move. "Why?" he droned.

Grabbing the flag, Huck made a mad dash for the exit, the enemy scrambling to catch him. He jumped, turned, and shot one down before taking a side hall into a little-known fake wall. "After Max, I just want to get a better hold on this."

"Then do it." Arkin stood up. "I'm hitting the gym."

Someone finally shot Huck dead, taking the flag. As the last man alive on his team, it was game over. He put down the controller. "You don't want to come with me?"

Arkin shook his head. "Ask Lilia if you want company."

Something was eating at Arkin and Huck didn't know what. One night, he was harassing him to text every hour or two that he was safe, and now he wanted to avoid him or sit in silence playing video games, talking only to growl at him for getting them killed.

Awkwardly staying seated, Huck watched Arkin grab his gym bag and head out. Doing these things alone wasn't a good idea. Not after last time. But then again, Valon didn't put off the same energy as Max. Still, alone was a bad idea.

"Hey, Lilia!" he shouted towards their shared wall.

Lʙʟɪᴀ ᴡᴀʟᴋᴇᴅ ᴄʟᴏѕᴇ to him the few blocks to Valon's studio downtown. She offered him smiles and encouraging nudges in the lobby. Her long blue hair tickled his arm as she sat so close while they waited.

"Don't let him trick you into doing something you don't want," she offered quietly.

Huck nodded. "I feel like I have to take a few risks, though. I have to reach out to this thing to understand it."

She cocked her head, taking his hand comfortingly in hers. "Why now, all of a sudden?"

Finally, someone asked! Huck took a deep breath. "A year ago this weekend."

She nudged him with her shoulder. "What is?"

Not once had he told anyone. Logan knew because he read the report. He'd never even told Holly exactly what happened in Coven Wood. The place no one could find. Almost like it didn't exist in this world. He didn't want to recount the entire story to Lilia. At this point, he wasn't sure how much of it was real. He swore every detail was true, but now so much had faded or been blotched out in his mind.

"My brother Mark took his life on our birthday," he whispered. "Holly found him in the bathroom. I was on a hunt with my best friend, Jasper." He cleared his throat, a thick lump forming there. "To distract myself, I took Jasper to a haunted place the day after Mark's funeral."

Lilia nodded, wrapping her arm around his for comfort.

"We went to this place I found online while we were researching." He frowned. "I can't find it now. It was called Coven Wood."

Lilia looked away, eyes frowning into the middle distance. "Why do I feel like I've heard of that name?"

Huck shrugged and nodded. "That's what the cop said who took my statement. Thought she knew it, but nothing came up. They scoured the woods. They didn't find... the bed-and-breakfast where it happened."

"Where what happened?"

"Where I..." His eyes stung. "Where I left Jasper to die. They killed him."

"Damn," Lilia breathed softly. "They never found him?"

He shook his head. "One year later and this *thing*, whatever it is, is getting worse. Almost like it awakened that day. I'm scared of what will happen if I don't figure it out."

"My boy!" The soft, carrying voice of Valon interrupted them. He smiled, his fingers gently steepled. "Come back to my office. Let's talk."

VALON'S OFFICE WAS DARK. Almost-black cherrywood lined the walls and matched the wood of the red-velvet furniture. Crystal balls, fake skulls, and other paraphernalia lined his book shelves. Valon signaled to a thick-cushioned, wing-backed chair for Huck, then went behind his desk. He reached into a mini fridge and pulled out two bottles of sparkling water. He opened them both and handed one to Huck.

"I'm so glad you came back," he said soothingly. "I've been thinking about you ever since our first meeting."

Huck took the bottle, glad to have something to fiddle with, but didn't drink it. "I don't know if that's good or not," he admitted. "I'm really desperate, so it's whatever."

Valon smiled kindly. "We tend to do foolish things while we're desperate. Tell me what you mean." He steepled his fingers on his desk. Huck noticed he still wore his black robes and the white collar underneath. It suddenly felt like going to confession.

Hoping confessing his desperation wasn't a foolish thing to do, he started. "The anniversary of my," he cringed. He didn't have a better word. "Of my awakening is coming up. It's getting worse and worse. I need a way to make it stop."

"Oh, Huck," Valon said slowly. "I can only advise you from my own experience." His face fell. "It wasn't easy. And may not have been the best thing."

"You stopped it?"

Valon sucked in his right cheek and leaned forward over the desk. "In a way. But it was the wrong thing to do, Huck."

"Why? How can making this stop be bad?"

"Because of what it requires." He sat back now, entwining his fingers and taking in the boy before him.

If he went on, Huck didn't hear him. His eyes buzzed and the taste of metal rose in the back of his throat. It was happening. He dropped the bottle of water and gripped the chair's arms. His peripheral vision turned to that dead, white-green light. Behind Valon, in a shroud of mist, a form stood. Not the kind like the shadow people or the thing that haunted him, but a man. He wore a band t-shirt from the 80s, a faded red jacket, and black boots. Focusing, Huck looked at the form, trying to penetrate the veil of the Front. That's when he spotted it.

Hanging from the man's chest was a thick chain. It dropped to the floor and slithered up the back of the chair, vanishing behind Valon.

"Huck!" Valon called.

Huck blinked, and it all disappeared. Valon stood before him, mismatched eyes filled with concern.

"You did it just there," Valon interjected. He leaned against his desk. "Was that involuntary?"

Huck nodded, then looked around for the ghost. "Someone is following you," he said quickly. "They're chained to you. A man in a Mötley Crüe t-shirt."

The calm, passive mask that normally covered Valon's face dropped away. His constant, light smile faded. The change gave Huck pause.

"I saw two chains on me," Huck offered, trying to prompt Valon to speak. "What does it mean?"

"How did you see them?" Valon asked. "You can't see your own, bound to you." Valon's eyes suddenly went wide, and he jumped up from his desk and ran to his bookshelf. "He's coming, isn't he?"

"Who? What?" Huck asked, gripping the chair again as if it might tip him out.

"How terrifying that you and I ended up so close. It couldn't be by accident." His fingers hissed over the spines.

Now Huck got up and followed Valon to his bookcase. "What are you talking about?"

Valon grabbed a familiar book off the shelf and marched back to his desk, bent over it. Huck recognized the book as the one his father gave him.

Having enough, Huck snatched the book away. "Talk," he ordered. "Tell me about the chained man."

A strange, dark glare creased Valon's eyes. "*You* talk, Huck. Why do you have two souls chained to you? Following you?"

Huck gulped.

Valon nodded. "That's what I thought." His face relaxed. "I was able to give up witnessing. That's what we call seeing into this thing you call the DarkFront."

The dead place, with the black floor. The place Max told him to open a door to.

The man went on. "The only way I found was to make a deal." He nodded to the book in Huck's hand. "I found that entity one night." He took a moment to compose himself. "Like you, I wanted the visions to stop. To close myself off from the DarkFront like everyone else. See, you and I, we're witnesses. We have the ability to see the specters, to open up that place. When we do, we open ourselves to it as well. However, those like us are beacons to the things that lurk inside there. I cannot begin to imagine what they want with us except that we can see into their world, go into their space. We're like a gateway for them to pass through. They can anchor to us."

Huck shivered. "But this one, I see it all the time."

Valon reached up and grabbed the book. He flipped it open to a page and pointed to a crude drawing of the shadow Huck saw.

"My personal demon," Valon said. "The one I made a deal with. Gormalech, the phoenix."

The name sent a chill down Huck's spine. "A demon?"

Valon shrugged. "Could be. I don't know what it wants. It came to me. Too late, I learned it was because I am a witness. They can see us, we can see them."

Now the pieces came together. "And you made a deal with it?"

Valon nodded. "I asked it to shut me off from the Dark-Front. Turn it off, so to speak. But I had to give something up. I agreed, no questions asked. Anything would be worth it, right?"

Huck nodded.

"No." Valon shut the book. "Tell me, did the man behind me have dark, curly hair? Deep-set, brown eyes?"

Huck nodded again. "A red jacket."

"Michael. My closest friend. Taken as payment." Valon sat down, looking weaker and smaller than ever before.

"But your show," Huck pressed. "You do this kind of thing for a living."

"All fake."

Exhaling in disbelief, Huck stumbled back. His spirit fell. "What am I supposed to do? This thing is coming after me. It knows I'll be weak. What does it want?"

"It could be drawn to your guilt, Huck," Valon said sternly. "Two chains. Who are they? Why are they bound to you?"

No way, Huck thought. No way were they Mark and Jasper. "Mark wasn't even my fault!" he shouted, pounding the book on the desk. "And there was no way in hell I could have saved Jasper! It's not my fault!"

Valon closed his eyes and shook his head. "I am at peace with my guilt and closed off to the Front. You are not. You have two bound souls." He tapped the book. "Gormalech will find you. I suggest you be ready."

A feeling of being trapped crushed in on Huck. Fear gripped his heart. He looked around, almost expecting the thing to appear. "Why me?" he asked, choking on the words. "What will it do to me?" His nose and eyes stung. A tear escaped his left eye.

A new kindness eased Valon's intense stare. "Be ready."

Desperate, Huck asked, "Can you help me?"

Valon scoffed cautiously. "No. I have done my part to stay away from such things. You're on your own. Unless…" He gripped his chin in thought.

"What?" Huck asked, almost begging.

"If you got a hold of your witnessing, just enough, and came on the show—"

Huck almost spat. "No, not after last time."

"We'd be ready this time," Valon pressed. "If I could see it—I don't know—maybe I'd think differently."

A familiar sense of being manipulated stung Huck. Just like Max, all Valon wanted was his horrible curse.

"I'll think about it," Huck sighed.

Chapter 26:
The Party

"There you are!" Lilia hiss-whispered, running up to Huck.

He'd been hiding out in the library for the last few days to avoid Arkin, only going to his room to sleep and grab his laptop charger. The alcove he hid in nestled behind some bookshelves in a little-used part of the building on the third floor. It had east-facing windows and got a lot of sun. The smell of the books calmed him and made him feel smarter than he thought he was. Plus, the chair here had very few signs of being used and looked cleaner than the rest, despite it being an old wing-back chair.

"How'd you find me?" Huck asked, stowing the book on specters Max had given him. He'd stared at it for days, but nothing mentioned being what they had called a witness. And the DarkFront was his name for the land of ghosts. No one else seemed to have a name for it.

Lilia sat on the floor near his feet and slung her pack off. Her long, blue hair reached the carpet. "Arkin said you hide here."

So his room mate *did* know where he hid. "Nice of him to

come get me himself," he mumbled. He pulled one knee up and rested his chin on it. "So, what do you want?"

She smiled up at him. Gently, she rested her hand on his shin. "I know this Friday is your birthday and the anniversary of Mark's death." She said it so gently, he couldn't get mad at her. "I was thinking it might be good for you to try this whole university thing. You've been very studious all semester. Even Miss Embers said something about it. So why not come with me to this warehouse party?" She smiled energetically, biting her bottom lip.

Huck grimaced. He'd never been very social when not performing. Sure, anyone in his high school would tell him differently, but most of that had been an act. It had been easier before. Plus, Jasper and Mark were the quiet ones. Being the front man came easier when there were people who wanted to hide behind him.

Lilia scooted closer to him, squeezing his leg affection-ally. "You shouldn't be alone, at least. You don't have to party. But it'd be a lot more fun if you did." She smiled, her teeth made brighter by her dark red lipstick. "Huck," she got up and sat on the arm of the chair when he didn't reply. "Just one night. Let loose. See what it feels like to experience a college party. Arkin said you wouldn't, but I think there's a party animal in here somewhere." She jabbed her finger into his black hair.

"Will he be there?" Huck asked.

She nodded. "Everyone on our floor is going. But it's a warehouse. You probably won't see him. Come and drink with me."

"I'll think about it," he promised. She left with a smile and a wink. He took out his phone and opened his various social media accounts to check on them. It had been some time and activity dropped drastically. He'd never been good at maintaining it. That had been Jasper's job. The last video seemed ages ago. He opened the recording app he used.

"Hey, guys, it's me, Huck," he said to the camera. "Sorry it's been a second. No ghosts yet, but I wanted to drop in for the anniversary of my brother's passing. In a few days, it will have been a year since Jasper's murder, too." He paused and looked away from the lens. "I don't know what he would have wanted. But I'm going to try something wild tonight. I'm going to this party, so wish me luck. I have no idea what I'm supposed to do at these things. Those of you who have followed me the last three years know I never go out. Well, tonight, we change that."

He added some effects and posted the video. Taking a deep breath, he pushed himself up and started the mental preparation needed for whatever the hell a warehouse party was.

THE THUMPING of the music shook Huck's ribs before he even got inside. He had to take a rideshare down to the fringes of the city, as parties like this would have been broken up on campus instantly. Lights strobed inside the broken out windows, matching the pulsating glow sticks and other flashing devices the partiers had. Once in side, he took in the metal rafters and haphazard decorations. Everywhere, packed almost shoulder to shoulder, students and other people he was sure were too old for the university, jumped and danced to the rhythm. He instantly regretted his decision to come.

"Hey!" Lilia shrieked, throwing her arm around his neck and dragging him down to her level. "You came! I'm so happy! First rule, get super messed up quick." She shoved a large, colorful drink into his hands. Her breath wreaked of vodka.

"I don't know if that's such a good idea," he shouted to her. "How many of these have you had?"

She pulled a weird half smile, half grimace. "I don't know, Huckleberry. I tend to lean into the buzz. Not really as drunk as I look." She stood up on her toes and gave him a quick peck on his cheek. "I really want some oatmeal, though. Oh, and watch out for Arkin. The footballers are ganging up on him."

Someone slammed into Huck from behind, knocking him forward. Lilia guffawed, falling to the ground. She managed to save her drink somehow, arm raised above her.

"Drink!" she shouted, dumping the beverage into her mouth. "You won't notice the annoying people then."

Still clutching the liquid she gave him, Huck inched his way around the ruckus to a small, open area with a tower of kegs. Being surrounded by the intoxicated crowd oddly reminded him of being trapped in the mausoleum. With that thought, the walls closed in. The faces of the party-goers morphed into hideous, ghostly masks leering at him.

To dispel it, Huck shot back the entire cup Lilia gave him, chugging until it was empty. He'd not eaten all day, and the too-fruity vodka hit his stomach like a rock. In just a few minutes, his head spun pleasantly. His arms weighed him down and his feet turned to lead. He panicked a little, but also felt like something wrapped a fuzzy blanket around him. Curious, he wondered what a second would do. Maybe if he could be this calm, he could focus on getting in and out of the Front.

Huck wandered into the crowd in search of a second, colorful drink, only to run into what had to be the entire foot-ball team. They chanted around a mess of kegs, just like

Huck had seen them do in high school. Some things never changed. The one Huck recognized as the quarterback landed from a keg stand and raised his arms, shouting like a maniac.

"Now our little man," the quarterback, Jack if memory served Huck right, shouted. Jack reached back and pulled Arkin out by the collar of his t-shirt.

Arkin raised his hands up, shaking his head.

"Don't pussy out on us... *again*," Jack hollered, almost drooling onto Arkin's shoulder from pure inebriation. "We've got nothing to lose anymore. Thanks to you." He wrapped his arm around Arkin's neck and roughly knuckled his hair. "Right, team? Whose kick lost us that last point?"

"Arkin!" they all chanted back.

Huck grabbed a second drink and shot it, watching the bullies. He didn't understand the game. He had no idea it was Arkin's kick that lost them that last game. The game that got them kicked from the running.

"Get his legs, boys," Jack order.

"I don't want to," Arkin shouted.

The team grabbed his long legs, tripping him. Arkin fell onto his chest. He struggled, but couldn't free himself.

"Why not?" Jack taunted, prepping a new keg. "Gotta get home to your gay-boy room mate?"

Huck glared at them. Did they mean him?

"Leave him alone," Arkin growled, sufficiently pinned by the team.

Jack chortled. "Get a good, deep breath, little man. We're not letting you up for air." He grinned grossly at his team. "Just how you like it."

"Shut up!" Arkin roared as the team gripped his shoulders.

Something in Huck snapped. Pushed forward by the liberating vodka, he marched into the circle of bullies. "Hey!" he shouted, shoving Jack from behind.

Jack turned. His watery eyes squinted at Huck. "I'll be damned! It's little man's little man." His hand flashed out like a vice, grabbing Huck's shirt front hard. "You here to stick up for your boyfriend? Because of him, I was made a fool in front of scouts. The freakin' Dolphins, man!"

"Get off me," Huck hissed. "And let him go." He swayed on his feet, trying to jerk away from Jack.

"How cute is this?" Jack crowed to his team. "Tell you what, little dude. Impress me. You do the stand and we'll let our prize loser off the hook."

"Back off, Jack," Arkin snarled.

"What's the matter, little man? Afraid your boyfriend likes bigger dudes?" He grabbed his crotch, obscenely thrusting towards Arkin.

Emboldened by Jack's taunts and the booze, Huck shoved him hard. To his surprise, Jack stumbled backwards. "Get me up," Huck snapped.

Roaring and cheering at the fun, two team members ran to Huck. He braced his hands on the side of the keg and leapt up. The footballers caught his legs and held him up.

"Twenty seconds!" Jack crowed. "Right, little man? Twenty seconds was all you had to hold."

"Huck, cut it out," Arkin called, but the team overpowered him again.

Ignoring him, seizing the opportunity, Huck clamped the keg spout in his mouth and counted the seconds with the chanting team. When he reached ten, the buzzing moved from his arms and feet to his skull. And it wasn't the good kind. The warm, booze-fueled tingles left and the metallic, haunting ones washed over him. The more he relaxed into the beer, the more it came. Soon, the warehouse vanished. His body went limp. The dead-light filled his vision. He stood right side up on the black, rippling ground. All sounds faded away.

He wondered if his body still chugged away at the keg. He felt stupid immediately. Why did he have to make such impulsive, dumb decisions? Taking a step onto the black nothing, he looked around. When he did, something like static shot over the DarkFront, making it hitch and flicker. The same sensation shot through his body. He gasped at the striking pain, doubling over, hand to his chest. But it disappeared just as quick as it had come.

"Must be the booze," Huck reasoned. It must have relaxed him enough to let him slip into the DarkFront, but it was like the connection was unstable.

When he looked up, a green door appeared. Not like a mysterious door. In fact, it looked like the door to the bathroom in their house. It even had the dent next to the handle where Holly had...

A clinking came from behind him.

Spinning around, Huck came face to face with his own visage. The only difference was this version had two blue eyes and a less upturned nose.

"Mark?" Huck shouted, diving towards his brother. "Holy shit." He gripped his shoulders hard, crushing him into a hug.

Mark shoved his twin off, then gripped the chains in his hands to stop them from clinking. Mark held a finger up to his blue lips, signaling Huck to be quiet. Mark pointed to the door.

Looking down, Huck saw the chains that went up into the darkness, fading into the shadows. Another came from Mark's wrist, coiled over the ground, and snaked up around Huck's own wrist. He gasped and raised his hand, making the chains clink.

"It's you," Huck breathed. "You're behind me. Like Valon's friend."

Valon was haunted because he killed his friend. Huck stumbled back.

"No, I didn't kill you."

Mark's face twisted in anguish.

"What was I supposed to do?"

Mark shrugged.

"Like what?" Tears poured from Huck's eyes. "And Jasper? Jasper!" he called into the darkness.

Mark raised his pale hand to silence Huck. The bloody cuts on his wrist still dripped.

"They killed him," Huck said.

Mark nodded.

Sobbing, Huck shook his head. "I didn't know what to do. What am I supposed to do?"

Mark looked at him sadly, tilting his head in sympathy. Even in death, Mark was the better twin.

Just then, the scent of hot, putrid brimstone filled the space around them. Mark jerked around to look behind him. He spun back to Huck. Eyes wide, he signaled for Huck to run.

"No," Huck begged, reaching out to his brother. "I don't want to leave you behind. How did I find you? Can I find you again?"

Mark backed away slowly towards the door, dissipating into the blackness. He shook his head. The chains clinked as the darkness enveloped him, then they vanished. Huck's wrist was left bear.

"Mark!" Huck screamed, his voice echoing.

"I GOT YOU," Arkin's voice said from somewhere to his right. "Huck, calm down."

Huck felt his fist make contact with something bony and fleshy. Someone grabbed his wrist, pinning it down. He coughed, his lungs stinging. Bile rose, and he puked. Choking on his own vomit, someone helped turned him to the side and pat his back.

"I told you to leave us alone," Arkin snarled to the crowd around them.

His vision coming back, Huck made out the shoes of the football team around them. He was on the floor. He gasped and panted like he'd been drowning.

"Hey, relax, it was a joke," Jack said. Huck noted the waver in his voice. Good. "How was I supposed to know this pussy was gunna suck the beer into his lungs? Rookie mistake."

"Should I call an ambulance?" Lilia's voice said. "He's not responding to us at all." She sobbed.

Huck reached a hand up to stop her. Arkin took his hand and helped him up into a sitting position. "I'm good," Huck wheezed. His lungs stung badly.

"See? He's a trouper," Jack said nervously. His hand jumped from his hair, to his belt, and back again. "You went hard, my man."

"Get the hell away from us," Arkin barked again.

Huck's head spun, but he felt Arkin's arm slide under his and they both stood up. He may have almost drowned, but he'd made a breakthrough. He'd gotten into the Front quickly and made contact with Mark. Could he do it again?

"Wanna go back to the dorm?" Arkin asked Huck. "You need a shower."

Drunk off his ass, Huck nodded.

Chapter 27:

Demon Hunters

The booze-fueled dreams came in and out of focus as Huck slept off his first ever hangover. He woke up at 3AM, dying of thirst, but didn't understand what his body craved. He lay in bed, positive this was what death felt like. His head still spun, even though they'd left the party hours before. The dreams he'd been having lingered. Red eyes watched him from above. With a hoarse scream, Huck shot up from his bed and dashed out the door. Fortunately for him, Arkin was prepared. When Huck stumbled through the common area, gagging only to puke into the trash can, Arkin appeared with a cold water bottle.

"First time?" he asked Huck, opening the bottle.

Afraid if he spoke he'd puke again, Huck just nodded and guzzled down the water. He swore he felt it splash over every parched organ in his body.

"I'll get you pizza for breakfast," Arkin promised, offering Huck another bottle and some painkillers. "But you also need to sleep. Best way to avoid the consequences of your actions."

Huck looked back towards the room. "It's in there," he whispered.

Arkin's head snapped to Huck's dark room. "What is?"

He gulped. "The thing that's following me." At this point, he knew he could tell Arkin anything. So he did. He told him about easily he slipped into the Front when his brain reeled out of his control. About Valon. And finally, about Mark.

They sat together on the floor. "You're, like, literally haunted?" Arkin asked softly. "Not this old-ass building?"

Huck couldn't pull his eyes away from the dark doorway. "I guess so. But I think I've found a way to get in."

"No, no," Arkin said quickly. "You don't want to go back in. Like you said: creepy shadow man following you."

"It's out here too," Huck cut in, taking another long drink. "I can't get away from it. Running is no good. I have to meet it on its own turf. It's in there with *them*."

He took the proffered pills from Arkin.

"Ok," his friend said with finality. "How do we lure it out? How do we…" He shrugged. "Trap it?"

Huck swallowed the pills. "I'm not sure. I might…" He sighed heavily. "I might have to call Max."

Arkin grimaced. "No way are you doing this alone with that psychopath."

He was glad to have Arkin's bravery, but he *would* have to go alone into the DarkFront. "First," he said, "I have to get back in there. Make sure I can go in and out." *Make sure they're ok.*

"Are there—I don't know—precautions we can take?" Arkin asked.

Nodding, Huck smiled. "You can help me with that. How do you feel about skipping class tomorrow?"

Arkin smiled. "I'd love to."

GETTING five pounds of salt in the middle of November was easy. Huck and Arkin went to the nearest hardware store and bought a bag, hauling it back to their dorm before going after the next hardest thing. A few people stared at them as they marched down the dorm hall with bags of road salt, but fortunately, most people didn't question things on a university campus. They also picked up large chunks of white chalk.

"If we draw one of these warding sigils wrong," Arkin asked, looking over Huck's shoulder at the book Max had given him, "what happens?"

"You know as much as me," Huck sighed. He tossed around his room for the talisman he'd made before school started. He'd never used it and wondered if it would work. He found it in the bottom of his suitcase.

"If I get possessed, I blame you," Arkin said as they headed out for the next item.

Huck knew he was trying to make light of a very heavy situation, but it wasn't working. His gut tied up in knots the more he thought about willingly trying to go into the Dark-Front. Seeking out the thing that haunted his dreams. Next, they headed out into the city on foot.

Arkin went on, unfazed by Huck's silence as they walked down the street, empty bottles in hand. "We're like real demon hunters now. Like the Ghostbusters."

This got Huck thinking. "What if we filmed it?" he asked, taking a turn to an older part of downtown. The sky outside had gone gray and a cold wind threatened early snow. He pulled his head into his hoodie deeper.

Arkin pulled a confused, slightly disgusted face. "Why? What if something goes really wrong?"

"I won't live-stream it," Huck replied quickly. "But… it could be really useful. When I go in, I can't see what's happening out here. And might be able to help others like me."

"Wow." Arkin whistled. "You're really serious about this."

"It's my life. I have to do something about it."

They stopped, looking down the gray, mostly empty street at their target. A beautiful, gray-stone, old-world cathedral stood at the end of the street. The rose window glowed between two ornate towers. Deep archivolts led to just as decorated wooden doors. A glowing sign, ruining the whole facade in Huck's opinion, read: St. Eleazar's Parish.

"Can we just walk in?" Arkin asked, whispering even though they still stood outside. "Who's Saint Eleazar?"

Huck shrugged. "It's a church. They let all types in, right?"

"Thieves?" Arkin gulped.

Rolling his eyes, Huck pulled his friend up the stone stairs. "Saint Eleazar will forgive us. It's for a good cause."

He led the way to the doors. Fortunately, there was a smaller door in the great wooden one. Huck pushed it open. The inside lay dark, glowing in golden candle light like the churches of old. The main space was lined with glowing stained glass windows. A few people whispered, eyes clasped shut on kneelers in front of the old wooden pews.

"It's right there," Arkin whispered, pointing to a tall basin just to their left.

Huck glanced around and saw what they looked for: a stone stoup hung off the wall to their left. "Shit, this feels so wrong," he whispered back, dipping the first empty bottle into it. He couldn't help but smile and suppress a laugh.

"This is *not* funny," Arkin hissed, handing him a second bottle. "I am so going to hell."

With the second bottle full, Huck screwed the top on and reached for the third and last. The book mentioned three as some kind of magic number, so he thought he'd increase his chances and work in threes.

"Can I help you boys?" a gentle, deep voice asked.

They both screamed, not even hearing the priest approach.

"Shit!" Huck gasped, holding the bottles behind his back. "We, that is, uh…"

The priest smiled, slightly amused. He was older, with a white ponytail and the crispest cuffs the boys had ever seen.

"Sorry," Arkin gasped, grabbing Huck and dashing out the door. "what the shit, Huck," he growled quietly.

"And blessed be," the priest called after them.

IN SPITE OF THE SITUATION, Huck smiled when they got back. "You were so scared," he laughed. "That was worth it."

They spent the rest of the day setting up wards they found in the book. They drew on the walls and floor with chalk, checking and double checking their lines, circles, flourishes, and accents. Arkin flicked the water around, reading a prayer from the back of the book while Huck set up his equipment. He tested the mics, showed Arkin how to read the EVP, and how the infrared camera worked.

"You get to wear this," Huck said, slipping a head cam over Arkin's blond hair. "Don't worry about angles and all that. Anything you see, it will. The rest will be static cams."

"Great." Arkin tapped the camera to find the light switch

on the side. "I feel like an old west miner. Why do you have cameras in the rooms?"

It almost felt like setting up an episode back in the day. The feeling warmed Huck when he replied. "I am finding that these things don't manifest right in front of us. My theory is they can pop out anywhere. I don't know how the Front works. Does it lay over our reality like a blanket? Is it like Dante's rings? Valon mentioned it's like an orb. Max said I have to 'go deeper'. I don't know what any of that means. So I want to be prepared and try to get some answers."

They stood back, looking at the insane scene before them. Black candles for banishing evil spirits—according to the book. Salt to keep them safe. Wards to help. Huck shook the longer he looked at it, the fear finally setting in. Seeing the tremors, Arkin nudged him.

"Do you know how to get out?"

Huck shook his head. "I saw an opening last time. I'm hoping if I go in with a clear head, things will be more obvious."

"How can I pull you out?"

A greater fear filled Huck now. "I don't know. Max said when I go in, my body is empty. The door to the Front will be open. I hope nothing goes in me while I'm out."

Arkin snapped his head to face Huck. "Ok, safe word then, so I know it's you."

He looked up at him. "Good idea. What did you have in mind?"

"Something only we know."

Huck wracked his brain. Then it hit him. "The first time we met."

Arkin tilted his head. "Oh, yeah," he smiled. "That was wild. Well, at least, I thought you were."

"Ok." He nodded, balling his hands tightly.

Walking to the center of the common area, he laid down in the middle of the symbol they drew. The flickering black candles looked closer from here on the ground. He looked up at Arkin.

"See you in a bit."

Chapter 28:

The DarkFront

Huck paid close attention to the ground. His shoulder blades pressed against it and the top of his backside started to go numb. He tried to recreate the feeling he'd had the other night in the warehouse: the empty-headedness, the relaxation, the spinning world. He'd been scared, but at ease somehow. Coming to Arkin's rescue had emboldened him.

His palms faced up, and he in hailed deeply, eyes closed. He started to feel stupid. The room was so quiet, even Arkin's breathing had vanished. Sighing, he pushed himself up. "This isn't work—"

The dead light surrounded him. He froze mid push and looked around. He could only see a yard or so beyond himself. Standing now, he could look down at his own body. Everything was frozen, though. The flames on the candles did not flicker. Arkin stood perfectly still. All this lay behind a thin, smokey, glass-like panel. Turning, the expansive Dark-Front loomed out before him. The dead light followed him, giving just enough light for him to see. Looking down, he took in the black, rippling floor. The chains around his ankles hovered over the ground now. Like the things they attached to were far away, pulling the chains taut. He could still move. This time, they didn't hit the floor, sending out more ripples.

Grateful for at least a little more stealth, he looked around. He had no idea where to go or start. So, he followed his chains. If his theory was right, he'd find Jasper and Mark on the end. Wherever the other end was. His heart pounded and sweat beaded in his palms, thinking he might see them again. Maybe it was the wrong thing to do…

Even though he walked towards the chains, they never went slack and he never saw the end. The space got darker until, finally, he saw a warm, reddish-yellow light ahead. It splayed out on the ground like the light through a kitchen door at night. Curious, he moved toward it. Looking down, a thin trail of blood ran under his feet and into the door like a path. He took a few steps along it like a tightrope before the loud, ghostly wail of a woman shot out from the doorway. He froze mid-step, listening.

"No, John, no!" the woman screamed, her voice shaking in terror. The shout echoed like in a dream. "John, why?" It sounded like she fought for her life.

Huck didn't know if this was real or what he'd stumbled onto if it was something in the Front. Was it another person in the Front? What happened if more than one came through? Checking over his shoulder, he saw the hazy entry way he'd come through. He could still see Arkin's blond head in the dorm. So he took a few more steps forward. The closer he got, the more movement he heard inside the kitchen door. He could see yellow linoleum on the floor now and hear old rock and roll coming from a crackling radio.

"John, please!" the woman wailed bitterly. "Why, John, why?"

A plate crashed, and someone ran, turning over a chair. Huck finally peaked in. Just as he did, the loud, deadly crack of a shotgun broke through the other sounds of a tussle. Red mist shot out from the doorway. Gasping in horror, Huck ran to the door and looked in.

Inside waited the stereotypical layout of an old kitchen from the 1980s. A woman lay on the yellow floor, half her face blown off from the shot. Her one remaining eye swiveled in her head. A man, Huck guessed John, stood over her, taking a long drink from a bottle, a shotgun held limp in his hands. He looked down at his wife, then over at an upturned bassinet in the corner. A tiny, pink hand stuck out from underneath, not moving.

"Holy shit!" Huck gasped, stepping back. He looked around the outside of the doorway. Nothing held the door in place. It just existed right there in the blackness of the Front. It stood like a monolith in the middle of nowhere.

"No, John, no!" the woman screamed again.

Thrusting his head back into the kitchen, the scene played out again. This time, Huck watched as John stepped away from the baby, his work done there, and turn on the woman. She ran from him, throwing plates, tried to escape out a window—which Huck saw showed a picture perfect lawn complete with a white picket fence—and then succumbed to her fate once again.

It played over again.

"What the hell?" Huck breathed, eyes wide.

"You him?" a hallow, echoing, gruff voice shot at Huck.

Eyes wide in terror, Huck looked up to see John finally notice him. Not realizing the ghostly replay could see him, he backed away, hands up.

"No," Huck panted, wondering if he should run.

"She cheated on me!" John roared. He flipped the barrel of the shotgun down and started to reload it. Behind John, the scene played out again, without him in it.

Seeing his chance, Huck dashed away from the mad John and his kitchen. He ran, his legs feeling sluggish against the black ground of the Front, but got far enough away that the kitchen light dimmed. He half expected John to follow him, but nothing appeared.

Steadying his breath, he walked farther, past the first encounter. Not a second later, then something appeared to his left, making him jump. Something white and misty slammed against the black floor. It didn't cause a ripple, but it made a sick, smacking sound. Nothing was there. Tossing his head around, he looked again. Then the thing fell again, smacking against the ground. Knowing now it came from above, Huck looked up. Nothing was there at first, then a white specter appeared, falling rapidly. It was a child. Its ghostly form hit the ground with that sickening smack. This one didn't make a shout, a call. It just leapt off some unseen cliff and fell to its doom.

The deeper he went, the more doorways and scenes he found. Almost like he walked through a haunted house of death scenes. Everything was fairly modern. No ghosts from the 1800s or ancient times like in the movies. At first, he didn't peek into any of the scenes, afraid someone like crazy John might chase him down. But the deeper he went, the more curious he got. Especially when nothing seemed to be touching or interacting with him.

Up ahead, a street light stood in the darkness. The pool of yellow light under it showed a man in a hat and duster. He was smoking a cigarette and looking up. Huck slowly made his way to the man. He didn't seem hostile. Could it see him?

Maybe I can ask for directions? he thought awkwardly.

"Can you see me?" he asked the thing.

The man didn't make any indication that he saw Huck. He puffed on his cigarette and looked around again. The man moved his duster aside to grab something off his belt. All sorts of tools hung there: a wooden cross, a silver stake, and a rosary among others.

"Oh, damn," Huck mused. "Either it's Halloween, or this guy thinks he's hunting vampires." This gave him pause. Max believed in vampires. Had said something about them when he was busy leaving poor Sal to die. Suddenly, Huck wondered just how much existed in this world that he'd not believed in.

Huck walked on past the streetlight. He decided to look into a few of the scenes he passed. One was just an old living room, maybe 1940s, with an old man in a chair facing a static TV. He didn't move at all. Another showed a woman rocking a baby in front of a great window bathed in moonlight. Huck didn't dare stay to watch that one.

Finally, he came to what he thought must be a crossroads. All around him were tiny lights and glowing scenes of deaths. Soft whimpers, shouts of pain, and every once in a while some other loud sound filled the once quiet air. He stood still, not sure what to do now. Perhaps it was time to get out.

Turning, he looked back the way he was pretty sure he'd come. He chewed the inside of his cheek, wondering if he faced the right direction. The DarkFront had no paths. The light always came from right above him. No wind moved. He contemplated so long, he didn't realize at first that everything dropped quiet, moving around him like a slow-moving tread-mill. Not a single sound rose now. Huck's blood froze. All the lights disappeared slowly, phasing out. Only one stayed lit. Turning to find the source of the light, his heart stopped all together.

Behind him, far away but visible, stood a stonework arch-way. Dead ivy, black and withered, grew up around it. Again, nothing held it on any side, but he could see through it.

Closing off the archway was a cruel-looking, sharp, bright red wrought-iron gate. Somehow, he ended up right at the front door of something he was sure was not good.

As he looked into beyond the gate, one of the chains on his ankle moved. He jumped at the movement and turned.

Far off in the distance stood a solid form. It stood with its head lolled to one side, blood dripping from its chest. He recognized its light brown hair and band t-shirt.

"Jasper!" Huck screamed. He made a mad dash toward the form. He ran as fast as he could, but still his movement felt slogged down whenever he wanted to move fast. "Is it you?" he called.

The vision held up a pale, dirty hand to its lips, signaling for Huck to be quiet. Huck stopped in his tracks.

"What is it?" he asked. Tears pricked in his eyes as he beheld his dead friend. "Shit, Jasper, I'm so sorry. I-I-" he stammered. His words wouldn't come. What was he supposed to say? He left him for dead in the worst way possible: bleeding out for ritualistic slaughter, surrounded by cloaked and hooded murderers. Ones who said they wanted *him*. But he'd not even thought to ask to switch places with Jasper.

Jasper's ghostly face held no expression. His eyelids dropped and his blue lips hung partly open. Taking his hand away from his lips where he'd signaled Huck to be quiet, he then pointed behind him to the hellish gate, then motioned behind himself.

Somehow, Huck understood. Something was coming from there and he needed to run.

"But I have to talk to you," he begged, walking towards Jasper now.

Jasper glared at him with filmy eyes.

"Jasper, please," Huck begged.

The chain linking them yanked Huck towards where Jasper had pointed. Against every fiber in his body, Huck walked past Jasper. The closer he got, the more horrified he felt. He saw the cuts on his friend's flesh. Blood smeared all over him. The gash on his throat was wider than he remembered.

Huck hadn't realized at first, but the closer he got to Jasper's body, the brighter the dead light glowed around him and the more ripples he put out. Almost like since the two of them stood here, the signals were stronger.

"Shit," Huck whispered out loud.

Just as realization hit him, the smell of sulfur polluted the air. Whipping back around, the red gate swung open. Nothing came out, though. Spinning around, wondering where the monster went, Huck scanned the darkness. In the midst of his panic, a hard, cold hand grabbed his wrist.

Huck screamed and spun to face Jasper. The dead boy, one hand on his wrist, used the other to point behind them.

"Is it…?" Huck looked back the way he came. "Is it going to the door? Is it going for me?"

Jasper dropped his hand's, dead eyes trained on the way back.

Cursing, Huck dashed back the way he came. This time, the heads of the dead people poked out of their scenes, looking towards his hazy opening. A few already lumbered towards it. The spirits must have been alerted to his empty, waiting vessel.

Even though he was slower, he moved faster than the dead in the DarkFront. He ran, the ripples and chains signaling to all around him where he was. He passed mad John, who fired a shot over Huck's head. Huck yelped in surprise but kept on running. Up ahead, he saw the opening.

Nothing moved still on the other side. Not sure how to close it, or if he'd let anything out, Huck dove through.

His body didn't move, but it felt like he'd been tossed onto the wooden floor with a thud, knocking all the air out of him. He groaned, holding his head, and looked up. He was back in his dorm. Nothing looked disturbed. The candles flickered, and the heat kicked on, hissing in the ducts above.

"Holy hell, Arkin," Huck started, sitting up. "I think I made some progress, but—"

Arkin lay before him on his back. Mostly. One arm contorted around so violently that it cradled his head from behind. One of his legs bent hellishly up under his back so his foot came over his head. His spine arched so dangerously it looked like it might be broken. But worse than the unnatural bending of his friend's body were his wide eyes. Arkin's blue eyes bulged so wide tears flowed freely from the dryness. His mouth gaped in a soundless scream.

Huck couldn't move, petrified. "Arkin?" he whispered softly.

A deep, monster-like roar rose from Arkin's throat, his eyes turning black as they honed in on Huck.

Chapter 29:

A Vessel

Arkin shrieked. Like lightning, he twisted his body around, stood on all fours, and launched himself at Huck. His jaws cracked open, and he snapped at Huck. The weight of his friend landing on him with such force dazed Huck so much, all he could do was hold his hands out in front of him, shouting.

"Arkin, stop! What happened to you?" he called over the snarls and grinding sounds of Arkin gnashing his teeth.

Suddenly, he froze. A tiny sliver of drool dripped from Arkin's open mouth down onto the bridge of Huck's nose. Panting, Huck looked up, pushing against Arkin's shoulders. In the stillness, he could see into Arkin's eyes; the whites had pitched to black and his irises burned red. Veins pulse all over his neck, face, and head. Sweat beaded on his body. Without having to ask, Huck realized what had happened.

Something came through with him. It jumped out before him, maybe even looking for him. Was it a ghost? Some spirit he'd run into on his way out? Or was it...

"Huck!" Arkin screamed, falling limp like a rag doll and rolling to the left. "It's-it's inside me!" He grabbed at his throat. An invisible hand made a heated impression on Arkin's flesh, strangling him.

Huck scrambled to his feet and looked around. "But we did everything right! Didn't we?" He turned back to his friend. "Hold on, there has to be something in the book about banishing or whatever."

Choking, Arkin reached out for Huck. "I… can't hold on. It's letting me speak." Arkin's eyes went wide as he tried to gasp for air.

Huck could see it almost perfectly now. The indent around Arkin's neck grew tighter. The flesh underneath started to burn. "It's here? It's talking to you?"

Eyes pleading, Arkin couldn't even nod. Then it happened again. Arkin's head snapped all the way back, and he screamed, but the cry was quickly overtaken by an infernal roar. Arkin bent his back so far, his head almost touched the floor. Using his arms and bent legs, he launched himself at the wall. When his face hit the plaster, bloodying Arkin's nose, it flipped over onto its belly and crawled backward up into a corner where it glared down at Huck.

In Arkin's voice, mingled with the guttural growl of the thing that possessed him, it said, "This body is wrong for me!" It roared in what Huck thought must be annoyance. It pounded the wall and bashed Arkin's head against the ceiling.

"Get out!" Huck commanded, but of course, nothing happened.

The thing rolled its head and then suddenly fell, landing in a painful heap on the ground. Arkin's normal voice groaned in agony.

"Get it out of me," Arkin whimpered.

The thing would keep hurting Arkin. It came out of the Front and got into a living body. Still not sure if it was a ghost or something worse, Huck realized the least he could do was immobilize Arkin, so the thing didn't end up breaking him. Quickly, he called Lilia and put the phone on speaker while he ran to his room to strip the sheets off.

"You all are being awfully loud over there," Lilia said over the phone.

Knowing she'd understand and there was no time to waste, Huck shouted, "Lilia, Arkin's possessed. Bring your hand cuffs—anything to tie him down!"

The phone beeped, showing she'd hung up. He knew she believed him and she was on her way.

As Huck tied Arkin's legs together with his bedsheets, the monster inside Arkin rolled its head and laughed monstrously. The thing didn't seem to know how human bodies worked and flailed as it tried to inflict more pain on its vessel.

Using Arkin's voice, it said, "Tie me, chain me, but I won't leave you."

But even as he finished with Arkin's legs and Lilia burst in, Huck took in his friend's body. Arkin's veins pulsed dark and his flesh turned sallow and clammy. Purple circles bloomed around his eyes and even his face looked thinner.

"This damned vessel is not right!" the monster moaned. Huck had gotten on top of Arkin, holding his wrists down.

"Lilia," Huck shouted as Arkin tried to buck him off. "Get his arms!"

Crying and shaking, having no idea what was going on, Lilia obliged quickly and without comment. With Huck's help, they got his arms behind him and fastened with her cuffs. Using a belt from Arkin's dresser, Huck bound the top of his arms as well. Once mostly immobile, the monster started to whip his captor's body, banging his head against the wall. Huck shouted for it to stop, placing his hand between it and the wall. Lilia jumped and thrashed through Arkin's duffel just inside his bedroom door. In a second, she reappeared, slamming his helmet over his head and fastening the chin strap.

"Huck!" Arkin's normal voice sobbed. "I feel… I feel so sick."

"Shit," Huck panted.

"It said he's not the right vessel," Lilia sniffled, running her hand under her nose. "What does that mean? Will it kill him?"

"Just hold on, Ark," Huck ordered, flipping through the book while on his knees.

Arkin moaned again. "I'm not. It's letting me out. It wants you to—Ah!" he screamed in agony, sobbing. "It wants you messed up. Wants you to panic."

Gripping his hair in frustration, Huck shoved the book at Lilia. "Look in here for anything useful." He stood up and ran into his room.

"What are you doing?" she cried. Black tear tracks ran down her pale face and her eyes already turned red from silent crying.

"Lilia?" Arkin's voice said in a deep, seductive drone.

She froze, turning to face him, eyes bulging in fear. "It knows my name?"

"Don't talk to it!" Huck ordered, dialing a number on his phone. He locked his eyes on Arkin's struggling body as the phone rang. He had no idea what time it would be in Connecticut or if Max had even gone home. Half hoping he was still in town, Huck started to pace. The time between rings stretched on like a lifetime. Finally, a ring got cut short.

"Hey, Huck," Max's voice came, low and monotone—almost bored. "Look, I know you want me to apolo—"

"I don't care about that!" Huck cut in as Arkin roared a piercing scream. "How do I banish a spirit that's possessed someone? Like you did for me in the cemetery?"

Max didn't miss a beat. "What? Who's possessed?"

Lilia screamed. Spinning around, Huck watched as Arkin snapped at her hands with his too-wide jaw. Lilia scrambled away, crying and raising the book to use it as a club if Arkin tried to bite her again.

"My friend," Huck panted, forcing the sobs down into his chest. "I-I went into the Front. I made it deep inside. I was practicing so I could…" He stopped. No, Max didn't need to know the details. "Something came out with me. I need your help, please!"

This time, Max didn't reply for a minute. Huck heard him breathing and moving, but he didn't say anything.

"Help me!" he shouted into the phone.

Behind him, everything went quiet. He turned again and saw Lilia shoved into a corner, holding the huge book over her head for protection, her knees pulled up to her chest. Arkin lay sill, his spine bent again, eyes wide and staring right at Huck.

"It's looking at me," he whispered to Max.

As Huck locked eyes with his possessed friend, Arkin's tongue slipped out between his teeth and slowly licked his lips.

"I need a witness," the demonic voice said. "Made for possession. Your body is mine, little Huckleberry."

Finally, Max said, "I heard that. It's not come out of him?"

Huck shook his head even though Max couldn't see him. "We drew wards from the book. Hoping it would protect us. But they didn't. It came out and got into him."

"But not you," Max added. "Sounds like you have it

stuck. Which is good." He sighed heavily. "Listen, Huck, even if I wanted to help, I can't. I'm back home in New England and it'd take me hours to get to you. Sounds like you have it under control."

"What?" Huck's guts turned to ice. "Just *tell* me what to do!" he begged. "Max, please!"

"Hey," Max cut in. "I thought you were stronger than this. But it seems…" He sighed again, this time sadly. "I can't say to you what I think will happen, Huck."

"What do you mean?" He panted, unable to get his breath.

Max blew into the phone. "I thought maybe you could help me with my research. That you were more in tune than you are. That'd you'd… work out. But when things don't work out, you got to move on. You don't keep things that are broken. I hope you understand."

Did he understand what Max was saying? "You mean me?" His voice came surprisingly steady. Angry. Hateful. "I'm broken. Not working. You wanted me because you thought I could slip in and out of this DarkFront. That I was a functioning—whatever you call it—witness? But now that you know I'm not, I'm *useless* to you. Is that it, *Max*?" He growled his father's name.

"Don't take it the wrong way, Huck. You're just not… useful to me. I don't keep things in my life that don't have value."

"Fuck you!" Huck screeched into the phone, the veins on his neck pulsing.

"What happened?" Lilia cried from the other room. Her eyes locked onto Arkin, who hadn't moved in a moment. "I think he's… settled down? I don't know."

Huck pulled up the past numbers on his phone. "Just hold on one more second, Arkin." He hit Valon's number.

"Hey!" Lilia called through a stuffy nose in the other

room. "I found something. It's called a locking ward. It can lock a spirit inside something. Maybe we can…"

But Huck didn't hear the rest of her sentence. "Go get a marker, Lilia."

She looked up, scared and confused.

"Do it! And draw it on his chest," he ordered.

Lilia gasped, crying anew. "I'm not locking that thing inside him!"

"We have to. We'll wash it off when we get to Valon's. Call a rideshare and pay them whatever the hell they want to keep quiet."

Sobbing audibly, Lilia ran into the room to get a marker.

"H-Huck," Arkin's normal voice croaked. "It's ok. I'll be fine."

He wanted to go back to his brave friend's side. But he thought getting close might open him up for possession. He was outside the wards they drew on the ground and Arkin was inside. It might have been the only thing keeping him safe.

Was he sacrificing a friend… again?

"Valon!" Huck gasped in relief when the secretary patched him through.

"Our father!" Arkin shouted gleefully in his demonic tone again, "who art in heaven, little Valon Gabriel took an angel's name. He thought that he'd be safe, but will still end up in flame."

"Oh, my god," Valon's voice whispered over the phone. "What have you done? That's a demon's voice."

Finally, having someone who understood these things and who might offer answers, the tiniest bit of relief flooded Huck. "Can you help us?" Huck begged. "We're locking it inside and can bring him down. I don't know what to do."

Valon waited a beat before answering. "This could be what I need."

"What?" Huck shot.

Lilia came back in and cautiously approached Arkin. He thrashed and tried to kick her away, but she got on top of him, shoving her forearm under his jaw to stop his biting and ripped his shirt down the front. Biting the cap in her mouth, she pulled the marker out and started to draw on his sweaty chest.

"I could get everything back I've lost," Valon said, nervous excitement filling his voice. "Let me film it—live broadcast his exorcism! That would shut the nay-sayers up."

Destroyed once again by the idea that he was just something to be used, Huck shouted in rage, hot tears pouring from the corners of his eyes.

"That's right, Huckleberry," Arkin snarled.

Huck turned to face him. Finished with the ward, Lilia had backed off. Arkin sat now, legs half crossed with his ankles tied, glaring at Huck.

"Weep, break, fail," the demon purred. "A phoenix can only rise from the ashes. I need you destroyed before I can take you completely." Arkin rolled his head, letting it fall too far to the back. "That curse no man can ever be free from anchors you to me. I will find you anywhere. You shine like a beacon. Cast me out now and I will return. You are far too haunted to be free of me."

Arkin winced in pain, making a small moan.

Huck swallowed hard. "Valon, do this for me and I'll do whatever you want after. I'll make it good. I'll find anything you want. I'll do anything. Please, it's hurting him."

Valon cursed softly. "All right, my boy, you don't need to go into all that." He sighed, and Huck heard him rubbing his chin. "I'll get the book of exorcisms and prayer." He sighed deeper. "I haven't done this in some time."

"You can do it," Huck encouraged him automatically.

A moment passed before Valon said softly. "Very well. Bring him over."

Chapter 30:

The Rite

Arkin struggled but Huck gagged him, and he and Lilia got him into the rideshare. The driver—the same one who had taken them home from the hospital—panicked but Huck assured him Arkin was just having a really bad trip and they needed to get downtown. The driver wanted to call an ambulance or take them to the hospital, but Huck again said they'd be fine. Lilia didn't speak, quietly crying next to him.

Valon met them outside his building. He held a bottle of vodka in one hand, unscrewing it quickly once he took in Arkin and the weeping Lilia.

"What's that for?" Huck asked as Valon tipped the vodka into Arkin's mouth.

"Helps him relax and, if I'm being honest, opens us up to that place you call the DarkFront far more easily," Valon said. A little bit of the vodka, saliva, and blood trickled out of Arkin's mouth.

Huck couldn't argue with that. He'd experienced that once and thought maybe it was just a fluke. But maybe he was on to something. Still, it seemed like a dangerous combination to mix spirits and liquor.

Valon led them up into his studio. "I've prepared an area in the filming room. Wards are down and salt is spread along the edges of the room."

A little hitch of fear stopped Huck. "I said you can't record this one," he barked.

He was going to go on, but a strangled, low growl in Arkin's throat stopped him. The muscles in Arkin's body tensed before Huck saw the change. He braced himself for another round of thrashing. Arkin's head snapped back, cracking into Huck's face just as he attempted to lower him into the leather office chair Valon had in the middle of the devil's ward. Blood exploded from Huck's nose and he swore he felt it crunch back into his face. The demonic voice laughed as Huck dropped his captive.

"Take this," Valon called to Lilia, handing her a bottle of holy water.

"Is this real?" she asked skeptically, but unscrewing it all the same.

"Are you all right?" Valon called to Huck where he rolled on the ground, clutching his face. He went for Arkin, heaving him into the chair before tying him down.

"Yeah," Huck panted, spitting a wad of blood out onto the devil's ward. He glared at the demon's eyes in Arkin's face.

"I want to lick the blood off your face!" the demon hissed, grinding Arkin's teeth. "Sweet blood. I'll spill it before I take your corpse for my own."

Arkin pressed against the arms of the chair to spring forward, but Lilia shouted, tossing a big splash of the holy water onto Arkin's chest. Arkin screamed and writhed, but it allowed Valon enough time to fasten him down tightly and remove the football helmet.

"Good reflexes," Huck complimented Lilia.

She nodded thanks, but started to cry anew at seeing

Arkin's blistering chest. The demon cringed, flailing and flinging his head back.

"I'll break this little boy before you push me out!" it snarled towards Valon. It stopped moving all of a sudden. Its eyes roamed up to Valon's face. "Still a witness. Still a beacon."

"Saint Michael the Archangel, defend us in battle," Valon started, pulling a huge metal cross out from under his black robes.

"Hypocrite!" the demon screeched. "Murderers! You cannot sail an anchored ship!"

Huck stood back as Valon started to rapidly spit words in Latin, stepping closer to Arkin. "What does it mean?" he asked. Before the words even left his mouth, the familiar buzzing in his skull vibrated his vision. His eyes stung as if he'd poured hot sauce on them. The pain mounted and his knees buckled.

"Holy shit, Huck," Lilia gasped. "You have blood coming out of your eyes."

Huck blinked and a red sheen overtook his vision, but the dead light rapidly encroached on his peripherals.

"I'm here for you, little boy," the demon roared. "You won't let go, I won't go!"

The thing twisted Arkin's entire torso violently. A snap cracked out over Valon's hurried verses. Huck saw Arkin's left wrist twist at an unnatural angle, something under his skin sticking out, dangerously sharp. The demon pulled back just for Arkin to scream in pain before taking over and laughing again.

"Hurry!" Huck called to Valon.

Panting, the older man stopped, signaling Lilia to douse him with the water again. "Something holds it here. Like it's bound to this place. I can feel it straining with every word."

As Huck's vision slowly slipped more into the Front, the chains behind Valon came into view. Like breath on glass, so did the ghost behind him. He locked onto the ghost as the deadlight overcame his vision. But the room did not disappear. He did not enter the DarkFront, he merely saw its presence over his physical reality. He cast around to take in more of the new sight.

Behind Arkin stood the thing he'd seen in his nightmares for months. The long, black body hunched over Arkin, its long, sharp fingers buried deep into his chest from behind. The longer he looked, the more detail appeared. The demon's long, double-bent legs ended in claws like a hawk. Black and burnt orange feathers covered its avian legs. Red eyes glowed perfectly round over a cruel, flaming beak. All around its body wavered heat lines, distorting the space. The image looked familiar. He'd read the demon's name, but he couldn't remember.

Realizing the monster was in the physical world, Huck looked over at Lilia with a plan. He was about to speak, but stopped upon seeing her. In this vision, people around him were just shadowy outlines. Arkin was a dull gray. Valon stood out in a blueish-green, almost like neon. So did he. But Lilia's form was entirely wreathed in what looked like dimly glowing, purple fire.

She faced him and gasped. "Are you hurt?" she asked, reaching for him.

"I'm fine," he said back, his voice sounding a million miles away. "I have to go in."

"To the DarkFront?" Valon cried, flipping to another page in his book of prayers.

Huck nodded. "I know what's anchoring him to me."

"What if the demon posses you while your body is empty?" Valon asked.

The demon shrieked and pulled against Arkin's broken arm. "Where are you going, little boy? Leaving me an empty vessel, are you?"

Huck glared at the monster. "No. You're trapped." He tapped his own chest to remind him of the binding ward on Arkin's.

"Not forever," the demon growled with a wicked grin. "I will destroy this meat sack. Once he gives up his ghost, I come for you. I need you weak, broken. From your ashes, I will rise."

Another tinkle of familiarity rang in Huck's ears at that. He sat down behind Valon's desk and closed his eyes, taking a long drink from the vodka bottle abandoned there. "Good luck, asshole," he snarled to the demon

ENTERING the DarkFront this time was like slipping down a water slide. Huck even felt himself land on the black ground, sending out a million tiny ripples. This time, he immediately followed the chains draping off his ankles. He wasn't ready to see what he found, only a few steps into the darkness. Like before, a pale light splashed out over the black floor; a doorway to a bedroom. One of the chains led to it. A woman's soft weeping came from inside, but this time it was muffled and distant. Huck recognized the room before he even got to it. Holly's familiar weeping stopped, then started again.

Slowly, Huck approached the room door. Inside, everything was tinged with the dead light. The items in the room—collectible figures, posters, a pile of unfolded laundry, a glass of water—floated in the room like it was submerged in water.

Finally, he forced himself to look at the figure in the center. A shadowy, gray image of Holly knelt on the floor, face in her hands before she gripped the body of a boy with Huck's face. She screamed a wailing sob over him, begging him to wake up. It was Mark.

Huck forced himself to watch the scene unfold again. Holly's gray form ran past to the door, stopped a moment, then screamed and ran into the bathroom he and Mark shared between their rooms. The wailing tore Huck's heart as Holly pulled Mark out of the bathtub, wrapping him in his black towel before hauling him out into his room. She dialed on her phone and wept incoherently into the phone before cradling her boy in her arms again.

The sobs infected Huck. He sniffled and looked away.

"I'm so sorry, Mark," he moaned through a stuffy nose. "I wish I could make it right. I wish I could redo it!" He gripped his face in his hands.

A chill beside him made him look up. Mark's ghost—dead, pale, milky eyes—appeared beside him. His black hair fell in front of his veiny face. Huck screamed and leapt back. Mark watched him, blue lips closed.

"You're here!" he cried joyfully. He gripped Mark's upper arm, but his brother didn't make any sign that he noticed. "What's happening? Why is that thing following me?"

Mark slowly inclined his head to the horrible scene that started again.

Huck didn't look. "Because of this. Is..." He choked on a sob. "Is your blood really on my hands?"

With agonizing calm, Mark shook his head.

"Then why are you chained to me?" he begged. "The ghosts that haunt me are drawing this thing to me. Why won't you leave?"

Mark's face twisted in sorrow.

Huck realized what he'd said. "I'm so sorry." He put his face in his hands again. "I'm so sorry. It was that night, wasn't it? The night you texted me. That's when you decided. What was it? Did you see what I do?"

Mark nodded, his face softening.

"Then why don't I follow you?" he implored his twin. "Why am I not overcome?"

At this, Mark pointed behind Huck. He turned and saw a different kind of opening. Like the adit to a cave, a rough-hewn entry way yawned open just a few steps away. A dark orange light flickered inside. Before he even stepped towards it, Jasper's voice cried out, begging Huck to save him. Huck winced, drawing his shoulders up to his ears, preparing to cover them.

"Oh," he whispered sadly. "I wasn't alone. I had Jasper." He turned to look back at Mark, to apologize again for leaving him alone.

But now Jasper stood next to him. Blood still covered Jasper's chest and face. The gash on his neck looked fresh.

"Jas!" Huck cried. "No one believes me! They can't find you."

Jasper slowly shook his head and shrugged.

A strange tickle alerted Huck to a wet sensation on his hands. Lifting them, he saw now that they were covered in blood. Jasper's blood. He gasped and stumbled backward.

"What was I supposed to do?" he shouted at his dead friend.

Again, Jasper replied with a shake of his head. It wasn't about what he was supposed to do, Huck realized.

"Can I take you back with me?" he tried.

They both shook their heads mutely.

"What can I do?"

Together, both pointed back the way Huck had come. Somewhere beyond, Arkin's voice cried out in agony.

Like lightening, an epiphany hit Huck's brain. "I can save him." He looked back at Jasper and Mark.

To his surprise, Mark smiled with just the right side of his lips, the way Huck did, and nodded. He flicked his head towards the hazy opening as if to tell him to get on with it.

"But…" He reached for his brother and best friend. "But I want to make *this* right."

Sadly, Jasper shook his head again.

Huck sobbed softly. "I'll never do it again. I'll never abandon someone. Never leave someone alone." His eyes went over Mark's shoulder to the death scene one last time. "It should never come to that. But I didn't know what to do. How to help."

Mark reached out and gently turned Huck towards the exit. He pointed. Softly, Mark mouthed, *Be there.*

He walked a few paces before turning around to look at them again. When he did, Huck noticed the chains had vanished. And so had they.

"Wait!" he called into the darkness. Even the lights from the doorways vanished. Everything turned black but the way back. *I wanted to see them just one last time!* he screamed in his head. But he'd already made his choice.

A GASP for air burst from Huck as he bolted up from behind the desk. Three voices shouted in the room before him. He couldn't make out anything going on. The chair where Arkin was tied down had tipped over onto the floor. Valon stood with his foot on Arkin's chest, chanting with renewed vigor, and Lilia held his head still, sobbing all over again.

"What's going on?" Huck cried, running around the desk to meet them.

"It's working," Lilia panted. "But it's been fighting so hard. It levitated, and it's hurting him."

The foggy over-lay of the DarkFront waned the longer and harder he breathed. The purple fire around Lilia now touched Arkin's temples where she clutched him. It almost looked like a protective barrier.

"Join me," Valon said. "Where three of us gather in purpose, the devil cannot stay!"

Holding hands, Valon chanted the last verse again of something Huck had never heard. "Say your piece," he instructed the others, "to finish the rite."

"So mote it be!" Lilia shouted with absolute conviction.

"Adios, asshole," Huck added, glaring at the red eyes.

Above them, the lights flickered and danced. A power surge shot through them, shattering every bulb. Even a few windows blew in, slashing the four of them in a rain of glass. The pressure mounted so high, their ears bled. For a moment, a blackness unlike anything they had ever seen filled the room, utterly blinding them.

Huck felt something caress the side of his neck.

I'll see you again, the deep, demonic voice whispered into his hear. He even felt its hot breath tickle him.

Then, the moonlight came through the shattered windows. Huck opened his eyes. On the floor between the three of them, Arkin coughed. A gurgle came up from his throat and he tried to moan.

Huck flew back to the desk and grabbed a sharp letter opener. He came back, ripping into the knots that bound Arkin. "Call an ambulance," he ordered Lilia.

She nodded and ran to her phone a few feet away, abandoned on the floor.

"Arkin?" Huck asked, gently tapping his roommate's face.

He didn't respond. He choked, fighting to breathe, but couldn't draw a breath. Huck pushed aside his tattered shirt and took in all the bruises over his ribs and chest. Gently, he held his broken hand to stop him from hurting himself further.

"Can you hear me?" he asked again.

Shaking, blood dribbling from wounds, Arkin tried to turn his head to face Huck. His face swelled up, and a lump formed on the back of his head. He shivered hard.

"They're coming," Lilia piped up, rejoining Huck. "What happened?"

Not leaving Arkin's side, Huck covered him with his hoodie. "I'm not sure. I went in and figured out what I'd done wrong. Realized I can't change what I've done. But I've got an opportunity to try again."

Behind them, Valon took a long drink from the vodka bottle, leaning hard against the wall. "It was brave to go in," he affirmed. "One day, you'll have to tell me what you did." He offered the bottle to Huck.

He took it and swallowed some before offering it to Lilia, who also took a long drink, her eyes glued to him. "This thing, Gormalech, if I remember correctly. Gormalech the Phoenix. It's drawn to people who are haunted. Most people aren't haunted. They think they are, but aren't. I was. But I did it to myself. I was keeping them here. Keeping them *there*." He sniffled and ran his hand under his nose.

"You let them go?" Lilia asked quietly, sitting next to him and leaning her head against his shoulder, eyes locked on Arkin.

"Something like that. Maybe it's not so much an opportunity as forgiveness."

The sound of the three of them panting filled the still office.

Valon nodded. "There are no second chances. There is only forgiveness and a vow to make a change."

Chapter 31:

Called

By the second week in December, Arkin was mostly healed and the three of them stood in the art studio. Huck and Lilia came down to get their projects before packing up and heading home for the holidays. Lilia proudly stood back, staring at her huge painting on one of the massive easels. Her hips stuck out to the side, and she rested her chin on her hand, smiling at her work.

"I call it Salem Revels," she announced to the boys. "It depicts a history that never was. Witches dancing free around the fire."

"Works for me," Arkin said, admiring her artistic addition to his arm cast. "I like a good depiction of female nudity."

Lilia groaned and smacked him before gathering her supplies. The other art students had been and gone before them. They hadn't moved to pack up, waiting for Arkin's strength to return. They had been busy helping him finish his classes from the hospital.

"You coming back next semester?" Arkin asked Huck.

"Oh?" Lilia interrupted. "Were you thinking you might not?"

Huck didn't answer right away. He looked for more things to gather in his art bag to avoid eye contact. "I don't know. I was thinking of either not coming back or switching majors. It wouldn't matter at this point."

"Why?" Lilia asked.

He stood up to finally meet their eyes. "This semester was terrifying. Who knows what might happen if I really dig into this? I feel like I should take the win and leave."

He caught the other two sharing a glance. "Go on," he groaned, sitting next to Arkin on the workbench.

Arkin spoke first, gently nudging Huck with his shoulder. "It's like I said earlier. Don't give up. This thing... won't leave you. Trust me, I know," he added when Huck slumped. "I heard that thing. It said stuff to me I'll never forget. Huck?" He waited until Huck looked him in the eye. "It's not going to leave you. You need something normal in your life. University can be that."

Huck wanted to argue, maybe even lie and say it was going to be ok. But he'd had an email from Valon the day before. "Valon said as much. Said this thing only comes when called." He pulled his phone out and opened up the email. He read, "'Gormalech is hell's dark harbinger. Those who practice the evil craft try to summon him, but he comes when the time is right, according to lore. He's a symbol of what's to come: destruction and rising from the ashes. Be careful and watch your back.'"

Lilia wrapped her arms around herself. "Sounds creepy."

"Creepy is inspiration!" Ms. Embers called, bursting into the art studio. Her arms were filled to bursting with rolled up canvas. "I thought all the students left days ago. It's winter break. What are you three still doing here?" She smiled at them from behind sheets of long, brown hair. Her patchwork skirt had road salt and water stuck to the bottom. It must be snowing out.

"Sometimes creepy is inspiration, Ms. Embers," Huck mused, hopping off the table to leave.

She smiled. "Elora, Huck. Call me Elora." She reached out and touched his shoulder. "Are you well? You look pale. Your aura is… different."

He nodded, used to her eccentric way of talking. "Just winter mood swings, I guess."

"Well," she handed him back his canvas with a grade scrawled on a sticky note, "you do good work. Hope to see you next semester. I know you don't have to take an art class, but your images are so haunting. It'd be a shame to throw away that talent."

"Maybe." Huck took the proffered canvas. "Not sure I'm coming back."

Elora looked up through her slipping glasses. "Oh, how sad. Well, I live in Henderson, the city on the other side of Boaz County. Maybe I'll run into you."

ARKIN NODDED ENCOURAGINGLY AT HUCK. The boys sat on the floor of their empty dorm, the game on the screen paused. "Call him. Stop whining about it and call him. Tell him everything you told me."

Huck looked away, pouting. "There's no point in calling Max. He made it very clear he's not interested in me. And that's putting it lightly."

Leaning forward, Arkin glared at Huck. "And your sister?"

Huck shoved him away, but Arkin gripped his upper arm. They locked eyes again.

"You're right." Huck shrugged him off, picking up his phone.

His roommate nodded. "It's not all about you, Hucky. Do this for her."

After Huck dialed, Arkin snatched the phone and turned it to speaker, dropping it on the floor between them. Huck glared at him, but Max picked up.

"Listen to me, Max," Huck said, cutting off Max's greeting.

Arkin smiled evilly, encouraging Huck.

"You didn't stick around for me. I had to find my own way. In more ways than one."

Max cut in. "What the hell are you—"

"Just listen to me for once," Huck snapped. He started to shake. Arkin grabbed his shoulders firmly. "You have to watch Celeste. You have to be there for her."

"She lives in Florida with her grandmother," Max reminded him.

"I don't care." Huck swallowed. "She's going to be like me now. Yes, she is!" he snapped when Max started to talk again. "It's got something to do with my blood. And my guts. You gave her my kidney, so she'll get my gift. It happened to Mark from a simple blood transfusion. It *will* happen to her if it hasn't already. Mark couldn't handle what he saw. I don't know Celeste and how strong she might be, but no one deserves to witness all that alone. This is your second chance, Max. To do what is right. Just because she hasn't perfected how to control it doesn't make her useless. She can see anything. Even demons. No one can handle seeing demons alone."

"You haven't seen demons," Max mocked him.

Huck's throat went dry. "If only you knew, Max. She's also going to be a beacon now. Spirits and all that crap are going to be drawn to her. She won't have a choice but to see them."

"No, listen," Max tried again. "Demons don't pop up. Maybe you saw a shadow entity. There are all kinds of specters. Demons have to be summoned. They can't come out like other specters. Someone has to call them."

Arkin's eyes shot up from the phone to Huck's. They both understood.

"Who would summon a demon?" Huck asked.

Max waited a beat before asking, "Huck, *have* you seen something?"

"None of your business. But..." Huck tapped the floor. "I might call you later."

"Good," Max sighed. "I was afraid you might cut me out. Thanks for the second chance."

"It's not a second chance, Max," Huck said. "It's forgiveness."

He hung up and pulled his knees up to his chest. Arkin scooted across the floor and sat next to him.

"Good job," he said softly.

A strange feeling warmed Huck and put him on edge as Arkin lightly touched him. He shook it off and just enjoyed the closeness of a true friend.

"Any chance you're coming to Boaz for the holidays?" he asked.

"Actually, yeah," Arkin said, suddenly standing up and going to his room. "Gramps wants me to hang out with him for the holidays and I can't blame him. He's crusty and lonely. Plus, I think he wants me to paint his living room."

Huck smiled up at his new best friend, knowing he wouldn't be alone for the break. His phone made a small tone. Picking it up, he saw a text from Logan.

It's cold, come down already.

"Ride's here!" Huck called to Arkin. He shoved the gaming system back into his backpack and the two of them ran down the cold stairwell to the parking lot.

Outside, Logan stood wrapped to his ears in a warm coat, scarf, hat and gloves. The hat reminded Huck of cowboys from the wild west.

"You look stupid," he smiled, opening the door to Logan's Camaro.

"I don't care how I look, I'm freezing!" Logan chided.

Huck helped Arkin dump all their things into the trunk before they both slid into the back seat. "Where's mom?" Huck asked.

They slipped into the car, closing the doors. The tinted windows cut out the gray sunlight.

Huck's phone beeped again. Logan kept talking, but Huck's ears rang, turning him deaf to the conversation in the car. The text, coming from a blocked number, was a picture of him, not seconds ago, walking out of the dorm doors with Arkin behind him. The shot came from across the street.

Huck whirled around and looked back, his heart flipping in his chest. He glanced back when his phone vibrated again.

The beldam watches. You will be prepared for the arrival of Gormalech, it read.

Bile rose in his throat. He choked, trying to swallow.

"You ok?" Arkin asked, elbowing him lightly.

Huck shoved his phone into his pocket, eyes watering. "Yeah. Sorry, where's mom? Is she home? Safe?"

"Cooking for you guys," Logan offered. "She thinks you wasted away to nothing here at the university and wants to make you something special. I said I'd come get you. And on the way home, we're going to go order parts for your car."

For the first time in months, excitement exploded in Huck, dabbing out the foreboding text. Whoever sent it was behind them. No cars tailed them. "You'll work on the car with me?" he asked, forcing joy to the surface again.

Logan nodded.

"Good," Arkin added. "Tired of walking everywhere downtown."

"Yeah," Huck joked. "Unlike real football players, kickers don't walk much. Wouldn't want to strain your precious legs."

"Shut up," Arkin smiled, punching Huck.

It felt good to be together, warm, and going home.

About the Authors: A.J.

A.J. Morgenstern is an aspiring writer of sorts. He mainly supports creative types through freelance work with graphics, emotional support, and the occasional story. He is a big fan of video games, football, and nature.

A survivor of some dark issues, he aspires to support and bring awareness to male trauma, childhood bullying, and the ever-growing presence of mental illness. A.J. is passionate about listening and being there for those who cry out for help.

Besides his work advocating, he hopes to one day skydive, own a ranch in the middle of nowhere, raise a family, and maybe find buried treasure once he owns a sailboat.

A.J. lives in Kansas, lurking in a dark office where he pens his stories in secret.

Find him online at https://www.facebook.com/blankman007/

About the Authors: Abi

Abi works part-time as a free-lance ghostwriter, editor, audio-book narrator, and is one half of the partnership that owns Altered Reality Magazine. She hopes to one day make these passions her full-time job while she hunts for the next bohemian adventure.

She has published works of fiction, poetry, academia, and even won awards for her short stories in science fiction and horror. Her novel, The Trial of Two, was named an Honorable Mention in the Writer's Digest 2021 self-publishing awards and won first place in the dark fantasy category in The BookFest Awards. Abi is also a proud mom of two ferrets. She currently resides in Kansas.

She is one of nine children--all who share the creative spark.

Find Abi online at: www.abigaillinhardt.com

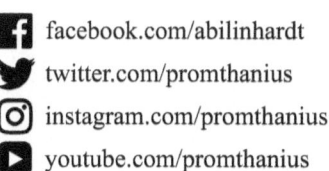

facebook.com/abilinhardt

twitter.com/promthanius

instagram.com/promthanius

youtube.com/promthanius

Also by Abigail Linhardt

Season of the Runer

Season of the Runer Book I: The Trial of Two
Season of the Runer Book II: Sojourn
Season of the Runer Book III: The Eldritch Hunt
Season of the Runer IV: The Father of Monsters (2023)

Stand-Alone Novels

Prince of MidWest
Why They Killed: A Waksha Virus Novelette
These Darker Streets
The Ghost of New Marseille (2024)

www.ingramcontent.com/pod-product-compliance
Lightning Source LLC
Chambersburg PA
CBHW020343180626
46812CB00001B/312